THE SECRET TO SEDUCTION

The Fontaines

EMBER CASEY

Charmaine –
Stay Wicked! ♥

xoxo,
Ember ♥
Casey

First printing, 2015
ISBN: 1-5089-0656-4
ISBN-13: 978-1-5089-0656-8

Cover Image © The Killion Group, Inc., used under license.

You can contact Ember at ember.casey@gmail.com.
Website: http://embercasey.com.

BOOKS BY EMBER CASEY

1

EIGHT DAYS UNTIL
CERTAIN HUMILIATION

"SCOTCH AND SODA, please."

The deep voice catches my attention immediately. I look up from my gin and tonic and sneak a peek at the man who just sat down beside me at the bar. He's a little older than me—maybe early thirties—and he has dark blond hair and a sexy spread of stubble across his jaw. As my eyes travel lower, I notice a little bit of a gut beneath his button-down shirt, but I tell myself that his broad shoulders balance out his shape quite nicely.

In any case, he's worth a shot.

I take a big gulp of my drink and turn toward him before I can chicken out.

"Scotch and soda," I say. "Good choice."

He looks over at me in surprise, as if he hadn't even noticed me sitting here. His eyes flick down to my drink—which is clearly *not* a scotch and soda—then to my body. I can't tell what he thinks. I'm definitely not a supermodel or anything, but I'm not completely atrocious, either. When I bought this top, my friend Amy assured me that I looked hot. But I'm not used to being "hot"—or even trying to be. Or whatever it is I'm doing right now.

"Do you like scotch, then?" he says finally.

"Actually, I've never had scotch," I blurt without thinking. When I realize I've just undermined my whole pick-up strategy, I rush on. "I mean, I've had whiskey. That's like scotch, right? Or…" *Oh shit. What am I even talking about?* "Or is scotch the same thing as whiskey? Or just whiskey that comes from Scotland? I know bourbon and whiskey are the same, and I like bourbon, and…" *Shut up, shut up, SHUT UP.*

The man looks less than impressed with my babbling, but he hasn't walked away yet, so there's that. My introduction might have been less than stellar, but this could still be salvageable. I take a deep breath—and a drink—and then turn to the man again.

"I'm Felicia," I say, flashing what I hope is a flirtatious smile.

The guy clears his throat. "Nice to meet you."

Before he can say anything else, the bartender arrives with his drink. I wait until the man's taken a couple of sips before I prompt, "And you are…?"

He pulls his glass away from his lips and gives me one more once-over, as if making a decision.

"I'm going to go sit with my friends," he says. And

with that, he slides off his stool and heads off through the crowd.

Fair enough. Maybe he came here for an evening out with the guys. My optimism lasts for about half a minute—right until I notice him sliding into an empty seat at the far end of the bar. No friends in sight. And to top it off, it only takes him about ten seconds to start chatting up the girl to his left. The bartender shoots me a look of pity as he wipes down the bar in front of me.

Ugh. It's bad enough getting shot down, but having a witness definitely adds to the humiliation. I almost think about calling it a night and just heading home, but I can't. I'm desperate. Desperate and more than a little tipsy. Aren't I the catch of the day? But I can't help it. I only have eight days—*eight measly days*—to get my shit together before I must declare myself Completely Pathetic. Okay, so maybe that's a little melodramatic. But there's more than just my dignity at stake here. My job is on the line. My dream job—as a staff writer at *Celebrity Spark* magazine—which I only got after *years* of "paying my dues" as an underpaid intern.

I take another long sip of my drink. I've never liked gin, but drinking it makes me feel more sophisticated. And much braver than my usual beer ever seems to. I need every bit of bravery I can get tonight.

I close my eyes as the alcohol burns its way down my throat. *Eight days.* I can still do this, assuming I don't wuss out now. I just need to up my game.

Three stools down from me, I spot a guy in a navy sportcoat. He looks young—not *too* young, but probably fresh out of his MBA program—and he's tapping his glass and looking around as if he doesn't know what to do with himself. Briefly, his eyes meet mine, and I glance quickly away, trying to be coy. That's how this flirting thing works, right?

I stare at my glass and count to three before shooting another glance in his direction. He's not looking at me. He's staring at some blond woman farther down the room. She laughs at something the man beside her says, and her perfectly-highlighted hair catches the light. She doesn't seem to notice Mr. MBA, so after a moment his eyes begin roaming again.

This time, when his gaze lands on me, I smile. Only for a second, but long enough that I hope he gets the hint. I was too forward with the first guy. This time, I'm going to let Mr. MBA come to me.

I look back at the bar and take another drink. *God, I hate gin.* It tastes like I'm sipping the blood of a Christmas tree. When Mr. MBA gets over here, maybe I'll ask him to order me my usual lager.

But a full minute passes, and no one appears at my shoulder. I glance down the bar again. Mr. MBA is still drumming his fingers against his glass, and now he seems to be studying the rows of bottles behind the bar.

Maybe he's waiting for someone, I tell myself. A friend. Or a woman.

Or maybe my smile wasn't clear enough. One of those articles on flirting I read this afternoon mentioned that the "rules" of seduction have changed so much in the past two decades that modern men aren't likely to approach a woman unless they have some overt encouragement. Maybe I haven't been obvious enough.

I try to watch him without being completely creepy. I just need him to look my way again. One look. One more smile from me. Easy peasy.

But as the minutes tick by and he doesn't even turn his head my way, I'm forced to consider that I might need to find another target. If he were the least bit interested, he'd at least *glance* my direction, right? I take another drink, and in my frustration it turns out to be a bigger one than I intended. I cough, nearly choking as my throat burns with the fire of a thousand angry fir trees, and somehow my hacking gets Mr. MBA's attention. He looks over, and I wipe the tears away from my eyes and fight back my coughs, trying to look sexy again. This is my chance, and I won't blow it. As soon as I have everything under control, I shoot him another smile. A big one this time. My eyes lock on his, hopefully making my intentions more than clear.

My throat still burns. Another cough tries to weasel its way out of my lungs, but I swallow it back. Mr. MBA hasn't looked away, so I keep smiling at him, even though it feels like he should have gotten the hint by now. He can't have any doubts that I'm interested in meeting him. So why is he still in his chair?

Maybe I should go over there. Maybe he still wants me to make the first move, I tell myself. But the other part of my brain is quick to talk me out of it. I've already made the first move. I'm smiling at him, aren't I? If he's interested in pursuing more, then he will.

Hopefully before my cheeks start to hurt.

But just when I think he's about to slip off of his stool, I'm suddenly aware of someone behind me.

"You're going to scare him off if you keep grimacing at him like that," says a deep, familiar voice in my ear.

I drop my glass. It hits the bar and tumbles over, spilling gin everywhere—including down the front of my shirt.

I jump up and spin around, but I don't have to look to know who sneaked up behind me. It's none other than Roman Everet, my boss and the whole reason I'm doing all of this in the first place.

He's not supposed to be here, in this bar. Sure, we're only two blocks away from the *Celebrity Spark* offices, but this place is about as hole-in-the-wall as bars come on this side of town. And Roman Everet is not a hole-in-the-wall kind of guy. He's a designer-suits kind of guy. A Ferrari-and-mansion-in-the-Hills guy. Which means he should be somewhere swanky rubbing elbows with other Hollywood bigwigs.

But he's here. And I can tell by the way he's looking at me that he's seen more than enough to convince him

I'm screwed. So I do what any self-possessed twenty-seven-year-old does when she realizes every last shred of her pride is on the floor.

I let out a squeak and run to the bathroom as fast as my discount-rack stilettos will take me.

And now, as I'm locking myself in a stall and trying not to hyperventilate, I guess I should probably explain what of all this is about.

2

AN EXPLANATION

I'M NOT NORMALLY a spaz, I promise. And I'm not normally the sort of girl who makes a fool out of herself trying to pick up guys at the local bar. Usually, I'm just Felicia Liddle, an all-around normal sort of person.

Except that I write for *Celebrity Spark*, one of the country's premier celebrity news publications. Working there has been my goal from the moment I graduated from college—where I doubled up in Journalism and Psychology—and my dream ever since I was old enough to read the tabloid covers at the supermarket.

Yeah, I'm that girl you've seen buying an armload of celeb magazines and frozen dinners at the checkout counter. And no, I'm not ashamed of it. I make no secret of the fact that I'm fascinated by celebrity culture (and fascinated by our culture's fascination with celebrity culture) even if it's not exactly something most people go around bragging about. But I worked my ass off to land this job. It took me five years of busting my butt at internship after internship (a.k.a. ferrying my weight in coffee to editors and making so many copies I'm probably personally responsible for the destruction of a couple of forests) but finally my hard work paid off. Six months ago, I was offered a position as a staff writer and junior editor for *Celebrity Spark* magazine. It was everything I'd ever dreamed.

And then, last week, everything came tumbling down. The sale of *Celebrity Spark* and its subsidiaries was finalized, and they started cutting jobs left and right. Even the Editor-in-Chief is on his way out, and in the meantime, Roman Everet, the CEO of the company that now owns us, has set himself up in the *Celebrity Spark* conference room to oversee the magazine's transition. Apparently he's the "hands on" type of mogul and likes to handle these things himself. In other words, he's a complete control freak.

I still remember the first time Roman Everet walked into the office. I'd heard his name a hundred times before—after all, it's my job to know all of the big names in entertainment, and his company has been hailed as one of the fastest-growing in the business—but I'd never seen the media mogul's face. People in my job see thousands of pictures of actors, musicians, heirs and heiresses, but we aren't typically clicking through photos of the people working "behind the scenes" in this town.

But naturally, I had a certain image in my head of

Roman Everet: middle-aged, silver-haired, slightly wrinkled from a life spent beneath the California sun— you know, just your typical CEO of a media company. Instead, the man who walked into the *Celebrity Spark* offices could have easily held a place among the inhumanly attractive celebrities that grace the covers of our magazine. For one thing, he was *much* younger than I expected. Mid-thirties, tops. His hair was the rich brown of milk chocolate, and his broad shoulders rivaled those of all of the athletes in this month's "Quarterbacks & Supermodels" roundup. He was, in short, most definitely drool worthy.

But then he started firing writers and editors left and right, and the glow wore off pretty quickly.

And the worst part of all? The day he showed up, I'd just bagged the biggest interview of my career so far. I'd been on top of the world, imagining how I'd catapult the feature into a better position at the magazine. But that sort of excitement dies pretty quickly when you suspect you're about to be sacked. Because even though I'd managed to get an exclusive interview with Emilia Torres—yes, *that* Emilia Torres, the star of the upcoming *Cataclysm: Earth* and the on-again, off-again girlfriend of megastar Luca Fontaine—I was still the magazine's most recent hire. And in spite of my years of interning, I knew I didn't have nearly the number of "sources" as some of the other writers at the magazine. The Emilia thing was just luck. A fluke. My landlady's brother's boyfriend is friends with Emilia's driver. I'm not an idiot. I know I can't build a career on miraculous connections like that.

But fluke or not, I'd gotten *something*. Something big. Something that could be used as leverage. At least that's what I told myself when I was called to the conference room for my inevitable meeting with Roman Everet.

He didn't look up when I entered. His head was bent over a tablet, his mouth a hard line as he scrolled through the document on the screen. There was a laptop to his left, two cell phones on his right, and various files stacked across the table. A large coffee and an untouched bagel sat by his elbow. I'd seen one of his assistants—of which there were at least four, by my count—bring those to him that morning. He seemed to keep them endlessly running around on errands. I was only in the room for a couple of seconds before one of the phones buzzed, but he took one look at the screen and then ignored the call in favor of whatever he was reading on his tablet. He still didn't bother to glance at me at all.

His distraction meant I had a moment to study him from the door, to ogle him without being noticed. He was perfectly groomed—not a hair out of place, not a speck of lint on his suit, not even the whisper of stubble on his clean-shaven cheeks. The last part made it all the easier to notice the strong cut of his jaw, as well as the slight indentation on his chin—which wasn't quite a dimple, and was a little off center, but somehow all the sexier for it—and I found myself suppressing a sigh. Shame I was about to get sacked. I wouldn't have minded having a little longer to stare at this guy, heartless bastard though he was.

"Sit down," he said finally without bothering to look up. His round baritone of a voice was as sexy as the rest of him, even if he did sound completely disinterested in speaking with me. "Felicia Liddle, is it?"

"Yes." I settled myself in the seat across the table from him and tried not to fidget. I knew where this was going.

"As you know," he said, still focused on the device in front of him, "I've decided to make some changes around here."

"Yes, Mr. Everet," I replied.

"It's purely a business decision," he said, as if he'd recited this little spiel a hundred times before—which, frankly, he probably had. "It's time *Celebrity Spark* fully embraced the digital age. It's a miracle the magazine has sustained the sales it has for as long as it has. But that won't always be the case. We'll continue to publish the magazine for as long as it remains profitable to do so, but our focus will shift to the *Celebrity Spark* website and our other digital outlets." For the first time since I entered the room, he looked up at me. His eyes were a strange shade of hazel—almost green—and I probably would have found them intriguing if I hadn't felt like I was about to throw up. In that moment, the lack of emotion in their depths only made everything worse. By his own admission, this was merely another "business decision" for him.

"As you can imagine," he continued in his matter-of-fact tone, "these changes require some restructuring here. There's no reason we need to keep a fully-staffed office, not when most of these jobs can be done from anywhere and most communications done via email. Subsequently, we'll be downsizing significantly. I've looked through your work, and you're a talented writer, but—"

"I got an interview with Emilia Torres," I blurted.

It was a stupid thing to say. *Of course* he knew about that already. But I was watching my dream job slip away from me, and I was desperate to save myself.

Roman Everet sat back in his chair, his hazel eyes assessing. "I'm aware of that. I've seen your notes. It looks like a good interview, as far as these things go."

He didn't have to finish. "But you're still firing me."

"Laying someone off and firing them are not the same thing."

"It still means I'm losing my job."

One of his phones buzzed, and he looked away from me and down at the screen.

"I'll be happy to furnish a letter of recommendation for you," he said, as he scrolled through whatever message had just arrived in his inbox. "Even put in a couple of calls, if you'd like. The interview with Emilia is a nice addition to your portfolio. I'm sure another magazine will be thrilled to find someone with such connections."

"But this magazine isn't?" My tone was more accusatory than I intended. But I was scared and angry enough that I didn't even think about the fact that I'd just barked at the man who held the fate of my career in his hands.

Until I saw his expression, that is. Then I was suddenly very aware of how I'd spoken to him. He stared at me, though I couldn't tell whether the way he slightly narrowed his eyes meant he was intrigued or merely shocked that I, a lowly staff writer, dared to address him that way. Mr. Sexy Mogul was probably used to people like me groveling at his feet. I held my breath, expecting him to throw me out without another word.

When he finally spoke, though, his voice was as calm as it had been a moment before. And there was a spark of something in his eyes that looked almost like humor.

"Emilia Torres might be a popular actress," he said, "but frankly, this magazine can do better."

I'm pretty sure I gaped at him. "Better?" I couldn't believe it. Emilia Torres is all anyone is talking about now. Her latest film, *Cataclysm: Earth*, has a larger budget than any movie in Hollywood's history—*and* costars Luca Fontaine, her former/ongoing/future flame and the highest-paid action star in the biz. The two have been fixtures in the tabloids for months—whether they're "on," whether they're "off," whether Emilia was spotted with a potential baby bump, whether Luca was seen with a mysterious brunette on his arm… it doesn't matter. The public eats it up. The issues fly off the racks.

"Tell me," Roman Everet said, spreading his hands, "when was the last time you saw Emilia on the cover of a celebrity news magazine?"

That had to be a trick question.

"Last week," I told him. "And the week before that. And every week this summer. Because her face sells magazines."

"No, her face does not sell magazines." His gaze was intense now, as if we'd entered some sort of interrogation. "Tell me, when was the *first* time you saw her face on a magazine?"

That was an even more perplexing question.

"I—I don't know," I said, uncertain. "A year ago? When she was cast in *Cataclysm: Earth*?"

"And is that cover-making news around here? When a B-list actress is cast in an A-list movie?"

"I wouldn't consider her a B-list actress," I countered.

He raised his eyebrow. "Not anymore. But she was most definitely B-list back then. Possibly C-list, depending on who you ask. But when did that change? I'll give you a hint—it wasn't when she was cast."

The way his eyes bored into me made me want to shrink back into my chair. But I wasn't about to let him beat me. Not when he was taking away my job. I straightened my shoulders. If I was going down, then I was going to do so with a fight. And I was *not* about to let him convince me that I didn't know what I was talking about.

"She became A-list news when she started dating Luca Fontaine, her A-list costar," I said. "She strengthened her position on the list when she and Luca broke up. And she cemented it when they got back together again."

He nodded, though his gaze didn't lessen in intensity. "Very good. You see my point then."

Frankly, I did *not* see his point at all, and my silence must have told him as much.

"Emilia isn't news on her own," he said slowly, as if explaining things to a child.

Ah.

"She's news because of Luca Fontaine," I said. Not only is Luca a huge star, but he's a *Fontaine*, and that name carries a lot of weight in Hollywood.

Another nod. "And how many times has Luca Fontaine given an interview in the past, oh, six months?"

I had to think about that. Because of my job, I make an effort to skim through every celebrity news magazine each week and to keep up with all of the biggest gossip blogs. But for the life of me, I couldn't remember anyone posting anything more than an occasional sound bite from Luca himself.

Apparently Mr. Everet could see the wheels turning in my brain, because slowly, the corners of his mouth turned up in the semblance of a smile, though his eyes remained as sharply appraising as they'd been the entire conversation.

"Emilia has been quite eager to speak with the press every step of the way," he said. "When she and Luca are together, she goes out of her way to talk about how much she loves him, to gush about the way he treats her, to make the whole world believe they're the perfect couple. When they break up, she's just as eager to discuss the drama. I'm sure that's what you discovered during your chat with her?"

He was right, of course. When I asked her about rumors that she and Luca had broken up again, she claimed that she wanted to keep the details of her love life private—but she threw out so many not-so-subtle hints about the matter that anyone with half a brain could have pieced together the story. She even warned me to watch out if I ever met him in person—apparently, Luca has a "weakness for dark-haired women." The whole thing is perfectly calculated, of course. I'm not *that* naive, and I've been studying this industry my entire life. I'm not sure how much of

Emilia and Luca's relationship is real and how much is manufactured to keep the attention of the press and public on their movie. And honestly, it doesn't matter. It's all part of the game, and real or fabricated, it still sells magazines and gets tens of thousands of website clicks.

That wasn't Roman Everet's point, though.

"I'm sure Emilia was eager to take the active role in this whole performance," he said. "It's simpler if only one of them is talking to the press, and Luca has a reputation for avoiding interviews. But by now everyone's heard Emilia's side of the story. I could probably write the answers to her next interview myself."

His condescension was starting to get to me again.

"Predictable or not, those answers still sell magazines," I reminded him. "I don't care if we've heard them a hundred times before. People still want to read them."

He looked almost amused by the fact that I'd dared to challenge him. Suddenly he stood up.

"My point isn't that they don't get sales or clicks *right now*," he replied simply, moving slowly but deliberately around the table. "It's that sometime in the near future they *will* get stale, and people *will* be tired of hearing Emilia talk about Luca. And we shouldn't wait until that point to seek out a bigger story. We should be working on that today. We don't want to follow the trends or the sales or the clicks. We want to *make* them."

His words were like a punch right to my gut. If *that* was what he was looking for, then no amount of arguing my case was going to save my job. I'd thought I'd hit the big time by snagging that Emilia interview. He was talking about something in another stratosphere.

"You understand, then?" he said, moving toward the door.

Yes, unfortunately, and even his sexy chiseled jaw and broad shoulders didn't keep me from wanting to kick him.

I knew that was my cue to get up. To go back to my desk and pack up my things and leave the office for the last time ever. To revamp my resume and start chasing that next dream job. Mr. Everet's hand was already on the door handle, his body half-turned toward mine, ready to usher me out. But the anger and desperation were still alive inside of me. And instead of moving, I heard myself say, "What if I can get that bigger story?"

His eyes widened slightly in surprise, and his hand froze on the door. After a second, that amusement that had been teasing at his lips spread into something deeper.

"What exactly are you proposing?" he said, and it was clear by his tone he was only asking me for his own entertainment.

I wasn't sure. Honestly, I think I was hallucinating a

little. So I said the first logical thing that popped into my mind.

"An interview with Luca Fontaine," I told him.

Now he gave me a true smile—but the sort of smile a cat gives its prey when it decides to play with it for a little while before devouring it whole. The kind of wicked smile that probably got him between his fair share of women's legs—it would certainly have done all sorts of twisted things to my insides under different circumstances.

"That would be a feat, considering his general attitude toward interviews," he said, walking over to the table and leaning against the chair next to mine. "How exactly do you plan to do it? I'm assuming he hasn't already consented?"

God, I hadn't realized how tall he was until he was towering over me. Between that and those eyes, my voice wanted to die in my throat. Besides—this was where my plan got sticky. But Roman Everet was asking me questions, which meant he was at least *entertaining* the idea of letting me try. I just needed to give him a reasonable answer and then I could work on the real plan later.

Unfortunately, no answer—reasonable or otherwise—was popping into my brain. It was hard enough to get Emilia to agree to an interview with me, as unimportant as I am, and as Mr. Everet so kindly pointed out, she was usually eager to talk to the press.

But as the silence stretched on and I saw the amusement in Roman's eyes start to fade, I knew I was losing him. I needed to say something—*anything*—to keep his attention.

"He has a weakness for dark-haired women," I blurted.

He sat up slightly. "Excuse me?"

"Luca Fontaine. He has a weakness for dark-haired women," I said quickly. "Emilia said so in her interview."

My answer must have intrigued him, because he was leaning slightly toward me. "And how does that matter?"

"I—well, I'm a dark-haired woman," I said. Though admittedly, having to point that out to him didn't say much for the potential effectiveness of my plan.

Nor did the way Mr. Everet immediately burst into laughter.

My cheeks went hot, and I considered bolting from the room. But something kept me glued to my chair. After a moment, he calmed himself again, but now humor pervaded his entire person.

"So you're planning to seduce him into an interview, then?" he said.

When he said it out loud like that, it sounded ridiculous. But I was still here, still holding onto my job by a thread, and I wasn't about to let go.

"Why not?" I said. "Women can seduce men into

doing all sorts of things. And it's not like I'm trying to get him to give up national security secrets or something." The more I spoke, though, the more I realized exactly how absurd all of this sounded. As I mentioned before, I'm not a troll, but I'm also not exactly movie-star gorgeous, either. I like my smile. And sometimes people will compliment me on my thick hair (a gift from my Greek heritage on my mom's side). I'm that girl who glides through life without most people noticing her one way or the other. I don't get catcalled walking down the street—especially not here in good ol' L.A., where I don't exactly fit the "look"—but it's not like I have people making snide comments about my appearance behind my back. I'm just... average. Just me.

Which was fine, at least until I told Roman Everet that I was going to seduce one of Hollywood's hottest bad boys.

The CEO looked like he was on the verge of laughing again. But he hadn't sent me from the room yet, and I took that as a good sign. Instead, he was now looking me up and down. His gaze moved slowly across my body—from the top of my head, to my breasts, then down my legs to where my feet were tucked beneath my chair—and I suddenly wished I'd chosen something a little more flattering to wear to work that day. Things were usually pretty casual around the *Celebrity Spark* offices, so most of the time I just threw my hair up in a ponytail and tossed on a button-down shirt and black pants. Not exactly the "honeypot" look. His expression revealed nothing about his opinion of what he saw.

"It's an… admirable plan," he said finally. His eyes met mine again, and I felt my flush deepen. It was one thing to meet his gaze when I thought he was just firing me. It was another after he'd just evaluated whether or not I was attractive enough to seduce Luca Fontaine. Someone with Roman Everet's looks and money certainly has his pick of women—and he's not even a famous actor. I knew I probably didn't even live up to *his* standards, let alone Luca's.

"Let's say you do have the… *ability* to convince Luca to give you a private interview," he continued. "How exactly do you intend to get close enough to do so in the first place? The *Cataclysm: Earth* set is closed to the press. And most members of the Fontaine family are quite adept at avoiding reporters when it suits them to do so."

The fact that he hadn't completely thrown out the idea shocked me. But now I suddenly had another impossible question to answer. My mind fumbled for a response.

And then it hit me.

"The *Hollywood Saves!* event next weekend," I said. "Many of the Fontaines show up every year." There would be a red carpet before the event, and my *Celebrity Spark* press badge could get me in. It wasn't an event someone in my position would normally attend—celebrities rarely haul out the drama and scandals at charity functions—but it would give me a good chance to get close to Luca Fontaine. I was pretty proud of myself for remembering it.

He seemed impressed by my answer as well.

"I can see you've thought this through," he said.

We both knew I hadn't, but I'd made my case. Either Roman Everet bought it or he didn't.

And for a long moment, he said nothing. He continued to look down at me, and I fixed my eyes on the bridge of his nose, trying to appear confident without actually meeting his unsettling gaze—or without getting distracted by that sexy little non-dimple on his chin. I needed to be steady, firm. He needed to see that I was serious about this.

"I'll tell you what," he said finally. "I like your creativity, so I'm willing to give you a shot."

I couldn't believe it. My desperate plea had *worked.* "You are?"

"It's a probationary period, of course," he continued. "I have a strict budget to adhere to, and I can't just keep an employee on a whim. You have until the day of the event, no longer. If you fail, you'll need to start looking for new employment. If you succeed, you can stay, though your longterm fate here will be left to the discretion of the new Editor-in-Chief. I should have one in place by then."

I nodded, still in disbelief that he was letting me go through with this. "I understand."

"I'll even give you a little freedom," he said. "Secure an interview for *Celebrity Spark* with *any* of the Fontaines and I'll say you've proved yourself good enough to stay. Does that sound fair?"

I continued to bob my head. "Yes. Yes, that's fair." And then, "*Any* of the Fontaines?"

"I know you're smarter than that. I mean the Fontaines of a certain…"—he waved his hand—"*level*, shall we say. A-list only. Second cousins and uncles and all that don't count." His eyes fixed on me. "If the average person on the street couldn't tell you which one it is, then you're on the wrong track."

"Okay."

"Good. Then that's settled." He indicated the door. "We're done."

I wasn't about to wait around to see if he changed his mind. I got up, thrilled beyond belief that I'd somehow miraculously been able to keep my job, and tried to ignore the way my skin prickled at the feeling of his gaze on my back.

It wasn't until about ten minutes later, when the glorious shine of my victory wore off, that I realized the *Hollywood Saves!* event was a mere ten days away. And that I was insanely, ridiculously, royally *screwed.*

3

EIGHT DAYS LEFT (AGAIN)

OKAY, SO THAT brings us back to me dry-heaving in the bathroom of a dumpy bar.

In the two days since my meeting with Mr. Everet, I've racked my brain for ideas of how I'm going to pull this off. And honestly? Against all odds, I've come to the conclusion that my best chance of getting an interview with Luca or any of the Fontaines will be to go with my original spur-of-the-moment (incredibly insane) plan to somehow charm my way in. I have nothing else to offer them—nothing they need, anyway. When you're Hollywood royalty, you're pretty much set in terms of money, fame, and connections. And the Fontaines are more than just royalty—they're a multi-generational dynasty. If you can name a position in the film industry, a Fontaine has been there. And won all the awards. And probably caused a lot of trouble—and broken a few hearts—along the way.

In other words, they are the wet dream of every

celebrity news outlet in existence. Except you don't become as big as the Fontaines without learning a few tricks about how to manage the press to your advantage. They're masters of the PR game, which means it can be nearly impossible to pin them down for an interview.

If I weren't already fighting an uphill battle, that's not my only disadvantage here. As I'm sure you've noticed by now, I'm not exactly "smooth" in the charm department. I don't have any experience seducing people. Hell, I can barely *flirt*. When I dated guys back in school, it was usually because we'd become friends in class first. Since then, I've tried online dating a few times, but for the most part, I've been focused on other things—not making googly eyes at someone next to me at the bar or chatting some guy up across the canta-loupes at the supermarket. I'm not even really sure how men and women interact these days outside of the internet.

Naturally, my first step was to try and learn. Since my meeting with Roman Everet, I've read every "How to Flirt" article I could find. But I knew I needed some real-world experience, which is why I came out here tonight. I thought I was ready to put the tips I'd learned to the test—with the help of some liquid courage, of course.

I was *not* expecting to have my first practice session crashed by the man who got me into this mess. I'm surprised that after witnessing that display he didn't fire me on the spot. I'm obviously not going to pull this off. He can save *Celebrity Spark* a week of my pay by canning me right now.

But what do I do at this point? I wonder as I stare at a bit of graffiti on the bathroom wall. *Hide in this stall until this place closes?* There's no way to get back to my car without walking past him. But while I could try to wait it out, hole up in here until closing time, sitting in this stall for a couple of hours doesn't sound very appealing—especially considering I'm going to have to face him at work on Monday anyway. What do I gain by being a coward now?

With a sigh, I leave the stall and go over to the sink. My initial assessment of my appearance in the mirror isn't *all* bad, at least. My cheeks are still a little redder than usual, but out in the dim lights of the bar, I'm not sure anyone will notice. My makeup is still mostly in place, though it could use a touch-up. Otherwise, I look just as I did when I walked into this place after an hour of careful preparations in the *Celebrity Spark* bathrooms: my dark, thick hair still holds its waves, my short skirt still hugs my hips, my black top still shows a healthy amount of cleavage. There's still a big wet spot down my front from my spilled gin, but it's not as obvious as it would have been if I'd been wearing a different color. I grab some paper towels and dab at it.

Still, after a couple of harsh rejections at the bar, my faith in my appearance has wavered significantly. I toss the paper towels in the trash and open my purse. My lips get another layer of plum-colored lipstick. My eyes another swipe of dark brown eyeliner. It's sultry without being vampy—or so I thought when I walked out the door tonight. As I study myself now, I'm not so sure.

But I'm also not going to think any more highly of myself if I cower in here much longer. At this point, I suspect the only thing that will help me is another drink. Something strong.

And so, after one last doleful look in the mirror, I leave the bathroom.

Roman Everet is still here. I spot him the moment I step back into the bar. It's only been a couple of days since I met him, and yet there's something unmistakable about his bearing, something instantly recognizable about him, even across this crowded bar.

He's not looking at me. He's not even looking in the direction of the bathroom. But I know he's waiting for my return. As I watch him, he takes a long sip of his drink—something dark and undoubtedly expensive, or at least as expensive as you can get at this bar—and then says a few words to the bartender. God, I hope they aren't talking about me. I'm sure I've provided plenty of entertainment for both of them tonight.

I shift my gaze to the door. I could leave if I wanted to. Just walk right out. But why delay the inevitable?

I straighten my shoulders and march over to the bar, sliding in right next to the man who is more or less my boss for the next week. I don't look at him. Instead, I smile at the bartender.

"Shot of tequila, please," I say. That'll make me feel better.

Mr. Everet doesn't seem surprised to see me suddenly appear at his side. I sense his eyes moving over me, analyzing me, and I'm thankful it's too dark for him to see me blush. I don't want to think about the opinions he's forming right now.

Unfortunately, he seems more than happy to share them.

"You're trying too hard," he says.

If I had a drink, I'd be choking on it. "What?"

"This." He waves his hand, indicating everything from my head to my toes. "This is too much."

"Excuse me?"

The bartender slides my shot across the bar to me, and he's giving me one of those pitying looks again. I glance away from him quickly, but unfortunately that means that I find myself looking right into Mr. Everet's sharp, penetrating eyes. He seems completely unconcerned that his assessments are making me uncomfortable. And completely oblivious to the fact that I couldn't care less about his opinion of me.

My cheeks are getting hotter. I grab my shot and throw it down, hoping the burn will chase away the humiliation coursing through my veins.

"How much have you had to drink?" he asks me.

I glare at him. "Not nearly enough." I wave at the bartender again. "Long Island Iced Tea, please."

I can tell without him even saying a word that Mr. Everet doesn't think that's a good idea. And maybe it's stupid to keep downing hard alcohol in front of the man who gets to decide whether or not I keep my job. But he already has too much power over my future. I'm not about to let this man dictate my drink choices, too. And there's nothing illegal about having a drink when I'm off the clock. Doesn't a big-shot CEO have better things to do with his time than hang out with his soon-to-be-ex-employee on a Friday night?

Under different circumstances, I might have found his unrelenting gaze flattering, or even arousing—I mean, *look* at the guy. There's no doubt that the body beneath that designer suit is extremely lickable. Or that those hands, which look so large around his glass of dark liquor, probably know exactly how to tease a woman into exquisite pleasure.

But these aren't circumstances where I can fully appreciate either of those things. He shouldn't be here in this grungy bar. He shouldn't have witnessed my laughable attempt at flirtation. He shouldn't be sitting next to me, studying me, when he has a company to run and fancy, important places to be.

He's silent as the bartender mixes my drink, silent as the glass gets passed into my hand, silent as I take my first sip. In fact, he's silent so long that my anger seeps out of me and I start to get nervous again. He obviously has something he wants to say. Why won't he just spit it out already and put me out of my misery?

Finally, I can't take it anymore.

"What?" I ask, ashamed by how my voice cracks on the word.

"I didn't say anything," he replies.

I really want to leave it there. To sip at my Long Island and pretend none of this ever happened. I don't want to hear about what I'm doing wrong, about all the poor decisions I've already made tonight. I'm already judging myself. I don't need his judgment, too.

But after a moment, he sighs, and I know I'm about to hear it anyway.

"Do you want my advice?" he says. "Or are you just going to get offended?"

Okay, so I guess he *did* notice that his comments were getting to me. And yeah, it would be easy to tell him that I don't care about his opinion. To put up a wall and ignore his criticisms. But let's be honest—I need the help, and we both know it.

"Fine," I say. "Tell me what I'm doing wrong, Mr. Everet."

"Roman."

"What?"

"Call me Roman."

Using his first name makes this worse. It makes it... *intimate.* At least when he was "Mr. Everet" I could sort of pretend he wasn't a real person. The formality made it safer. Easier. But that's not exactly something I can explain to the man in front of me.

"Okay," I say. "Roman. I'd like to hear what you think I'm doing wrong."

He doesn't respond immediately. Instead, he takes a long, slow drink, and I can't decide if he's giving me one last chance to walk away or if he justs likes to watch me squirm. Finally, he puts his glass down.

"It's too much," he repeats.

"What is?"

"Everything. The way you're dressed. The way you try to get the attention of these men. It's coming off as desperate."

"Desperate?" *Oh, God.* I mean, I know I *feel* desperate, but I didn't realize everyone else could see it.

But Roman isn't finished.

"Don't get me wrong," he says. "The approach you take is up to you. In fact, I'd venture that there are many men who'd be happy to accept what they believe you're offering. But I don't think you'll be getting the results you'd like. And I'm fairly certain this strategy won't help you win the attentions of any of the Fontaines. Luca and his brothers have women throwing themselves at them all the time. You'd just be one more."

I can read between the lines, as much as it pains me to acknowledge what he isn't saying.

"And I'm not sexy enough to stand out from the rest," I say.

"That's not what I said. I'm only suggesting that the odds would be against you."

That's not exactly reassuring. I run a finger through the condensation on the side of my glass. "What am I supposed to do, then?"

"Your current method might get you a smile and a few polite words, but not much more. Certainly not an interview. You need a far subtler approach."

A far subtler approach. Could he be any more vague? I take a long sip of my Long Island Iced Tea through my straw, waiting for him to continue. To explain. But when I sneak a glance at him, he seems to be waiting for me to speak.

"How... How do I..." Looking him in the eyes makes it harder to ask the question, so I drop my gaze back to my drink. "I obviously don't have any idea what I'm doing. You're going to need to be more specific."

He swivels toward me on his stool, and before I realize what's happening, he takes me by the shoulders and turns me back to face him. Our knees bump together beneath the bar, but he doesn't seem to notice. I, on the other hand, am aware of everything—from the way the fabric of his pants rubs against my bare legs to the heat of his hands through the satin of my shirt. If I thought using his first name made things too personal, him touching me takes things to an entirely new level.

Especially because he's holding me so I can't easily look away. I'm forced to meet his eyes, to face this sexy devil of a man who may or may not be my worst nightmare right now. My heart thumps.

"Felicia," he says, "you can't let your nerves about this situation get in the way of your common sense. You're acting like you've never spoken to a man before in your life." He cocks his head. "You're not a virgin, are you?"

My cheeks are flaming. "No! Of course not."

The look he gives me tells me he doesn't quite believe me. When does humiliation become so acute that you explode into a thousand little pieces? Because I'm pretty sure I'm almost there.

"But you've spoken to men before?" he asks me. "Dated them?" I'm reminded of the intensity of the interrogation he gave me over Emilia Torres, like this is one more business problem to solve.

"Yes. Yes, I've dated," I manage. "But I never… I mean, we were always friends first. I've never had to approach them."

"It doesn't matter who approaches. It's about the conversation that follows."

"Well, in that case, no. I haven't had a lot of experience in that area." I realize I'm fidgeting, bouncing my knee against his. I force myself to be still. "I—I mean, I don't exactly have men fighting over each other to talk to me." Admitting that to a guy who could be an underwear model isn't exactly easy.

"But you could. It's all about the presentation." He drops his hands from my shoulders, and suddenly I feel as if I can breathe again.

Still, it takes me a moment to find my thoughts. I gesture at my outfit. "And this is the wrong presentation."

He sits back. "It's not just about what you wear, though that certainly plays a role. It's about what you say, how you engage, and most importantly, how you make him feel. You have everything you need, Felicia, but you aren't putting it to proper use."

I'm not sure whether that's a compliment or not. I swivel back toward the bar and grab my Long Island. At least he doesn't think I'm completely hopeless. Still, his dark, scrutinizing gaze continues to unnerve me. It's like a tickle on my skin, and I suppress the urge to shiver. I don't like being analyzed this closely, especially by someone like *him*, who's probably never had trouble seducing anyone in his entire life. On the other hand, what do I have to lose? My dignity's already out the window. This is about saving my job. Period.

"What would you suggest I do?" I ask him finally.

There's a hint of wry humor in his expression. "I don't have a step-by-step guide, if that's what you're looking for."

"Then you can't help me?" I ask, and if I had any pride left, I'd be ashamed by how disappointed I sound.

"I didn't say that."

This is the point where I realize that he's dragging this out on purpose—that he's actually *enjoying* watching me squirm. I see it in his eyes, and that devilish smile that stretches across his lips confirms it. I start to turn away in disgust, but he reaches out and grabs my arm. His fingers feel too warm on my already alcohol-flushed skin. Or maybe I just feel exposed, considering my humiliation here tonight.

"It's not impossible to teach someone seduction," he says, his voice dropping low, "but it isn't simple, either. There's no guide, no preset rules. In fact, some would say there are no rules at all. The question is, are you willing to learn?"

Something about his tone makes my heart beat a little faster—though I'm sure the fact that he's still touching me doesn't help. I pull my arm out of his grip.

"Are you offering to teach me?" I ask.

That smile of his widens. "Perhaps."

I frown. "Don't you have more important things to do?" I mean, he's the freaking CEO of a growing media company. He just bought the largest celebrity news magazine in the country. This guy probably regularly puts in hundred-hour weeks.

"I think this is very important, Felicia. Do you not?"

I'm certain that he's teasing me now, and part of me thinks I should just walk away. He's clearly getting some sort of sick joy out of this, and I'm not sure how I feel about being some big shot's "entertainment" after a long week of work.

But walking away now would mean giving up on this Fontaine interview, and I'm not prepared to do that just yet. I knew when I got into this business that I'd need to be tenacious. That I'd need to push myself outside of my comfort zone. Besides, I still have most of a Long Island Iced Tea to finish. And it's making me bolder with every sip. In fact, I'm feeling pleasantly warm right now.

"Okay," I say, surprising myself with how steady my voice sounds. "Let's do this. What do I need to do?"

Something gleams in his eyes. He's altogether too pleased by this.

"As I said before, there isn't an instruction manual," he says. "But I'll tell you what. Pick a guy. Show me what you can do, and I'll help you refine your technique."

Wait—he wants me to do *what*?

"You've already seen what I can do," I remind him. Or what I *can't* do, more accurately.

"Not up close. Not with a chance to truly study you. And this time you know you need to be subtler. Let's see how quickly you learn and adapt."

"Right now? Here?"

"When else? There's plenty of opportunity. And we don't have much time before *Hollywood Saves!*"

This is ridiculous. I didn't come here to put on

some sort of show for Roman. I don't deny that I need the help, but how am I supposed to get better with this guy watching my every move?

But how am I supposed to get better if I don't try?

Another gulp of the Long Island goes down my throat. It's making me feel fuzzy-headed and reckless. I glance around the room. This bar is filled with men. Some young—college-aged—and others old enough to be my grandfather. There are men in T-shirts and men who look like they just got off work. None of them are dressed as nicely as Roman—which makes me wonder again why he had to wander into *this* bar—but that doesn't help me one way or the other when it comes to getting their interest.

Finally, I look back at the man beside me. Roman looks perfectly calm and perfectly amused. Is this what media moguls do for fun on their nights off? Why isn't he in some swanky club or out on his yacht with a couple of models on his arm? This man could be sitting with any woman he wanted right now. Instead, he's sitting here with me. Asking me to go hit on someone so he can watch. Maybe he gets off on this sort of thing, the sicko.

I think I need another couple of shots.

But damn it, a part of me—the alcohol-fueled part—really wants to prove myself to this guy. To show him that I'm not as inept as he thinks. To prove that I've got the gumption to work for *Celebrity Spark.*

"Okay," I say. "Let's get this over with."

His hazel eyes flash. "Very good." He glances around the room once more. "Well, who is it going to be, then?"

"*I* have to pick?"

"Would you prefer I choose your target?"

Okay, maybe not. I bite my lip and take another look at the men around me. Who should I approach? Someone alone, preferably. I don't think I have the skills to get a guy away from his friends. Maybe that guy over by the dart board who looks barely old enough to drink—he's got a frat-boy look, and if I know anything about frat boys, they'll respond to anything with breasts. But Roman might think he's too easy a target—seducing him won't prove anything. Besides, Frat Guy seems to be checking out that table of young women by the door. If I go over there and get rejected by *him*, I'm not sure I'll ever live it down. *Next!*

My eyes fall next on an older man—probably in his mid- to late-fifties. He's nursing a beer by himself at a table in the corner. But as I watch, he straightens and lets out a huge belch. Nope. *Next!*

On my third glance about the room, I finally spot someone who seems like a good candidate. He's sitting by himself at a table near the bathrooms, and he looks only a few years older than me—maybe thirty. He's dressed casually but nicely, and he seems to be focused on the game playing on the TV above him. To top it off, he has a basket of chili cheese fries in front of him. Any guy who likes chili fries is cool in my book.

"Him," I say, indicating my target.

Roman looks over at the man. His eyes narrow slightly, but I can't tell what he's thinking—or even whether he approves of my choice. But it doesn't matter. I've made my decision, and I don't wait to hear what my new "teacher" thinks. I take one last sip of my Long Island and slide off of my stool. *You can do this*, I tell myself. *Think of it as a game. A challenge.* I'm tipsy enough now that those words actually pump me up a little. *I've got this. I can be a master seductress.*

On my way across the room, I remind myself of Roman's advice: *Be subtle. Don't be desperate.* As I wind my way through the tables, I yank the neckline of my shirt a little higher. No need to have the ladies on full display. I can do this on my own.

I hope.

But my confidence fades as I get closer to the table. What's my opening line? Should I just walk up to him and say hello? Will he think it's strange if some girl just appears next to his table and starts talking? *What the hell am I doing?*

By the time I'm standing next to him, full-blown panic has taken over. It doesn't help that I can feel Roman watching me, waiting to analyze my inevitable failure. His gaze is practically burning a hole into my back. Why, oh why did I think this would be a good idea?

Just be subtle, I remind myself. *Be friendly.* Easier said than done, though. Especially when my target with the chili fries looks up at me in confusion.

"Uh, the other girl's waiting on me," he says.

Oh, God. He thinks I'm a waitress.

"Oh, no, I'm not—I don't work here," I say quickly. This is the part where I should explain who I actually am and why I came over here—or, you know, the *pretension* of why I came over here—but suddenly my mind is blank. Why did I charge right up to him without going over a couple of introductory lines in my head? That Long Island has turned me into an idiot.

I can almost *feel* that bastard Roman laughing at my sudden paralysis. If he wanted entertainment, he's definitely getting some right now. Oddly enough, the annoyance that rises with that thought seems to restore the feeling to my tongue.

"Hey," I say. *Remember—be subtle.* "You watching the game? Who're you rooting for?" I almost let out a breath of relief after the words have left my lips. That sounded normal, right?

"You like baseball?" he says, surprised.

Normally, I wouldn't openly lie to a guy, but since this is just practice, I know it's my best shot.

"Sure," I say. "I'm a huge..." *Oh, fuck—what's the name of L.A.'s baseball team?* I look quickly up at the television, scanning the screen for a name. But I quickly realize I'm screwed. L.A. isn't even playing—the game appears to be between Atlanta and New York. How am I supposed to know who he's going for?

"I'm a huge New York fan," I say finally.

"Figures." He sounds disappointed. "Most people are."

I'm not sure how to respond to that, except, "You're not?"

"Nope."

He's no longer looking at me, and his initial enthusiasm seems to have waned. *Damn.* I should've picked the other team. But I'm running on alcohol and I'm not going down that easily.

"There's nothing wrong with a little friendly rivalry, is there?" I ask, feeling bold.

He glances over at me again. "I guess not."

"I'm Felicia." I hold my hand out to him.

"Chuck." He gives my hand a shake. "Want to watch the game?"

Did he just… Am I really… Did I pull this off?! I grab a chair and slide in next to him at his table. As I do, I throw a glance back over my shoulder at Roman.

And immediately realize that was a mistake. His hazel eyes are piercing, even at this distance, and though he's smiling—he even gives me a nod of approval—just meeting his gaze instantly makes me feel nervous again. I can almost hear his rich baritone in my ear: *You have everything you need, Felicia.* But those words don't keep my hands from shaking.

I lace my fingers in my lap and quickly turn back toward Chuck. He's looking at the TV again, absorbed in the game. My eyes follow his to the television screen. We bonded—sort of—over baseball. If this is moving to the next level, then I need to keep up the charade.

I know the basics of baseball, of course. I haven't lived under a rock. But my brother Matt was always more into football growing up, and I was more interested in books and magazines than I was in sports, so I can only somewhat follow the game playing out above us. Instead, I try to take my cues from Chuck— though that's tricky in its own way. At one point, Chuck lets out a cheer, and I start to clap as well—until I remember that I'm supposed to be supporting the other team.

Yeah, this is definitely why you don't lie when you're trying to seduce someone. This is why you don't go into a seduction without a game plan. But most of all, this is why you don't down a bunch of alcohol before trying to prove to your sexy boss that you know what you're doing. Your sexy boss whose very presence makes your blood race a little faster and your nerves spiral out of control.

Chuck's not much of a conversationalist. Or maybe he's figured out that I couldn't name a single profession-al baseball player if my life depended on it. Either way, he doesn't say a word to me. And I, panicked and confused as I am, don't say a word to him. I feel like I should comment on the game, to at least *try* to make this work, but I know that I'll reveal my lie as soon as I open my mouth. And all I can think about is how Roman is watching me, waiting for me to make my move. The pressure is building with every passing second. I need to say something. Anything.

"What else do you like?" I ask him.

He's still looking at the TV. "Hm?"

"What else do you like? Besides baseball, I mean. And chili fries."

He shrugs, still watching the game. "Football. Basketball. Not really into hockey."

"Ah." Is he making this hard on purpose? Is he not interested in me after all? If not, then why did he invite me to sit down?

I have the urge to look back at Roman again, as if somehow his expression will tell me what to do. My focus is torn in two directions—between the man in front of me and the man behind. I need to focus on Chuck, as hopeless as it seems. Maybe I just need to drop a bigger hint.

My eyes fall on his glass. "Their beer selection here is good, isn't it?"

He nods. "Pretty good, yeah."

Okay, then. An even bigger *hint.*

"I'm really thirsty," I say, "but I'm not sure what I should get."

Chuck shrugs. "The waitress can bring you a menu."

And we're zero for two. It's clear that this approach is getting me nowhere, but I'm not sure what I'm doing wrong. I mean, I've got absolutely no game, but I'm not *completely* socially inept. I don't think. Maybe I need to crank things up another notch.

Though my gut tells me this is a bad idea, the Long Island is telling me that I've got nothing to lose. I grab the bottom of my shirt and tug it downward, pulling the neckline back to where it was before. Let's see what the ladies can do.

I lean across the table. "I've always wanted to try their chili fries. Mind if I steal one?"

He gives me another shrug. "Sure."

I reach over to the basket and take my time selecting a fry. When I finally find one I like—with enough *stuff* to be delicious, but not so much that it will be messy—I slowly bring it to my mouth and take a bite.

"Mmmm," I say, perhaps a little too enthusiastically.

It's an objectively awful attempt at seduction. But it gets his attention. Suddenly Chuck's eyes are no longer on the game. They're on me. Or, more specifically, on the girls falling out of my top.

"That was delicious." I lean forward across the table, and I watch him struggle with where to look. "What do you think?"

"Hm?" His eyes fly up to my face again.

"About the fries? Yummy, aren't they?"

He shifts in his seat, and suddenly he seems to want to look everywhere but me. I fight back a smile. *I've got him.* The twins have done their job.

Of course, that leaves the question of where I go from here. I'm not interested in going home with this guy—or teasing him unnecessarily. Again, I curse myself for walking into this without a concrete plan. My objective was to flirt, to seduce him—but how do I know when I've accomplished that?

Chuck's eyes have drifted to my breasts again. I need to do *something* while I have his attention. Something to prove to Roman that I'm not completely hopeless. Something like… getting Chuck's number. Or giving him mine. That's harmless, right? That's doable.

Especially when Chuck's eyes seemed fixated on my bazongas.

I lean forward a little more and reach for another chili fry. His eyes follow my fingers as I select a fry from the basket and raise it to my lips, but as soon as he meets my eyes, he looks away again. This guy's as nervous and skittish as I am. In spite of Roman's warnings to be subtle, if I wait for *him* to make a move, I'm going to be here all night. I've been at this table for at least half an hour already, and I'm sure Roman's getting impatient.

"I should probably go," I say, surprised and pleased at how casual I sound. "But maybe I can call you sometime?"

Chuck sits up straight. "Call me?"

"You know, so we can meet up again." I give him what I hope is a sweet—and not desperate—smile. "If you want that, of course."

The poor guy looks so nervous that I suddenly feel terrible—it was never my intention to put him on the spot, or to make him uncomfortable in any way. But I'm too far in. It's now or never.

"Will you give me your number?" I ask him before I can chicken out.

His eyes widen, and he shakes his head quickly. "No. No, I'm sorry."

The bottom drops out of my stomach. I wasn't expecting such a quick and violent refusal.

"I'm sorry," he says. "I shouldn't have let you sit down. I thought you just wanted to watch the game."

"Oh." I'm already sliding out of my seat. My neck is on fire.

But then he drops the real kicker: "I didn't mean— look, I'm married." He holds up his hand, and sure enough, there's a gold band around his finger. I can't believe I've just spent the last thirty minutes trying to pick up a *married* man.

But that's not even the worst part. The worst part is that Roman is waiting for me. Roman has witnessed this entire scene. And now I have to walk back over to him and explain how, yet again, I've made a complete ass of myself.

Or I can hide in the bathroom again. That seems like a really good idea right now.

In any case, I need to get away from Chuck as quickly as possible. No wonder he looked so uncomfortable. No wonder he didn't offer to buy me a drink or ask for my number. I stumble back across the room.

Roman looks like he's trying not to burst out laughing. I want to melt into the floor and disappear.

"Well," he says, "that wasn't exactly subtle, was it?"

I sink onto my barstool without answering and try to get the attention of the bartender. Maybe he'll give me a free drink out of pity.

Roman is still sipping casually at his liquor. "Don't look so bereft. We might have our work cut out for us, but I still believe you have potential."

I give a short laugh. "You're not ready to give up on me yet?"

"Certainly not. Quite the opposite."

I glance over at him. Does he really think I have a shot at seducing Luca Fontaine, or does he just want to prolong this for his own amusement? I can't tell from the way he's looking at me—I only know that, as usual, his gaze seems to see right into me.

"Trust me," he says in a tone I suspect has led many women to do just that. "I know just what you need."

But you know what? Even with my Long Island goggles on, I don't trust that smile he gives me one bit.

4

SEVEN DAYS

F I FELT like an idiot at the bar, I feel even worse the following morning. My head is *killing* me. Yeah, that's definitely the last time I trust the promises of a Long Island Iced Tea. That bitch.

It's Saturday, which is when I'd normally sleep in, but for some reason I told Roman I'd meet him for lunch so we can discuss my strategy. I still have no idea why I agreed. Oh, right—I was drunk and stupid last night.

As I pull on my jeans, I consider calling and canceling. The thought of facing him after last night makes me want to throw up—but on the other hand, that might just be the hangover. With my luck, I'll take one look at him and get sick all over his shiny designer shoes.

The more I think about it, though, the more I realize that for some weird reason, I *want* to go. It doesn't matter if Roman actually believes I can pull this off, or if he's only doing this for his own pleasure. This is my chance to show him how far I'm willing to go for this job—and to learn a couple of things along the way. If it has even the slightest chance of helping me get ahead in this industry, then I'm willing to try. Last night was a low point for me. That means I can only go up from here, right?

If I'm going to do this, though, that means diving in with both feet and giving it my best effort. First things first: jeans aren't going to cut it. At least not *my* jeans—which are comfortable as hell but baggy in the butt and knees. I want to show Roman that I'm approaching this project like a professional—and if I can feel like less of a slob next to him in his perfectly pressed, ridiculously expensive clothes, even better.

It only takes me an hour, but after trying on (literally) everything I own, I decide on a simple blue sundress and black strappy sandals. It takes me another forty-five minutes to do my hair and makeup. After trying a bunch of styles, I decide to put my hair in a ponytail. By the time I'm reasonably happy with my look, I'm late, so I don't have time to overanalyze the final results.

Roman is already at the bistro when I arrive, and I stop dead in my tracks when I see him. He's not wearing a suit today, only a button-down and gray slacks—which is, I suspect, as "casual" as this man gets—and the effect is, well, most definitely pleasing. Does this man ever look less than perfect? The nerves

I'd managed to push away instantly come rushing back. Learning how to seduce someone will be challenging on its own. Learning from someone who's devastatingly attractive? That's a whole new level of awkward.

Maybe this is a good thing, I tell myself as I force my feet to start moving again. *And after all, the Fontaines are all insanely attractive as well. I need to get used to flirting with someone who makes my insides all fluttery.* I don't want to worry about getting tongue-tied on the big night.

He doesn't look up until I'm at the table. I thought his eyes were hazel when I saw them back in the *Celebrity Spark* conference room. But in the natural light let in by the bistro's large windows, they look much more green. Green with a touch of blue—and even a little gold. A girl could get lost in those eyes if she isn't careful.

Focus, I remind myself. *And don't forget that you work for this guy.* I realize that I'm gripping my purse so hard my nails are leaving indentations in the leather. I need to calm down.

"Good morning," Roman says after I've stood there an awkwardly long amount of time. "Please, sit."

I start to take the seat across from him, but he shakes his head.

"Here. Next to me." He indicates the chair to his right.

"*Next* to you?"

He nods. "It will make things easier."

I'm not exactly sure which "things" he's referring to. But at least if I sit right next to him, our conversation will be a little more private. I slide into the chair and glance around. Anyone looking at us would assume we're on a date—if they could get past the idea that a man who looks like Roman might be interested in an ordinary girl like me.

Our waitress arrives within seconds. "Good morning. What can I get you to drink?"

Roman already has a drink—something the color of amber. A little alcohol would definitely calm my nerves right now.

"A mimosa, please," I tell her.

But even as the waitress nods and scribbles it down, Roman says, "I don't think so."

I turn to him. "What?"

"No alcohol."

I'm pretty sure I'm gaping at him. But he just gives a little smile and a shake of his head, as if I'm making a big deal out of nothing.

"Give us a moment, please," he tells the waitress.

She walks away, shooting me a worried look as she passes.

"Are you being serious?" I say as soon as she's out of earshot. "I can make my own decisions about what I drink."

"I'm not forbidding you from anything, if that's

what you're thinking," he says calmly. "By all means, have a drink if you want to. But I think it will be easier if you're sober this time around. I don't want you to use alcohol as a crutch."

I'm not sure which is worse—the fact that he apparently thinks I have a drinking problem, or the fact that he actually has a point.

"I'm not an alcoholic," I say softly.

"I never said you were," he replies. "You're nervous, and you think the alcohol will make it easier. It won't. And there won't be any alcohol available to you on the night of *Hollywood Saves!*, so unless you're planning on smuggling a flask beneath your gown, you might be in trouble." He taps a finger against his glass. "I must admit, though, my knowledge of women's clothing is somewhat limited. Perhaps you've thought of something I haven't."

Oh, I doubt very much that this man's knowledge of women's clothing is *limited*—and I don't even want to think about his suggestion that he's thought about where I might hide a flask on my body—but he's more than made his point.

"It's not that I *need* alcohol," I tell him. "It's—it's the principal of the thing. What do you think the waitress thinks of us right now?"

"Frankly, I couldn't care less. And neither should you. In fact, that's my first bit of advice if we're going to do this—you have to stop being concerned about what other people think of you. Trust me, it will make everything a lot easier."

I almost argue that I *don't* care about what other people think of me, but I know that's a lie.

"But doesn't that defeat the whole point?" I say. "Just last night you were telling me I shouldn't let people think I'm desperate."

"Understanding how others might perceive you and *caring* about it are two very different things. The first is imperative if you wish to be successful, while the latter will hinder you."

I let that sink in while he beckons the waitress over again. I order a soda without looking at her, doing my best not to imagine what she might be thinking about me—or Roman—right now. Easier said than done.

When I look back at Roman, he's watching me. Probably trying to decide whether or not I'm taking his advice. I quickly glance down at my menu.

"There's no need to drag this out," I tell him. "I'm here, I'm sober, and I'm ready to hear your analysis of my performance last night."

"Analysis?" I hear the smile in his voice, even though my eyes are fixated on desserts. "That's such a cold, formal word."

I'm suddenly self-conscious again, suddenly over-whelmed. Maybe it's his gaze. Or maybe it's that I'm already realizing this is an impossible task. I'm getting the cold sweats just asking him for help—it would take a miracle to make me stop caring about what other people think in just seven short days.

"It doesn't matter what you call it," I say, trying to push through the feeling. "I'm here to learn."

"You make all of this sound so serious," Roman muses. "Like this is some sort of class you've been forced to attend. Don't think of it as an obligation, or as something you're forced to endure. Instead, think of it as an *opportunity.*"

I give a nervous laugh. "An opportunity to humiliate myself?"

"I was thinking more along the lines of an opportunity to... expand your horizons a little."

There's a suggestiveness in his tone, and it makes panic rise in me anew.

"Tell me," he says, "do you think you're attractive?"

That question doesn't make this any easier. "I—I mean, I don't think I'm hideous."

"That's not what I asked."

"I... I'm pretty enough," I say. "I mean, I'm not going to be winning any beauty contests anytime soon, but I'm not afraid I'm going to die alone or anything." *Not yet, anyway.* "One day I'll meet a nice guy who thinks I'm beautiful no matter what and we'll settle down and have perfectly average little babies."

Roman looks thoughtful. "Is that really what you believe? That you're just 'average'?"

"Don't say it like that." I fiddle with the edge of the

tablecloth. "Objectively speaking, it's the truth. And I'm okay with that."

"I politely disagree. *Objectively speaking*, you're well above average. I'm surprised you haven't realized that."

My neck goes warm. "You don't need to—"

"You think I'm just flattering you?"

"I'm not an idiot." Now my whole body is hot. "There's no reason to pretend that I'm on the same level as the women Luca Fontaine normally dates. That's not helping anyone."

He doesn't respond. Instead, he just continues to look at me, as if somehow he might change my mind with his stare alone. If I wasn't self-conscious before, I am now. I didn't come here to pick myself apart, or to listen to him lie to me in some twisted attempt to calm my nerves. It's insulting. *I can't do this. I can't...*

I start to rise, to run, but his hand is suddenly on my arm—not gripping, not forcing, but gently urging me to sit back down.

"No need to get up," he says. "My, but you're jumpy. Remember what I've told you—you need to relax. Stop thinking and worrying so much."

Slowly, I sink back into my seat. But his hand remains resting gently on my arm, as if he's afraid I might try to run off again. And honestly, I just might.

"I want you to try something for me," he says softly, as if coaxing a frightened animal. "Try to keep an open mind."

Agreeing to that might be dangerous, but his hand is still on my arm, and I find myself unable—or unwilling—to move. I remind myself that I've committed to giving this my full effort, and finally I nod.

"I want you to take a few deep breaths," he tells me, his voice deeper than it was a moment ago. "Try to relax your body. You're going to need to grow a thicker skin if you want to improve."

"My skin is plenty thick."

That's such an obvious lie that he doesn't even bother responding.

"Close your eyes for a moment," he says. "Close your eyes and just breathe."

I'm not sure where he's going with this, but I obey. Right now, that sounds much better than having to face those intense eyes of his.

"Now let your shoulders relax," he says. "Try and let the tension flow out of your body."

Easier said than done. Especially when his fingers still rest on my arm. Has he forgotten he's touching me? *I* certainly notice, and it makes me nervous. My entire arm tingles at the contact, and I'm finding it hard to think straight.

"Very good," he says, even softer than before. "Keep breathing. Try to find your heartbeat."

What is this—some kind of New Age nonsense? But there's something almost hypnotic about his voice, something that makes me want to try to do as he says.

He's right—between the stress about keeping my job, the disaster that was last night, and my current embarrassment, my whole body is tense. His fingers on my arm aren't helping things, but I don't have the ability to ask him to take them away.

"Good," he says, and the approval in his voice sends a strange rush of pleasure through me. "Try to listen to your body. Feel your breathing. Feel your heart. What are they telling you?"

That this is ridiculous. That I'm in way over my head. That it would be a lot easier to calm down if I weren't so aware of his touch, of his body so close to mine, of the way his voice keeps changing subtly... *Oh, Felicia... what are you doing?*

"I don't understand," I tell him without opening my eyes. "What does this have to do with anything?"

"It has everything to do with it. You need to understand your own body if you want to understand how to control someone else's."

My eyes pop open. "*Control* someone else's?"

"What do you think seduction is?" he answers. "It's manipulation in its finest form. You say or do things with the express intent of inducing a specific response in someone else."

"I'm not trying to manipulate anyone," I insist.

"Of course you are. And that's how you need to think of this if you want to have any hope of being successful. Everything you say or do has an effect, and you must be in control of yourself first if you want to control how others respond to you." He regards me for a moment before adding, "Don't look at me like that. Everything we do, every human interaction, is based on this sort of communication. Most people just aren't conscious of it. Is it wrong to choose the alternative? To take responsibility for such things and make deliberate choices about how we engage with people?"

"I… I don't know."

"People use techniques like this in business all the time. Every successful businessman does it—it's what makes him a master negotiator, or helps him motivate his employees, or gives him the upper hand in a dispute. Seduction is no different. It merely adds a… *sexual* component to the negotiation."

"That makes it sound so, so…"—is it just me, or have his eyes gotten a little darker?—"*clinical.*"

"It may seem that way right now, but trust me— understanding the truth behind seduction does little to hamper the results. In fact, you'll find that it rather enhances them."

I've no doubt that he's had his fair share of practice at this particular art, so maybe he's right. And maybe it's better that we take a clinical approach to this. If I treat it like business, like something formal and impersonal, then it will help. Maybe I'll avoid spending the next week acting like a flustered idiot next to this man. I certainly didn't come here expecting a master class in manipulation—but while part of me wants to reject the very idea, if I'm being honest, the whole thing intrigues me more than I want to admit.

Though, admittedly, that would be significantly easier if he stopped touching me.

Roman must see the interest in my eyes, because he's smiling a little now. He wants me to be in control of my body, to be conscious of every move I make and the response it elicits in others. I have no doubt, looking at the man in front of me, that he is in perfect control of himself. Every movement, every expression, every glance seems measured and certain, a conscious choice. But I'm not sure he can fully understand *my* reactions to him. I hardly understand them myself. Is he aware of what his smile is doing to my insides? Is he aware that the touch of his fingers against my arm—the way he's just brushed his thumb against my skin—is sending a little shiver of sensation all the way through me?

His thumb moves a little more—back and forth this time, the smallest of caresses.

And then the waitress is back with my drink, and my heart leaps in relief.

"Are you two ready to order some food?" she asks us. She looks at me first.

"Uh, sure," I say, eager to take my attention away from Roman for a moment. I grab my menu—with my right hand, since Roman's fingers still rest on my left arm—and quickly scan the options.

"The roast duck salad," I say. Normally I'd go for the burger, but my stomach's a little queasy after last night—and, if I'm being honest, our conversation so far today.

"And for you?" the waitress asks Roman. I might be imagining things, but her tone sounds a little clipped, and her smile seems forced. I don't think she liked the way Roman made me change my drink order earlier.

But she smiles anyway, because she knows how customers react when she doesn't, I realize. *She knows if she's pleasant, at least on the surface, she'll probably get a better tip.* How she really feels doesn't matter. Maybe she made some assumptions about my relationship with Roman after our earlier conversation—hell, maybe she thinks his grip on my arm, light and gentle though it is, is further proof of her assumptions—but it doesn't matter. She behaves a certain way to get a certain result. Isn't that exactly the sort of everyday manipulation Roman was describing?

I don't even hear what he orders. But as soon as we're alone again, I'm once more aware of his attention on me. I'm aware of my breathing and my heartbeat as well, and both remind me of exactly how anxious, how uncertain I feel right now.

He leans toward me, and if we were on an actual date I'd assume he was about to kiss me. My stomach tightens, my whole body reacting to his sudden nearness. What is he doing?

There's a flash of something in his eyes, and the corner of his mouth tilts up. "How long have I been touching you?"

I pull back. "What?"

"How long have I been touching you?" His thumb brushes against my skin once more. "I know you're very much aware of it."

"I-I don't know," I say.

"I think you do," he says. "You were aware of the moment I touched you, and you've been aware of my fingers every moment they've remained on your arm. Am I wrong?"

I want to lie, but I know there's no point.

"You grabbed my arm when I tried to stand up," I say finally.

"Grabbed it?"

"No—not grabbed. I mean you took my arm. You just… just set your hand there."

He nods. "And then?"

And then *what*? I don't know where he's going with this, but I'd be squirming if his eyes weren't pinning me to my seat.

"And then you left it there," I say. "You didn't move it."

"I didn't move it at all?" His voice is even, objective, like he's quizzing me on my homework or something. Somehow, that makes this interrogation worse.

"You moved your fingers a couple of times," I say

after a moment.

"Which fingers?"

"I don't know."

"I think you do."

He's right, I do. But I'll be damned if I admit it to him. Cheeks flaming, I jerk my arm away from him, and he sits back, seemingly unperturbed.

"Touch is a very powerful tool," he says. "And very intimate. Humans are biologically designed to respond to it. It usually signals attraction or affection—or aggression, but we're not concerned with that here. The key to using it successfully in your case is to be subtle, as I suggested before. If you were to march up to a man right now and grab his arm or run your hand down his chest, he'd certainly get the hint. But most people aren't comfortable with such blatant attention from complete strangers—they don't trust it."

Oh, I understand that much. I don't trust *him* one bit.

"That's why you have to take your time," he continues. "Be slow but deliberate. Keep him guessing." He leans toward me, close enough for me to see the gold in his eyes. "Find an excuse to touch him that *isn't* openly sexual. I touched you when I was trying to coax you back into your seat, but maybe you'll brush your hand against his when you're passing him his drink, or maybe you'll touch his side when someone squeezes past you in a crowded bar and forces you to stand closer together. If you can *keep* touching him after the initial contact, even better. Pretend you've forgotten that you've left your hand on his sleeve. Don't make any quick or obvious motions to remind him that you're touching. He'll remember on his own. He'll start to wonder if *you* remember, whether the touch is intentional or a mistake, whether he should say something to you or pull away. That helps keep his focus entirely on you."

I don't know whether to be impressed or unnerved that he successfully tricked me in this way. It's so simple, and yet I know through my own experience that he's absolutely right. I can still feel the echoes of his fingers on my skin.

"It's easy enough to spot the signs of his response, assuming you know what to look for," he continues. "Dilated pupils, faster breathing, reddened cheeks. Classic signs of anxiety and arousal."

Arousal. He says it so casually. This time I can't help but shift in my seat. Oh, yes. He's very aware of what he's doing. He's not content to entertain himself with my flirting mishaps—he seems to enjoy making me squirm just as much.

But you need his help, I tell myself. *He knows what he's talking about.* If the last ten minutes have taught me anything, it's that if anyone can help me seduce Luca Fontaine or one of his brothers, it's this guy.

"Your first assignment will be to put this into practice before our lunch is over," he tells me.

"What? Here?" He can't be serious. It's one thing to try and flirt with guys in a dark bar—I mean, people go to those places to mingle. But we're in a fancy bistro. What does he expect me to do? Sit down at another table and pretend to pick lint off of some poor guy's shoulder?

"Don't look so frightened," he tells me. "I don't bite."

I suddenly get it.

"You," I say. "You're asking me to practice on you." That sounds even worse than trying this on some random dude. At least I'll never see a stranger ever again.

His eyes flash. "That's precisely what I'm asking."

"But you know what I'm trying to do," I protest. "The whole point is that I'm supposed to keep you guessing."

He gives a shrug. "But it will give me the chance to observe and critique you."

This sounds like a nightmare. But I came here seeking his help, and it's silly to refuse to even try.

"Fine," I tell him. "I'll see what I can do."

"Remember—subtlety is the key."

I'm not sure how to be subtle with him right next to me, waiting for me to act. He seems to be aware of everything I feel, of each and every reaction I have to him before I'm even aware of them myself. How am I supposed to pull this off?

The waitress reappears with our food, and I jump.

She shoots me a concerned look, and I force myself to smile at her. I can't explain to her why I'm actually so nervous. I'm not sure I can adequately explain it to myself.

We eat in silence for a few moments. Already, my mind is racing. When am I supposed to start? How am I supposed to make that first touch look like an accident? Is this all just part of some game for him? But I force the panic down and focus on my salad, waiting for him to speak.

As time goes on, it's clear he has no intention of breaking the silence. Every five minutes or so, his phone will buzz on the table, and occasionally he'll pick it up and respond to whatever messages or emails have popped up on his screen. For a few minutes, I'd almost managed to forget how big of a deal this guy is—and that his work doesn't end on the weekends. Roman Everet wasn't born to riches. He has a reputation for being ruthless, for working around the clock to build what is quickly becoming an empire. And yet he's sitting here at lunch with me, trying to teach me how to flirt like a normal human being. I guess even a workaholic needs his distractions—though I'd have thought someone of Roman's means and reputation would have preferred higher-end forms of entertainment. My ineptitude must *really* amuse him.

Or maybe, just maybe, he's doing this because he thinks it might actually help me score an interview with one of the Fontaines. If I pull this off, if I get *Celebrity Spark* an exclusive cover story, then it definitely kicks off his ownership of the magazine with a bang. It's in his best interest to tutor me to success, to turn me into a ruthless reporter who can seduce secrets out of celebrities. I'm an investment.

I'm letting this idea sink in when he finally speaks again.

"Close your eyes," he says.

I swallow. "Again?"

"Yes."

I do as he asks, curious as to what sort of lesson he's going to teach me now. I hear him shift in his seat, hear him lean toward me, and my whole body braces for his touch, or for the rich tones of his voice in my ear.

But he doesn't touch me, and when he speaks, he's not close enough for me to feel his breath against my ear.

"I want you to answer a few questions for me," he says.

I nod, trying to push down the odd sense of disappointment I feel. "Okay."

His phone buzzes on the table, but he seems to ignore it.

"What color is my shirt?" he asks.

I'm not sure what sort of questions I was expecting, but certainly something that was a little more relevant to our situation at hand.

"Blue," I say after thinking for a moment. "Grayish-blue."

"Very good. And my pants?"

"Dark gray."

"And my watch?"

That one stumps me. I rack my brain, trying to remember what his watch looked like, but I can't. I don't remember a watch at all.

"I don't know," I tell him finally.

"What about my eyes?"

My face goes hot. "Uh… hazel, mostly."

"Mostly?"

My fingers find the edge of the tablecloth again. "They're greener today."

"Mm. And what did I order to eat?"

That question seems a little out of left field, and anyway, I never heard him order. Heck, even though we've been eating for a full ten minutes now, I've been so focused on figuring out how to touch him I never even looked at his plate.

"I…" I should probably just guess. "Something meaty, maybe?"

"Meaty?"

Hearing the word repeated by him makes it sound obscene. But he doesn't give me a chance to wallow in embarrassment.

"Was I holding the fork in my right or left hand?"

"I… have no idea."

"When I touched you, did I use my right or left hand?"

"R-right," I say, properly flustered now.

"Felicia," he says, "open your eyes."

I do, and find myself looking right into his. My gaze drops quickly to my salad.

"You need to be more observant," he says. "And not just of things that arouse you."

Arouse. There's that word again, and with it, the stomach-churning rush of humiliation.

"In addition to maintaining control of yourself," he says, "you need to pay attention to him, to his response to you and your advances. You can't let yourself get distracted by your own reactions to him."

If lightning ever felt like striking me down, now would be a pretty good time. My mind whirls, trying to move past what he's implying—that I'm *aroused* by him, and that he *knows* I'm aroused by him.

"How does the color of his shirt have anything to do with his response?" I say quickly.

"It doesn't, not directly. But what a man is wearing can tell you a lot about the man and what he might—or might not—respond *to*. Take, for example, the man you approached last night. If you'd taken a moment to observe him more closely, to notice what he was wearing on his left hand, you might have saved yourself a lot of trouble." His fingers thrum against the table. "Not that a wedding band automatically means your efforts will be fruitless, but I'm not sure you're at that level just yet."

"Point taken," I say without looking at him.

"Noticing these things might take a bit of practice at first," he says. "Most of us pick up on some body language cues subconsciously, but as a rule, we're out of practice. Technology has dulled our skills—and even made such observation impossible in some cases. You can't see someone's expression when you're talking to them over the phone. You can't watch what they do with their hands when they send you and email or text. Of course, such technologies can help you tremendously if you're inexperienced or suffer from certain social anxieties—they make it much easier to hide your insecurities. But they're a disadvantage if you're a seasoned negotiator. Being able to read other people in person is key."

I steal a glance at him, but his expression is as inscrutable as always. My emotions might be plain for him—or anyone—to see, but Roman is a whole other animal. And, I suspect, Luca Fontaine is no different.

"What if someone is hard to read?" I ask. "I mean, I can look at his clothes and his food and all that, but... Luca Fontaine is an actor. He fakes emotions for a living. How am I supposed to know what he's really feeling?"

"With practice. Everyone has their tells."

"I have a week. And then one night of actual interaction. How am I supposed to practice?"

"With what you have," he says, spreading his hands. "Tell me, what do you know about me from what you observe here?"

He's put me on the spot again, and I quickly shove another bite of salad into my mouth, hoping to give myself a moment to think. My eyes roam over him, from his watch—which is on his right wrist, and made of silver or platinum—to his shirt, to his face. That ridiculously attractive face, with a jaw that could cut glass and that irresistible indentation in his chin. He's watching me study him, and though I'm only doing it because he told me to, it still makes me feel like I've been caught staring.

"In a normal situation," he says, clearly enjoying himself, "you might not want to study him so openly. It will show your interest, certainly, but it might scare him. However, since we're learning here, we can make an exception."

I want to point out that *he* stares more than anyone I've ever met, but I don't. I let my gaze slide over him one more time—trying not to blush any more than I already am—before I return my focus to my lunch.

"You're dressed well," I say. That's safe enough. "You're obviously wealthy. And you're perfectly groomed. You put thought into how you present yourself. You pay attention to detail."

Roman nods and gestures for me to go on. "And?"

And... "You're obviously a busy man." I jut my chin

in the direction of his phone. "But you're focused on what's in front of you."

"And?"

"And…" I'm not sure where he wants me to go with this.

"What does this tell you about me as a potential target for seduction?"

I twist my napkin in my lap, thinking.

"That you're a man who likes to be in control," I say finally. "That you wouldn't easily let a woman seduce you. If anything, you'd probably prefer it to be the other way around."

His eyes have darkened slightly, and I suspect I've hit the nail on the head. "Go on."

"You… you're attractive. And you have money. So you probably have women approaching you all the time. Beautiful women. You could have your pick of any one you wanted. And as I said, you like to be in charge, so you like having the power to choose."

He's no longer laughing, but there's an odd look on his face as he regards me. Did I insult him?

After a moment, he leans toward me.

"Tell me, then," he says, "how would you go about trying to seduce me?"

I knew this question was coming, but that doesn't make me any more prepared for it.

"I-I would be subtle," I tell him after a moment, though I know that's too obvious. "Pretend I wasn't interested in you at all. Not in *that* way, I mean. Obviously I'd have to show *some* interest or have some excuse to interact with you…"

When I don't go on, he raises an eyebrow. "Is that all?"

"I guess… I guess I'd need an excuse to get close to you," I say. "Maybe something work related. Or… or something else non-sexual. I don't know. Isn't this what you're supposed be teaching me?"

"Understand, I'm not doing this to put you on the spot," he says, straightening. "I'm doing this because no matter which of the Fontaines you approach, you're going to be facing a similar challenge. These are men who have their pick of women. It's not going to be as simple as seducing an average guy in a bar."

And I can't even do that.

"Well," I whisper, "what am I supposed to do, then?"

"You'll have to figure that out as we go along," he says. "For starters, though, you might begin with that assignment I gave you earlier. You might have touched me a dozen different times by now, and yet you haven't."

Shit. I'd forgotten all about that.

"I was waiting for the right moment," I mumble.

"And if you wait too long, you'll miss your chance completely."

What does he want me to do? One minute he's

telling me to take my time, to be subtle about it, and the next he's accusing me of not being aggressive enough. There's no winning with this guy.

"Don't overthink it," he tells me.

Don't overthink it. And yet he also tells me I need to be paying more attention to him. To be analyzing his appearance and movements. My head is throbbing just thinking about all the things I'm supposed to be doing—though admittedly, my lingering hangover isn't helping. Neither is the way he keeps looking at me—doesn't Mr. Observant realize that it's harder to concentrate when his eyes are boring into me like that?

I wiggle in my seat again. Beneath the table, my leg bumps against his, and I quickly pull it away. Out of the corner of my eye, I see Roman smile, the way he always seems to when he can tell he's making me nervous. And something clicks in my head.

I've been going about this entirely the wrong way.

He's right—I've had a dozen different chances to touch him, a dozen opportunities to "accidentally" instigate contact between the two of us. I can play to his expectations, act the way he expects me to act, and use that as my opening. I squirm in my seat once more, but this time it's not an involuntary act of anxiety. My leg is touching his now. Just slightly—in fact, I can hardly feel the fabric of his slacks against the bare skin of my knee—and I'm not sure he notices it at all. If he does, he gives nothing away. But *I'm touching him.*

"How do I keep from overthinking it?" I ask, twisting my napkin around in my hands, trying to keep myself under control.

"Again, it just takes practice," he says. "But that's why we're here."

"Oh. Okay." He still hasn't given me any sign that he's noticed my attempt to complete his assignment to touch him, but maybe that's on purpose. Maybe he wants to give me the chance to pretend this is real, that he doesn't know exactly what I'm doing.

"This isn't an exact science," Roman says. "It will become more natural as time goes on. But I have a feeling you will more than rise to the challenge."

Something about the way he says that sends a tremor of response through me. Is this his way of acknowledging my touch beneath the table? Or something else?

"So I'm not a lost cause?" I say. My voice trembles on the last two words—something that isn't entirely unintentional.

"Not in the least," he says, and there's something in his eyes that makes me think he means much more than he says.

I grab my fork. His leg is still touching my leg, mine still touching his. How long am I supposed to keep this up? Is he waiting for me to do something else? To press closer? To brush my foot against his?

How would you go about trying to seduce me? His question burns in my mind, keeping my entire body on edge. He and I both know I could never seduce someone like him, and pretending to try makes me feel ridiculous. But I'm trying—whatever else he thinks of me, he can't deny that I'm doing my best to heed his lessons. My leg remains perfectly still beneath the table, touching-but-not-touching, and I do my best to breathe. I'm so aware of everything: of the texture of his pant leg against my skin—so much rougher than the pants he was wearing last night—of the heat of his leg through the fabric, of the easy way he continues to eat, as if nothing is happening between us at all. Maybe, on his end, nothing is. He's so calm, so collected, and I'm as nervous as I was when he was touching me. Isn't it supposed to be the other way around?

The rest of the meal is torture. I don't move my leg an inch. We make small talk as we finish our food, and it's hard for me to offer anything but short answers. I'm on edge, still hyper-aware of every move he makes, and he still acts as if nothing has changed.

When the waitress brings the bill, he grabs it before I even have a chance.

"This is a business meeting," he says. "And that means the business pays for it."

I almost laugh at that. He's right, of course. But this—whatever this meal was—didn't feel like business at all.

But I don't say anything. And he never says a single word about my leg, though his knee remains right against mine until the moment we rise to leave.

5

SIX DAYS

THE FOLLOWING DAY, I'm still not sure what to make of my lunch with Roman. I have no idea whether my first "lesson" went well or went poorly—or even if my self-appointed teacher believes I've made any progress.

What I *do* know is that I need to continue to up my game before the *Hollywood Saves!* event, so I've taken it upon myself to do some extra research on my potential targets. It's not unusual for me to spend my Sundays with a pile of celebrity news magazines, or combing the popular gossip blogs for the week's biggest stories, but today my reading is a little more focused. Today is all about the Fontaines.

I've been intrigued by the Fontaine family since I was a little girl, since the very first time I saw a picture of Giovanna and Charles Fontaine on the cover of a magazine at the supermarket. They looked so beautiful, so glamorous—the perfect, classic Hollywood couple.

After that, I inhaled everything I could find about them—every magazine article, every biography, every movie he'd directed or she'd starred in. And my fascination soon spread from the happy couple to include the rest of the family tree as well. And trust me—that is one huge, complex, and utterly fascinating tree.

Charles is the youngest child of Nicholas Fontaine (yes, *that* Nicholas Fontaine, the one with every filmmaking award in existence), and Giovanna was at the height of her acting career when they met on the set of a film Charles was directing. Their marriage wasn't the first major relationship for either of them—before meeting Charles, Giovanna was in a passionate five-year affair with Arron Rex, the rock god. And Charles had a famous relationship of his own back then—he was married to Lavinia Hampton, the tennis star who died tragically in a car wreck two years after their wedding.

Still with me? Yeah, I know it's a lot to take in. These Hollywood dynasties can get pretty complicated, and this one's got a lot more branches than most of them. But don't worry—I won't go into detail about Charles' three older siblings and *their* kids, even though I find those parts of the family just as fascinating. Honestly, these days most people only really care about Charles and Giovanna and their sons.

And oh, their sons.

When two beautiful people like Charles Fontaine

and Giovanna Agosti come together, they naturally make beautiful babies. They brought four—yes *four*—beautiful Fontaine sons into this world (for which we mere mortals will be forever grateful): Dante, Luca, Raphael, and Orlando. All exceedingly attractive, all fond of making trouble. And the world can't seem to get enough.

When I was younger, I used to pretend that I was one of their kids, too. I'm roughly the same age as Luca, after all. I'd dream that I was part of that glamorous family, that I was beautiful and rich and famous just like them. Giovanna and Charles seemed so much in love—and so different from my own parents, who divorced when I was eleven. At home I was an ordinary girl from a broken family. In my head, I was part of the perfect family. If not as a flesh-and-blood daughter, than perhaps by marriage—I'll totally confess to having some fantasies about those Fontaine boys.

And now, some years later, I have to try and seduce one for real. My cheeks go hot just thinking about it.

Luca Fontaine is the second of Charles and Giovanna's children together, and he's arguably the most famous. He's the only one to go full movie star (so far at least), and he's managed to snag roles in a few huge blockbusters, including the upcoming *Cataclysm: Earth*. He's got dirty-blond hair—the same shade as his mother's when she was his age—and the sort of bad-boy, devastatingly gorgeous looks that make girls want to throw their panties at him. I've seen pictures of his smile that made me want to weep. Seriously. The idea of flirting with him, of touching him? Makes me so nervous I think I might be sick.

You could always go after one of his brothers instead, I remind myself. The other Fontaine brothers appear in the tabloids just as often as Luca. They're certainly big enough to satisfy Roman's terms.

And they've certainly got their own charms, too. Luca might be the movie star, but his older brother Dante is actually more of my type. If Luca is a golden god of a man, then Dante is the dark, brooding Lord of the Damned. He has dark hair and eyes like his father and grandfather, and there's a fierce intelligence about him. Shadows, too—I've often wondered what secrets he's hiding behind that burning gaze. He's never done much acting, but rather followed in his uncle's footsteps and pursued screenwriting. But in spite of his efforts to stay off the screen, he still has quite the fan base. In all of my silly daydreams, he was usually the one I imagined marrying.

And then there's Raphael, the third son. He's all over the place—one day he's showing up in a movie, the next he's competing in a motocross competition, and next he's the face of an international modeling campaign. He's the dark horse of the bunch—and also the one with the longest criminal record.

Finally there's Orlando, who's currently taking a

leave of absence from his grad program at Harvard. Last year he directed an independent movie that was panned at all of the festivals, and ever since, he's been gallivanting around the world—one week a photo emerges of him in Monaco, the next in Bali. I suspect he won't be at *Hollywood Saves!* with the rest of his family, but you never know. I need to be prepared to flirt with any of them.

I sigh as I flip through my magazine. Every single one of the Fontaine brothers is gossip gold. And every single one is completely out of my league—even if I'm only trying to get an interview.

My research on the family does little to convince me otherwise. More than once I have to push the magazines aside and close my eyes and fight back the panic, but as soon as I have myself under control again, I dive back in. If I'm going to have *any* shot at this, I need to learn as much as possible about these brothers—not that I didn't know much about them before, mind you. But now I find myself paying attention to different things— like the women who appear in the tabloids with them.

As Emilia Torres told me, Luca does seem to like dark-haired women. But I'd have to drop a few pants sizes and go up a few bra sizes to look like any of the women he's dated.

In the middle of the afternoon, my cell phone beeps with an incoming text message.

It's from Roman.

Meet me at the Celebrity Spark offices ASAP for your next lesson.

I suppose I shouldn't be surprised that Roman is at the office on a Sunday. I am, however, surprised that he should want to see me again so soon. I must entertain him more than I thought, if he's so eager to continue. Or he's *really* determined to procrastinate on his "real" work—whatever it is that media moguls do when they aren't buying out magazines or making employees feel awkward.

And aroused, I remind myself. Roman made it clear he knew exactly what he was doing to me yesterday. And I, the anxious, flustered mess that I am, didn't have the first clue about how to fight down those feelings. *Better now with Roman than Saturday with one of the Fontaines*, I tell myself. If I can't control my body's reaction around my boss, how am I supposed to do so around some of the most attractive men in Hollywood? Guys I've been idolizing since I was a child?

A second text message from Roman comes through.

It is absolutely crucial that you get here as quickly as possible. Please reply and confirm that you have re-ceived this message and will be here within half an hour.

He's not very patient today, is he? I shoot off an affirmative response and climb off of my bed. Roman's only given me thirty minutes to get to the office—that's not a lot of time. As anyone from L.A. will tell you, traffic in this town is a bitch, even on Sundays. And I haven't even bothered to get dressed yet today. But if my hours of research have shown me anything, it's that I have work to do, and I can't risk missing any lessons. I toss on jeans and a blouse, run a brush through my hair, and jog down to my car.

I make it to our building with three minutes to spare. The elevator seems to be stuck, so I take the stairs instead. By the time I make it to our floor, I'm out of breath, but I stumble into the conference room right on time.

Roman's in the middle of something. At first I think he's talking to his assistant—who's going through some papers at the end of the long table—but then I spot the headset clipped to Roman's ear and realize he's on a call. For a moment, they don't seem to notice me in the doorway, and I wonder if I should step out. But then Roman looks up, right into my eyes.

"Steve, I'm going to need to call you back," he says.

His assistant seems to realize that this is his cue to leave. He stacks all of the files in front of him and gathers them up, and he shoots me a strange glance as he leaves the room. I suddenly wonder if I should be worried.

When I turn back to Roman, I find him looking me up and down. He frowns slightly.

"Did you run all the way here?" he asks.

"Just up the stairs." I grab my hair, suddenly aware of how much of a mess I must look. My hair tends to go frizzy under the best of conditions, and when I reach up, I realize that sprint up the stairs didn't help. I quickly comb my fingers through the strands, trying to tame them and wishing I'd had the foresight to grab a hair tie or at least a couple of bobby pins.

Roman has risen from his seat, and he walks slowly over to me while I try to make myself presentable. When he gets to me, he reaches out—and my breath catches as his hand moves past my breast and under my arm, as if he means to draw me toward him.

Instead, half a second later, his hand draws back, a polka-dotted sock clutched between his thumb and forefinger.

I'm pretty sure I let out a gasp. I grabbed this blouse out of a basket of clean laundry—I hadn't thought to check it for any static clingers. My face burns as I snatch the sock out of his hand and shove it in my purse.

"Turn around," he says.

I do. And then I feel the brush of his fingers against my back, the shift of fabric against my skin as he peels something else off of my blouse. Did I bring my whole damn laundry pile with me?

This time, though, it's so much worse than a sock. When I turn around, I find him holding a pair of my underwear between his fingers. And not just any underwear—a lacy, wine-red thong. I grab it so quickly

I nearly take off his hand.

"I was in a hurry," I mumble, cheeks flaming. "You didn't give me much time to get here."

"You still might have been a little more professional," he says, then shakes his head. "But it doesn't matter now. We don't have enough time to worry about it. Come on."

I follow him back toward the elevators. "Why? Where are we going?"

"I've gotten a tip that Dante Fontaine is having an early dinner meeting at Hallevern's. We need to hurry if we don't want to miss him."

"Wait—*what*? You're taking me to meet Dante Fontaine?"

"More or less. I'm taking you to practice everything I taught you yesterday."

The bottom drops out of my stomach. "You want me to try and *seduce* Dante Fontaine? Today? Right now?"

"I want you to try."

Oh, God. "You—you could've told me in the text. I would've… dressed up." I wasn't prepared for this, not today. "I'm not ready."

"That doesn't mean it isn't good practice. Come on, I'll drive."

He doesn't even try to convince me that I have the skills to pull this off. We both know that I don't, not yet. Does he just want to give himself a good laugh?

What a sick bastard.

I'm feeling pretty sick myself, but I follow him down to his car. I can't believe we're doing this. I can't believe that in a few minutes, I might be face-to-face with Dante Fontaine and trying to... what? Flirt? Get information out of him? I thought I had plenty of time to come up with a game plan before *Hollywood Saves!* Now, I'm so nervous that I'm shaking.

"How... how do you even know he's there?" I ask.

"As I said, I received a tip. A man doesn't get very far in this town without his fair share of contacts."

I should have known. Most people who work in media have developed a network of "sources" and other contacts throughout the years—second-cousins of celebrities, club owners, drivers, and others who keep reporters and other interested parties in the know in exchange for a few dollars in their pocket. I've asked all of my friends and even my brother to keep their eyes and ears open for me—even talking to a waitress who once waited on a pop star might lead me to an important connection. But someone like Roman is probably operating on an entirely different level—he wouldn't concern himself with working-class contacts. Why, he's probably dealing directly with PR firms and managers and the people who are *really* running this industry.

He seems to read my mind.

"*Celebrity Spark* isn't a tabloid," he says. "It's a celebrity news magazine. I don't want anyone confusing the two. And I don't want us chasing after ridiculous rumors or harassing celebrities—I want *them* to come to *us* when they want or need publicity. The industry runs on visibility, and those with successful careers use that to their advantage. It's our job to give them that visibility under terms that are agreeable to all parties, and we do that by forming relationships—first with those managing the celebrities' careers, and then with the celebrities themselves."

"And that's where the seduction comes in?"

He smiles. "That's one way of going about it, yes. I want celebrities to find it a pleasure to work with us."

Roman must have a really bad memory because I'm pretty sure my recent attempts at flirting haven't been exactly pleasurable for those involved. If he's looking for someone to be awkward and pathetic, though, I'm his girl.

At least you haven't harassed anyone, I tell myself. *Celebrity Spark* had its share of over-zealous reporters in the past—in fact, the week I was hired the entire office was abuzz with gossip about a man named Asher Julian, a former *Celebrity Spark* employee who'd been fired after getting arrested for assault. I've never been interested in stalking celebrities or invading their privacy—I want the environment that Roman described, one that involves all of us working together.

Actually achieving that, though, is another thing

altogether. I can't believe I'm about to meet Dante Fontaine. Right now. When I desperately need a brush and when minutes ago I had a thong stuck to my back.

We've reached Roman's car—which is a Ferrari, of course—and I've started to sweat in a bunch of awkward places. I don't say a word as I slide into the passenger's seat, but I immediately flip down the mirror and inspect my appearance. I don't look *bad*, not really. But I definitely don't look like I hoped to look the first time I met Dante Fontaine—or anyone famous, for that matter. Hell, when I had my interview with Emilia Torres, I spent almost three hours getting ready. I wasn't even trying to seduce *her*.

Maybe you're worrying over nothing, I tell myself. *Maybe he'll be gone by the time we get there.* How long does it take someone to eat?

And that gives me an idea.

"Hey," I say. "Can you stop at a drugstore or something? I'll run in and grab some lipstick and a comb."

He doesn't answer immediately. His eyes are on the road—which is probably a good idea, considering how fast he peeled out of the garage. After a moment, he shakes his head.

"Not enough time," he says. "Don't worry. You look fine."

That's not what he implied back at the office, but it doesn't matter either way. My plan to stall didn't work, and the knot in my stomach tightens.

"What am I supposed to do?" I ask. "What am I supposed to say to him?"

"You remember our lesson yesterday, don't you?" he says.

"Yeah, but that doesn't help much. I have no reason to go up to him while he's eating. Unless you want me to open with the fact that I'm with *Celebrity Spark.*"

"Do you think he'd respond well to that?"

"No."

"Then you'll have to come up with a better opening line."

"You're the one who's supposed to be teaching me what to do," I remind him. I'm in a full panic now. My fingers are squeezing the handle on the door, as if somehow the car might save me. Who knows? Maybe we'll get a flat tire or something.

"As I told you before," Roman says, "there isn't exactly a step-by-step process to this."

"So you can't give me any advice? Anything?"

He's silent a moment, then says, "I think you're smart enough to make a reasonable attempt on your own."

That is just ridiculous. "Have you seen me? Or were you watching some other girl make a laughingstock of herself in the bar the other night? You've seen what I can do, and it isn't good. We both know that."

Another long silence from him, and then, "I've also seen that you're a quick learner. And you're more resourceful than you give yourself credit for."

At any other time, I would've enjoyed that compliment, especially from him. Right now, though, it only makes my panic worse.

"I can't do this."

"You can. Think of it as a challenge."

Why do people always say that when they're trying to convince you to do something you know you can't do? But it's clear that no amount of begging will get me out of this, not on Roman Everet's watch. I throw another glance in the mirror and run my fingers through my hair again. Up ahead, Hallevern's restaurant has already come into view. We definitely made good time.

Please, please, please, don't let him be there, I pray. Maybe he's a fast eater. Or maybe Roman's tip was incorrect. I'm due for some good karma from the universe, aren't I?

But any hopes I have of escaping this "lesson" are dashed when I see the photographers lingering outside the restaurant's doors. There are only half a dozen of them, but it's clear they're waiting for someone. A couple of them appear to be trying to snap pictures through the glass.

I'm nearly hyperventilating. I try to calm myself, try to breathe deeply, but I only succeed in giving myself the hiccups.

Maybe he won't be able to find parking, I think. Everyone knows how hard it is to get a space in this part of town. And Roman can't just kick me out of the car and expect me to go in on my own—not if he intends to pass this off as any sort of lesson, and certainly not if he's doing this for his own amusement. If he tries it, I'm running off and calling a cab to take me back home.

But as luck would have it—and it looks like I'm having some horrible, rotten luck right now—a car pulls out of its spot just as Roman turns onto the cross street. I hold my breath as he parallel parks, debating whether it makes more sense to lock myself in the car or to hop out and make a break for it. Both of those options sound completely childish, but I'm terrified enough that I don't care.

Almost.

If I've learned one thing about this job—and this industry in general—it's that guts go a long way. Audacity and shamelessness will get you a lot further than exquisite writing skills or perfect grammar. This is yet another chance to prove myself to the magazine's new owner. If he sees that I'm willing to try, to step outside of my comfort zone in the name of getting a major story, then maybe he'll let me stay, whether or not I actually get the results he wants. He admitted himself that I learn quickly. I just have to prove that I'm willing to try.

Still, my legs feel like lead when Roman finally kills the engine. He gets out and goes over to the parking meter, and it takes all of my energy to drag myself out of the car.

I can do this, I tell myself. *I can walk up to Dante Fontaine and… and… I don't know what.*

I smooth out my clothes, and I do a quick search for any stray socks or panties that Roman might have missed. My fingers go back to my hair, desperately trying to tug out any tangles or creases before I meet what is arguably one of the sexiest men in the world. A man who've I've spent years dreaming about. *A man who will probably look right past me, as most men do.*

I'm so absorbed in trying to make myself presentable that I don't notice Roman is back until he's right in front of me. His shiny black shoes come into view next to the crack on the sidewalk where I'm staring, and when I lift my gaze, there's concern in his hazel eyes.

"You'll do fine," he says, almost gently.

My eyes drop back to that crack on the sidewalk. "I'm not ready for this," I say, my voice no more than a whisper.

"Yes you are. And stop worrying about how you look."

Something in his voice makes me look up, but that's a mistake. I didn't quite register how very close he was to me, and those eyes seem even more intense when his face is so near. My breath freezes in my chest. I glance away again, and my fingers resume their frantic combing of my hair.

Suddenly his hand is on mine, gently pulling my

fingers away from my frizzy waves.

"I shouldn't have said anything about your appearance back at the office," he says. "I've made you second-guess yourself."

There's a tenderness in his voice that I've never heard before. But that's not nearly as shocking as the fact that he's started touching my hair, arranging the thick locks hanging down around my shoulders.

"I… It wasn't anything you said," I tell him without looking up from the sidewalk. It's my previous awful attempts at seduction that have made me second-guess myself. "I just wasn't prepared for this."

"Yes, I see I should have been clearer about our plans for today when I texted you," he says, though he doesn't sound the least bit apologetic. "Very careless of me."

I let out a small laugh. "It would've been nice to at least known to put on some mascara."

"You don't need makeup."

"I wasn't fishing for a compliment. It's just…" It's just that I spent the entire afternoon analyzing the sort of women Dante Fontaine dates, and while he doesn't appear to have a specific "type" like his brother Luca, every girl who's appeared on his arm has been absolutely gorgeous. And at least had on some lip gloss when they were out in public together.

"You don't need makeup," he repeats. "Not with those eyes and those lips."

My heart skitters and my eyes snap back up to his. But he's looking at my hair, which he's still touching, still arranging around my face. He must still be trying to make me feel better. Before I can come up with an appropriate response, he's speaking again.

"I think being fresh-faced is an asset in this situation," he says. "This is your chance to trust entirely in your own merits. There's no hiding behind alcohol or lipstick or a low-cut shirt. Trust me, those things matter little when you do this right. A woman in sweats can be just as enticing as one dressed to the nines."

"That assumes she knows what she's doing."

His fingers slow their movements in my hair, and if I didn't know any better, I'd almost think he was caressing the strands. Yesterday's lesson pops into my mind. *Is he doing this on purpose? Touching me longer than he needs to?* He's standing so close to me. Anyone passing on the street would think we were lovers, the way he's touching me. But his hazel eyes give nothing away. His gaze is intense, but there's no tenderness there—in fact, he looks like he's assessing some sort of work problem. Which, I suppose, he is.

"I'm not going to demand that you do this," he says suddenly, dropping his hand. "It is not, nor has it ever been, my intent to force you to do anything you don't want to do. But you've expressed an interest in learning, and you have the chance to do that right now, if you'll take it."

This wasn't what I expected him to say. And when he puts it like *that*, I don't really see how I can refuse.

My heartbeat is still erratic, my breathing uneven and shallow. I'm sure he notices.

"Okay," I tell him. "Let's do this."

Roman's mouth curls up—his first smile of the day—and he gives me a nod. "Lead the way."

I turn and head back toward the restaurant before I have a chance to lose my nerve. Roman follows, a shadow on my heels. I'm not sure whether his presence reassures me or makes this harder. I can almost still feel his fingers in my hair, touching me so delicately, so deliberately. Better not to think about that right now or I'll never work up the courage to approach Dante Fontaine.

When we get to the front of the restaurant, Roman reaches around me and grabs the door.

"I thought I'd get us a table," he says in a low voice. "It will be easier to watch you, and you'll have a place to sit if you need a moment to collect yourself. Besides, I haven't eaten since breakfast."

I nod, hardly registering his words. My eyes are on the photographers we just passed. One of them is leaning against the wall and smoking a cigarette, and his eyes rise to mine. I quickly look away and follow Roman into the restaurant.

I can do this, I tell myself. I just need a game plan. I don't want Dante Fontaine to think I'm some sort of creep. He's probably just trying to have a meal in peace.

When I spot him, though, I realize things are going to be even more complicated than I originally anticipated.

"He's not alone," I hiss at Roman, grabbing his arm.

And indeed, Dante Fontaine is dining with not one but *two* other people. Both men, thank goodness—I don't know what I would have done if I'd had to interrupt a date or something—but that's two more pairs of eyes, two more complications.

"I told you it was a dinner meeting," Roman murmurs to me, his hand closing over mine. "You're a smart girl. I'm sure you'll think of something."

He leads me toward the hostess stand, his hand still wrapped around mine on his arm. It's almost like we're on a date. You know, if a date involved hitting on a celebrity.

It's not until the hostess turns to lead us to a table that I regain my senses enough to peel my arm away from Roman's. Being that close to him isn't helping. I think I notice the hint of a smile on his lips when I pull back from him, but I don't have the ability to analyze that right now. My eyes are locked on Dante Fontaine.

And, oh God, I don't think I'll ever be able to look away again. Even across the restaurant—Dante and his party are seated at the far back, I suspect by request—the mere sight of him makes me go breathless. He's as gorgeous in person as he is in any of his pictures—more so, maybe. He has the kind of looks that draw your eye as soon as you set foot in the room. If I were a cartoon character, my eyes would be bugging out of my head right now.

He's wearing glasses—*real* glasses, not sunglasses—but they don't do anything to detract from his stunning appearance. If anything, they enhance it, adding to the fierce, dark intelligence that always drew me to him in photographs. There's something mysterious about him, something about him that makes me think he might be as intense as Roman—perhaps more so. But while the glasses might say "sexy college professor," his physique says something different altogether. His shoulders are as broad as those of his action-star brother. This man is no stranger to the gym. Or, I imagine, to carrying women up the stairs to his bedroom, or to pushing them up against the wall, or…

I push that thought away quickly. My pulse has quickened just looking at him, and I'm feeling suddenly light-headed. How am I going to pull this off if I let myself go all giggly and start imagining him naked?

He *would* look good naked, though, what with the way his arm muscles bulge…

Nope. Not going there. Not now at least. Tonight, when I'm safely alone in my apartment, I can let my imagination run wild. Right now, I'm just going to—

Suddenly my foot catches on the leg of a chair, and I pitch forward. Strong hands grab me—Roman's hands—before I land on my face, but I'm still a little stunned as he helps me back to my feet.

"Try to keep your head," Roman says. He's standing close to me, pretending to help—one of his arms is around my waist, and the other hand is on my arm—but I know he just wants to make sure the hostess doesn't hear. He tilts his head down close to my ear. "You're quite attracted to him, aren't you?"

No, shit. It's only Dante Fontaine over there. What the hell did he expect?

"He's just another man," Roman says in my ear. "We're all the same, at the end of the day. Fairly simple creatures."

"I… I'll try to remember that," I say softly.

Roman doesn't respond. Instead, he leads me after the hostess, who's waiting next to an open table for us. Roman keeps his arm around my waist the entire way there, as if he's afraid I might tip over again at any moment. It's strange, having his arm so tightly around me, and it doesn't help my lightheadedness.

My eyes skim past Roman's arms back to Dante and his two companions. Neither of the other men is anyone famous—at least as far as I can tell from here. They look like ordinary guys. One of them, like Dante, has his laptop out on the table, and the other has a notebook. Maybe going over Dante's latest script. Or making changes for *Cataclysm: Earth*—which Dante penned himself.

Not that it really matters *why* they're here. It's not like I can just waltz up and start asking questions about it.

Roman guides me into my seat, then takes the chair just next to mine. It gives him a perfect view of Dante's table.

"Try not to stare," he murmurs as he puts his napkin in his lap. "He might notice. And that will make your task more difficult."

He's right, but it's hard to be sensible when there's a creature of inhumanly good looks in the same restaurant. I bury my face in my menu and try to form a plan.

Beneath the table, my leg is shaking. I don't even notice until Roman's fingers come down on my knee, stilling me. A jolt of sensation shoots up my leg, but I hardly have time to catch my breath before he draws back his hand again.

"Remember what I told you about trying to relax," he says. "Close your eyes if you need to. Breathe deeply a few times."

I obey, if only so I don't have to look him in the eyes. It would be easier if he were sitting on the other side of the table, away from me. This is hard enough without Roman making me all fluttery and confused.

"Don't worry about getting an interview today," he says, and I hear him lean closer to me. "Just talk to him. Practice what I've taught you. You need to grow more comfortable talking to men you find attractive." He touches my hand gently, and I try not to react. He's close enough for me to smell him. For me to feel the heat of his body. For him to kiss me, if he were so inclined.

But he doesn't. He sits back, and I open my eyes again and try to regain some control over my thoughts.

I don't need to get an interview, I tell myself. *I just need to talk to him. I can do that. Baby steps.*

Dante's table is over by the bathroom. That at least gives me an excuse to walk over there—and a place to run if I start to freak out.

But I won't freak out. I can do this. I just need to play to my strengths. Which are… what? Being a nervous wreck? Having no game whatsoever? Tripping over chairs because I can't take my eyes off of the insanely attractive celebrity on the other side of the room?

Actually, now that I think about it, I can use *that* to my advantage. I think.

I don't tell Roman what I'm doing. In fact, I don't say a word to him at all, just slide out of my seat. I can't risk looking at his face. Those hazel eyes of his are too intense, too unsettling. I might not have a level head right now, but I won't do anything that might make the butterflies in my stomach even worse.

I stride across the restaurant toward the bathrooms. *You've got this*, I tell myself. But why, oh why did my first real-life brush with a Fontaine have to be with *Dante*? The one who was always my favorite? The star of most of my silly schoolgirl fantasies? At least I know that his brother Luca has a thing for dark-haired women, but I don't have that advantage here.

Don't think too much, I tell myself. *Just keep going.*

I focus on the back of one of the other men at the table. He's wearing a gray shirt with white stripes. Just an ordinary man with an ordinary shirt. There's no reason to be anxious. I'm just a normal girl walking past a normal guy on a very normal bathroom trip...

Until my foot catches on the leg of Striped Shirt's chair and I fly head-over-heels forward, landing across Dante Fontaine's lap.

It's a perfectly executed landing. Hell, a little *too* perfect—as I start to sit up, stunned and thrilled that I managed to pull this off, I realize that my left hand is right on Dante's crotch.

I freeze. Dante Fontaine's cock is right beneath my hand. *Dante Fontaine's cock.* This is... This is... terrifying. Thrilling. Insanely awkward. Absolutely amazing.

And I have no idea what the heck I should do.

I'm definitely touching it. Oh, God—it's right beneath my fingers. If I try to get up, I'll be pressing against it. If I move my hand at all, even to pull away, my hand will brush right over it. He'll think I'm trying to feel him up. I'm *already* feeling him up, even though it's an accident. And now I've been frozen for an ungodly long amount of time and he probably thinks

I'm some sort of freak.

There are hands on my arms. *Dante Fontaine's* hands. He's trying to help me up, trying to get me back on my feet.

"I—I'm so sorry," I say quickly. "I'm so sorry." God, his hands are so… *firm.* Not quite as big as Roman's, but probably just as strong. And then I look up, and I find myself gazing right into his eyes—those dark, beautiful, mysterious, melted-chocolate eyes. Maybe it's okay that I didn't march in here with a plan. I wouldn't have remembered what to say anyway.

"Are you all right?"

It's not Dante who speaks, but one of the other men—Striped Shirt. The one whose chair I tripped over.

"I'm okay," I squeak. "Okay."

I'm still partially on my knees, still half across Dante's lap, and still mesmerized by his eyes—and I'm still sort of touching his crotch. Oh, God.

I jerk my hand back. What do I do now? I spoke to him—kind of. I touched him—perhaps a little too intimately. But what next?

I can feel Roman's eyes on my back, and my stomach twists. Did he see how long I had my hand on Dante's junk?

But I don't have time to think about it right now. Dante's still trying to help me to my feet, and I let him. He still hasn't said a word to me, and he's frowning slightly. He probably thinks I'm a crazy fan. Or worse. I tear my eyes away from his as I find my feet.

"I was just on my way to the bathroom," I blurt, trying to smooth over the situation. "I tripped."

"It is a little crowded in here," he says. He doesn't sound angry, at least. And his voice is just as sexy in person as I imagined it would be—almost as delicious as Roman's.

"I'm sorry," I say again. Somehow, in the process of getting up, I grabbed his arm. I can feel his hard muscles beneath the fabric of his shirt, and I'm tempted to squeeze them—but I don't. I quickly yank my fingers away before I completely lose my senses.

It's then, only then, that I glance back at Roman. His eyes are locked on me, and even across the room, his gaze seems to knock the breath right out of me. I stumble back a step and almost fall right into Dante's lap again.

"I—I should get to the bathroom," I say. But even as I back away, I'm already thinking of all the things I should be doing right now. I should have let my touch linger on Dante's arm. I should have used this opportunity to observe him up close, to look for anything about his appearance or manner that might give me an opening for seduction. Instead, I can hardly look at him at all. I can hardly think about anything but getting out of here.

And then I notice that my purse is still at Dante's

feet.

"Oh," I say, kneeling down at the same moment Dante bends over to grab my things.

Our foreheads bump against each other. Once again, my initial reaction is to go completely still in shock—and Dante does as well. For a full three seconds, my face is right next to his. He smells divine—like sandalwood and cinnamon. I can hear his breath—*feel* his breath. Our cheeks are nearly touching. If he turned his head, his lips would brush right against mine. My heart is galloping, my breath a knot in my throat.

I should move. Grab my things and get up and duck into the bathroom. But my body doesn't seem to remember how to obey me. Maybe I should say something. Assure him again that I'm not some sort of creep or stalker. My lips move, trying to form a sentence.

But instead of words, the sound that escapes my lips is much, much closer to a moan. And we're not talking about a moan of frustration or embarrassment—either of which would have been justified in this case—but rather something that sounds a lot closer to the sound a woman makes when she's experiencing some sort of great pleasure.

Oh God oh God oh God. Suddenly I can move again, and I scrabble desperately for all of my things. I shove what I can reach into my purse and clamber to my feet.

"I'm so sorry," I tell him again. "I didn't mean to

disrupt your meal. Or to… I mean…"

This time, Dante gives me a smile—a small one, but a *smile*. It's all I can do not to giggle like an idiot. *Dante Fontaine* is smiling at me. After I touched his cock and bumped heads with him and made a very inappropriate sound when his face was only inches away from mine.

"No apology needed," he says.

Part of me wants to stay and talk, to see where I might take things from here. I haven't offended him. He's *smiling* at me. But the other part of me has noticed the way the other men at the table have started to look at me funny. One of them is glancing between me and Dante with something that can only be described as suspicion. It's probably best to make my escape before someone calls the cops on me.

"I'll leave you to your meal," I say with a nervous little laugh. I almost turn and go back to my table—to Roman—but then I remember I'm supposed to be heading to the bathroom. But I've only made it two steps in the correct direction before I hear Dante's voice behind me.

"Wait."

Hope rises in my chest as I turn around. My heart is skipping.

Dante is bent over, scooping something up off the ground. In my mad rush to get back up, I must have missed something. I smile as I step forward, already imagining how I might brush my fingers against his as he hands it back to me, but then my eyes fall to the object in his hand.

Shit.

It's my press badge. My fucking *press badge.* With "*Celebrity Spark*" printed in clear letters right on the front.

There's a frown on his face now.

"You're a reporter?" He looks up at me.

Oh, shit. Just… shit. I've blown it yet again. But there's no lying. No escaping the truth.

"I… Yes," I say, shuffling forward and continuing to curse silently at myself. "But obviously not a very good one."

Before he can reply—*oh, God, I don't want to hear his reply*—I snatch my badge out of his grip and turn and run into the bathroom.

For the second time in a handful of days, I lock myself in a bathroom stall. I'm shaking, but I can't even blame it on nerves this time.

I'm pissed at myself. For a moment, I actually thought I'd accomplished something. But in my carelessness—one stupid moment of carelessness—I completely blew any progress I made. I stumbled right at the finish line.

"Arrrgh!" I slam my hand against the door of the stall. I'm so stupid. So… *hopeless.* There's no way I can seduce one of the Fontaines. Not on Saturday. Not ever.

The press badge is still in my hands. I want to tear it

up. Throw it in the toilet. Flush it away. What am I doing? Why am I even trying? You can't teach someone to be a seductress in a week. I know that. And Roman must know it, too. So why is he even bothering to give me these lessons?

I brush my hair out of my eyes. It's still a frizzy mess, but there's no point in worrying about it now. I shove my press badge back in my purse and try to fight back the tears that burn in my eyes.

Look at you, Felicia. You're a mess.

The bathroom door swings open. I allow myself one final sniffle before straightening and trying to compose myself. I'm not going to let myself have a breakdown in front of someone else, even through the walls of a bathroom stall.

The other person's footsteps stop right outside my sanctuary. Suddenly, there's a tap on my door.

"Felicia?"

Shit. "Roman? What are you doing in here?"

"Are you crying?"

"No!" None of the tears actually spilled over onto my cheeks, so it's not actually a lie. "I don't think you're allowed in here."

"We're alone. It doesn't matter. Will you come out?"

"Not with you standing there." And then, in an attempt to recover *something* of my pride, "Did it ever occur to you that I might actually need to *use* the bathroom?"

He ignores my question. "How did it go out there?"

"You were watching, weren't you?"

"Yes, but I couldn't hear anything that was said. And for a moment you and Dante both disappeared beneath the table."

I lean my ear against the door. I'm not ready to relive the entire incident just yet.

"How do you think it went?" I ask him softly. "You're the expert, after all."

He's silent for a moment, and I hear him step closer to the door. When he speaks, his voice is as soft as mine.

"I think it went better than you believe. You tripped on purpose, didn't you?"

My eyes fall closed. "Yes. Was it that obvious?"

"I had a suspicion. But it wouldn't have been obvious to anyone who didn't know you."

I press a finger against the door. "You don't know me."

My voice is only a whisper, but I know he hears me. After a minute, he sighs.

"Felicia," he says, "will you open the door?"

I wish I could hide behind it a little longer, but I know I'd be doing just that—*hiding*. And somehow, after everything, I still want to impress this man, to show him I'm not a complete coward.

I open the door. Roman is standing directly on the other side, his eyes full of something I can't name. I don't let myself look into them for very long. Instead, I step past him and go over to the sink.

"I would consider this a very successful outing," he says, coming up behind me as I try to wrangle my hair into submission. "I thought you were quite creative in your approach. And you were able to speak with him, however briefly. Even a few days ago, I suspect you would have been too tongue-tied to string more than a couple of words together. That was our only objective today—to help you learn to push through your nerves."

He's standing too close to me, but I don't say anything. It's easier if I try not to notice his body at all.

"These things take time," he continues, his hand rising to touch my arm. "And I must say, you've shown a lot of promise so far. Which isn't to say there isn't room for improvement, but if you continue to be such a willing pupil, I have no doubt you'll make great progress." His fingers slide down toward my elbow.

I don't know what it is—the utter dejection I'm feeling, his unbearable nearness, or the sheer insanity of the idea that I might still pull this off—but a bitter laugh escapes my throat. Suddenly everything seems so ridiculous. So... stupid. And once I start laughing, I can't stop.

"Well," I say when I can speak again, "at least I got to touch his cock."

Roman's fingers freeze on my elbow. "What?"

"When I tripped," I explain. "I fell right into his lap.

It wasn't intentional, but my hand ended up right on his… on his…" Suddenly repeating the word "cock" in front of Roman doesn't feel right. I rush on. "It was only for a few seconds, I guess, but it felt like forever. I didn't know what to do, and he didn't move away… Maybe he didn't notice. Or maybe I wasn't touching what I thought I was touching." Which is silly, of course—I knew *exactly* what I was touching. And I might not be a man, but I suspect that a man knows exactly when he's being touched *there.*

Roman still hasn't moved or spoken. Maybe he's reevaluating his opinion of how it went.

"He didn't seem mad," I say quickly, suddenly wanting to justify myself. "I mean, he smiled at me afterward. Not *right* after. Not like… I mean, a few minutes later, he seemed fine. He didn't make a big deal out of it. He was only upset when he saw my press badge." Another laugh bubbles out of me, a little more strained than the last one. "I guess you can consider the whole thing a roaring success. How many seductresses manage to get their fingers around a guy's cock in the first ten seconds?"

He doesn't seem to find my joke very funny. His fingers drop from my arm, and in the reflection of the mirror, his eyes are suddenly hard.

"I'm not sure if that's the appropriate approach in this situation," he says, his voice flat. "You're only trying to get an interview, after all."

I'm afraid to turn around and face him. I shouldn't have said anything about my accidental groping, but at the same time, I never expected Roman to react like *this*.

"Well," he says, "I suppose there's no reason for us to linger around here. I have a lot of work to do today." He steps back and indicates that we should head back into the restaurant.

I take two steps and then stop. "I… That is, maybe we should go separately. If we leave together people will think that we were… well, you know."

His eyebrows rise slightly, and then his frown deepens. "I told you to stop worrying about what other people think of you."

"This isn't…" I don't know what to say. Fortunately, I don't have to go on. Roman gives a shake of his head, but his mouth is still a hard line.

"Fine," he says. "I'll go out first. You can follow whenever you're ready."

And then, once again, I'm alone in the bathroom.

I don't know what's gotten into Roman, but I don't like it. He seems angry with me, but I have no idea what I've done. *He* was the one who dragged me here and told me to flirt with Dante Fontaine. *He* was the one who, just moments ago, was telling me the whole incident went better than I thought.

Those thoughts circle through my mind as I make one last attempt to fix my hair. When I've finally gotten myself under control, I turn and walk back out into the restaurant.

I have to walk right past Dante Fontaine if I want to leave. For a moment, that thought freezes me in my tracks, but then I shake my head and force myself to move. There's no escaping it, and I might as well get it over with.

I walk quickly around his table. *Don't look at him, don't look at him, don't look at him...* I keep my eyes trained on the floor. The last thing I want to do is trip over another chair and repeat the incident all over again.

But I've only just made it past Striped Shirt when I hear Dante's voice behind me.

"Wait, Ms.—I'm sorry, I didn't get your name."

I stop. Should I turn around? Or should I run to the door? I can see Roman just on the other side of the glass, waiting for me.

But I remind myself that I'm trying to be less of a coward. Facing Dante Fontaine again is my chance to prove myself. Slowly, I turn toward him, biting back the urge to apologize again.

"Liddle," I say. "Felicia Liddle."

To my surprise, Dante doesn't look as pissed as I expected. He looks, well... if not *friendly*, exactly, then at least somewhat understanding. Not like someone who's going to take my name straight to the cops.

He sits back in his chair, his chocolate eyes looking me up and down. It's different from the way Roman looks at me, but no less embarrassing. I stare down at the floor.

"You know," he says after a moment, "if you're trying to get an interview with someone, it's usually better just to ask."

My head snaps up. "I—I wasn't aware you did interviews, Mr. Fontaine. You have a reputation for avoiding them at all costs." Wait—where did *that* come from? When did I get so bold?

To my surprise, Dante smiles. Again. *Two smiles from Dante Fontaine in one day.* Sixteen-year-old me would have died of happiness.

"That's true, I guess," he says, still studying me. "Though my publicist thinks I should be doing some to promote *Cataclysm: Earth.*"

I can't believe this. "So you'll do an interview?"

"I never said that. I just said that you'd have a better chance of getting one if you asked."

I can't decide whether that's an invitation or a rejection—*why can't men ever just give a straight answer?*—but before I have the chance to ask him, he says, "Have a good day, Ms. Liddle."

That's a dismissal if I've ever heard one. Maybe I should stay and try to convince him to answer a few questions—but I'm not that skilled. Not yet. Besides, this probably isn't my one and only chance—he should be at *Hollywood Saves!* this Saturday with the rest of his family.

"Thank you," I say. "Have a good day." And then I

spin back around before he can see my grin. I can't believe it. I might not have officially scored an interview, but my heart is full of victory.

I'm still grinning when I reach Roman outside.

"What is it?" he asks.

"I did it," I say. "Almost, at least. On my way out Dante stopped me and told me I should ask him for an interview." I can hardly contain myself. "I mean, he shot me down this time, but he made it sound like he's open to the possibility of doing something in the future. Maybe to promote *Cataclysm: Earth.*"

For the first time, I allow myself to look at Roman, but to my surprise, he doesn't look particularly impressed by what I've just told him.

"Either you secured an interview, or you didn't," he says. "There's no in-between. He was probably just brushing you off politely."

His tone leaves me cold. All of my excitement, my sense of victory, rushes out of me.

"Come on," he says. "I need to get back to the office."

I'm speechless. In the bathroom, he acted like I'd actually impressed him with my clumsiness and ridiculous attempts to flirt with Dante. Why would he suddenly turn cold when I tell him I was *this close* to achieving an interview?

It's almost like he's jealous, I think. Under different circumstances, there'd be no question. But this is

Roman. The man who, just yesterday, pointed out that he knew he aroused me and yet made no attempt to do anything about it. Who never said a word about my leg touching his beneath the table. Who's spent the last few days teaching me how to pick up *other* men. I don't know what his problem is, but I hope he figures it out before Saturday. Like it or not, this man is my only hope.

And that's *my* problem, I realize, remembering the way his touch affected me—I like it a lot more than I should.

6

FIVE DAYS

I'VE BEEN AT work for six hours and twenty-seven minutes, and Roman hasn't said a word to me.

Counting the minutes is a little obsessive, I know. But I sent off the final version of my Emilia interview this morning, and I've had a hard time concentrating on my work ever since. I know we didn't exactly end things on a good foot yesterday, but there's no reason for him to ignore me now. He's walked past my cubicle half a dozen times today—not that I've counted—and he hasn't even acknowledged me.

I lean and look around the edge of my cubicle. I can just make him out through the blinds on the conference room window. He's bent over his laptop, and he's got a headset in his ear. He appears to be on a call. After a couple of minutes, he starts shaking his head violently, as if arguing with the person on the other end of the line. He says something to his assistant, and the young man jumps up and dashes out.

Maybe it's for the best that he's ignoring me. It doesn't look like he's in a particularly good mood today.

And anyway, I should probably be focusing on *real* problems—like how I'm going to turn that brief but promising interaction with Dante Fontaine into a real interview. I got my foot in the door, and now I have to go in for the kill. I still can't believe I pulled that off—even thinking about it makes me all giggly and light-headed again. I know, I know—the ridiculous fangirling will have to stop if I'm going to make it in this business—but a girl can let herself have a few minutes to freak out over her interaction with Dante Fontaine, can't she? I mean, I *touched his junk*, after all. I'm pretty sure that's a scene straight out of some of the Fontaine fan fiction I wrote long ago.

I'm improving, that much is clear. Yeah, I freaked out a little in the bathroom yesterday, but I must have done *something* right if Dante was open to the idea of an interview. This past weekend at the bar—or even yesterday morning, when I realized I was about to face Dante Fontaine with crazy hair and zero makeup—I never would have believed it possible. It still seems like nothing short of a miracle. But somehow I feel... *stronger* this morning. Like I can take on the world.

Of course, that only makes my next few steps that much more important. I'm so close to scoring an interview I can almost taste it. I need to be ready to kill on Saturday. And that means preparing myself both mentally and physically.

I pull up my bank account on my computer. I've got exactly $238.42 left at my disposal after I mentally subtract what I'll need for rent and food this month. That's only $238.42 to spend on making myself look gorgeous for *Hollywood Saves!*—a ridiculously small amount, considering plates at the event start at $15,000 for attendees. I might not need a ticket, but I don't want to look like I wandered in off the street or something.

You can do this, Felicia. I've got a friend who does hair out of her apartment. She can help me tame my locks for a decent price—probably thirty bucks or so. If I throw in an extra fifteen dollars, she'll do my makeup, too. That leaves about $180 for a gown. Sure, I've got a couple of dresses I use for weddings and first dates and the occasional funeral—basically anything where I need to look nice—but those won't do. Not for this.

A few minutes later, I'm clicking through some of my favorite websites for the perfect dress. It's clear right away that my $180 isn't going to get me very far, but I'll worry about my budget later. Right now, I just need to find something appropriate. Something classy but sexy. Something that will make me look like a professional but also make Dante Fontaine want to jump my bones.

I'm so absorbed in my search that I don't even hear the footsteps behind me. Suddenly, there is a touch on my shoulder and the rush of warm breath against my ear.

"Working hard, I see," says a voice I know all too well.

I nearly jump out of my skin. I click away from the page of fancy evening gowns, but it's too late. Roman has seen everything.

I swivel around in my chair.

"This *is* work," I say, though I know my guilty reaction and red cheeks don't help my case. "I was looking for a dress for Saturday."

If Roman accepts that explanation, his face doesn't show it. If anything, he looks kind of smug—like he's just caught me posting vacation photos on social media or something.

"Really," I say. "I've got nothing to wear. And you can't tell me *Hollywood Saves!* isn't work." After all, he called our lunch at the bistro *business.*

He's smiling now, but in his usual infuriating, bemused way.

"Well," he says slowly, "since this is work, perhaps I should oversee your progress. Show me what you've found so far." He leans over me, toward my computer. He's close enough that I can smell his aftershave—or cologne, or whatever it is that men wear that makes them smell so damn good—and I lean away. My hand fumbles with the mouse, and I scroll back up the page.

"I… I was thinking of something black," I say, trying not to smell him. Or study that not-quite-a-dimple in his chin up close. "Something long. Classic."

"Mm," he says. His face is blank. Even his amusement is gone, and his brows are drawn slightly together, as if he's thinking. What the heck does that mean?

"Something short didn't seem formal enough for the event," I say, trying to justify my choices. "And black would be the most professional."

"Mm," he says again. This time, he gives a little nod as well. But he still has that little furrow between his brows, so I'm not sure what to think.

"I'll make sure it's sexy," I add. "But like you said, I don't want to be too obvious."

Roman doesn't respond. But he's still leaning over me, staring at my computer screen. The bottom edge of his suit jacket is resting against my leg, and I'm reminded once more of our little lesson over lunch. It can't be an accident that he's touching me—or is it? It's just his jacket. But then why else is he leaning so close to me? Is this another test?

I swear, this man is going to drive me mad.

"Let me show you another one I was thinking about," I say. I move the mouse, clicking away to another site. As I do, I move in my seat, letting my leg brush against his and my arm slide briefly past his side. My arm doesn't linger—I'm not quite that brazen yet— but I leave my knee resting lightly against his thigh. There can be no doubt this time, not like at our lunch on Saturday—this is no pseudo-touch beneath a table. And I'm certain he feels it.

One second passes. Two. And then suddenly Roman straightens and steps away from me.

"Well," he says, "I should be getting back to work."

I'm not sure what to say. Is he just going to ignore what I tried to do? Or is this a subtle way of showing me that I was being inappropriate? It's one thing to touch him when he's asked me to during a "lesson," but it's another to do so here in the workplace. For all that he's calling our lessons "business," there's still a professional line—and maybe I just crossed it.

Roman is straightening his jacket.

"I'll be interested to see what you choose," he says, "but I don't think you're quite there yet. If you'll forgive me, I have to return to work."

He turns to go, but only makes it two steps before stopping and looking back over his shoulder at me.

"Don't pick something black," he says, then turns away again.

"Wait—what?" I call after him. "Why not?"

He looks back at me, his expression cool. "I just don't think it's right for this particular project."

Like *that's* not completely vague. "Then what should I wear?"

He comes back to stand next to my desk. His eyes drift over to my computer screen again before fixing on me.

"I'll tell you what," he says. "My meeting this evening was just canceled. Perhaps after work I might take you to find something appropriate."

The absolute last thing in the world I want to do is drag *this* man around with me as I try on a bunch of dresses.

"I... I was just going to order a couple of options online and return the one I didn't like," I tell him.

He frowns. "Felicia, *Hollywood Saves!* is less than a week away."

"And we live in a world where one-day shipping exists."

"Do you really want to represent yourself and this magazine in something you ordered off of some discount site?"

I *know* I shouldn't be getting prickly over this, but I can't help myself.

"Not all of us are billionaires," I hiss, praying my few remaining coworkers around here aren't listening in. "Some of us aren't even sure if we'll have a job next week, and we can't afford to blow our entire savings on a dress. Not if we want to make sure we can eat next month."

For a second—a split second—he looks properly admonished. Or maybe that's just my overly optimistic imagination, because just as quickly, his expression is as controlled as it ever was.

"This is a business expense," he says. "*Celebrity Spark* will foot the bill, of course." His eyes drop to my computer screen. "But not if you're ordering something of questionable quality. I'm not going to make your choices for you, Felicia. If you wish to buy one of the dresses you've just shown me, then go ahead. I can't dictate what you wear. But if you wish to let this magazine cover the expense, I'll need final approval. I must oversee this company's spending."

He doesn't wait for my response. Instead, he turns and begins to walk back to the conference room.

I want to be stubborn—to spend my own money, to shop where I want to shop, to pick a black dress just to show him—but let's be real. This is a pretty amazing offer, and beggars can't be choosers. I might desperately need that $180 next month if all of this explodes in my face.

"Fine," I call after him. "What time?"

I'M AFRAID TO touch anything in this boutique.

Seriously, based on my track record, I'll probably brush against a gown and knock its thousands of little crystal beads loose. Or sneeze and somehow set the place on fire.

When Roman offered to take me shopping, I thought we'd end up at one of the higher-end department stores—not a fancy-schmancy shop like this where they try to shove champagne in your hand the moment you step through the door. (For the record, I turned down the champagne—it's a bad idea to give me alcohol in a boutique where the gowns cost more than my rent.)

Still, I can't seem to take my eyes off of the gowns around me. Everything in here is gorgeous. Roman shadows me as I walk down the length of the room, and I can feel him watching me as I study my options. I pause to look at a beautiful purple silk gown, and he stops behind me.

"See anything you like?" he asks in my ear.

Honestly, I'm afraid to like anything in here. There's no reason I need a gown like this, not even for *Hollywood Saves!* I'm just a member of the press. And it feels too strange, having Roman here with me, ready with the credit card. This isn't something magazine owners do for their employees. This is something billionaires do for their mistresses.

And before I can stop myself, I find myself asking, "Have you done this before?"

"Done what?"

I'm glad he's behind me and can't see my face. "Bought a dress for someone?"

There's a short pause. "Not in a professional capacity."

But in a personal capacity? I find myself glancing toward the salesclerk, who hovers just within earshot, ready to come to our assistance. *She* probably believes this is a personal errand, as close as Roman is standing to me.

"So you buy your girlfriends expensive things?" I ask.

His laugh is low and warm. "That's a personal question, isn't it?"

So is the way he's speaking into my ear, but I don't mention that. But in spite of his objection, he seems willing to continue.

"I don't see anything wrong with spoiling a woman," he says. "If she wants expensive things, I'm willing and able to give them to her. I've never had a woman complain about my lack of generosity."

For a moment, I let myself imagine what it would be like to date this man—to be lavished with expensive gifts, to be taken to fancy restaurants, to be treated like a queen. I can't decide if that's something I'd want— though, admittedly, I'd have no objections to trying it out for a while. I let my fingers trail across the purple gown. I should enjoy tonight while I can, even if this is "business." It's not like someone like Roman would ever actually date someone like me.

But my curiosity about Roman's dating life gets the better of me. "So what else does Roman Everet's girlfriend get? Unlimited access to your yacht? Surprise weekend trips to Paris? Do you take her to all the big industry events and introduce her to her favorite celebrities?"

He's still behind me, so I can't see his face. But I hear the smile in his voice when he speaks.

"I don't have a yacht," he says. "I get horribly sea-sick. I learned that the hard way on a private sailing cruise in the Adriatic. As for surprise weekend trips, I'm afraid those are out—unless I have some business in our destination. But usually that means I'm headed to New York or London. I haven't been to Paris in years." He steps around to my side. "And as for industry events, I have been known to take women to those on occasion. But I don't know as many celebrities as you seem to believe. I've formed working relationships with a handful of actors and musicians over the years, of course, but most of my business is with people on the back end—the managers, producers, agents, PR firms. You get the idea. Which is why I need every employee at *Celebrity Spark* to continue to make those connections."

"Ah." I don't look at him. Instead, I turn and study the gown to my left. It's a gorgeous dress with a plunging neckline and crystal-lined straps. Unfortunately, it's also black.

"What's so wrong with black anyway?" I ask. "It's classic. And you can't tell me it's not sexy."

One corner of his mouth tilts up. "And every other member of the press is going to be wearing something similar. Do you just want to blend in?"

Normally, my response would be *yes*. But I know that's not the right answer today.

"Then I should pick something bright yellow? Or red?"

"You don't have to go quite so extreme," he says. "But I don't think any man has ever complained about a woman in a red dress. It certainly draws the eye."

I'm not sure I'm ready for a red dress, whether or not Roman likes the color. I continue down the length of the boutique.

"Do you give your girlfriends this much direction when you're buying them gowns?" I ask.

"You're very curious about my girlfriends."

"And you're avoiding the question."

He gives an exasperated sigh. "If I'm buying a dress for a woman I'm seeing, then I let her choose whatever she likes. But if that woman seeks my opinion, then I'm more than willing to share my thoughts." He pauses. "You, however, are not my girlfriend, so I'm not sure why it matters. This is a business purchase, and I will give it the proper attention."

Ouch. That was blunt. I want to assure him that I wasn't suggesting he should treat me like a girlfriend, but I'm having trouble moving my tongue right now. So I keep moving through the dresses, still refusing to look him in the eyes. Roman, however, isn't finished.

"We live in a town and work in an industry where appearances matter," he says. "And I don't just mean attractiveness. I mean that simple things—like what color you wear—can make a huge difference in how people see you. A man is perceived differently depending on whether he walks into a business meeting in a

blue shirt or a red shirt. A pop star is perceived differently if she arrives at an awards show in an orange dress
than if she arrives in a white dress. Different colors
suggest different things to our subconscious minds. A
smart person uses that knowledge to her advantage."

I've found another black dress that I think is lovely,
but I don't bother asking him what he thinks. He's
right—I can't blend in. Not on Saturday. I'm still not
sure I'm ready for a red gown, though, no matter what
he says.

"Of course," he continues, "it's about far more than
perception. The exact same gown can look very different
on two different women. It's about their coloring, the
way they carry themselves, their attitude. Many things
come into play."

I'm not sure I have the *attitude* or anything else to
pull off some of the bolder, sexier gowns in here—
maybe this is his way of giving me an out. He doesn't
say anything else as I look through the gowns, so I guess
he knows he's made his point. Maybe it would be easier
to just let him point out a handful of gowns that he
thinks are appropriate and work from there.

After a few minutes, though, I find myself standing
in front of a beautiful beaded silver gown. The fabric
looks so delicate that I can't resist reaching out and
running a finger down the strap.

"What about something metallic?" I find myself
asking him. This gown might not be bright red, but it's

certainly showy.

Roman doesn't say anything for a long moment, and I risk a glance over at him. He's studying the gown closely, his brows drawn together. After a moment, he shakes his head.

"Silver wouldn't suit you," he says. "I'd put you in something gold." He glances around, then indicates a pretty gold gown hanging on the nearest wall.

"So I have the attitude to pull off a gold dress, but not a silver one?"

He seems to find that amusing. "As I said before, many things come into play. It's about personal coloring as well." He turns to me. "Hold out your hand."

"What?" Still, I find myself lifting my hand automatically, and he grasps my fingers in his, turning my wrist so my palm is facing up toward the ceiling.

"You have a warm, olive undertone to your skin," he says. "I'd guess that you have some Mediterranean heritage. Italian, maybe. Or Greek. Maybe even Spanish."

"Greek," I say, trying to ignore the warm feeling his touch is giving me. "On my mother's side."

"I thought so." He looks up at my face. "You'll want to wear something that compliments that. Gold or bronze would do." He pauses as his eyes roam over me. "It would work well with your hair, too. If you wore black, everything would blend together. But the gold… It would be striking. Memorable. And that's what you want—for these men to stop and take notice of you. To remember you."

"Striking" and "memorable" aren't words I'd normally use to describe myself, but the way Roman says them makes me almost believe it's possible.

"A gold dress could do that?" I ask softly.

There's a dark gleam in his eyes. "There's only one way to find out, isn't there? Why don't you try one?"

I nod, but he's still holding my hand, so I can't move away just yet. He's still studying me, still pinning me in place with that gaze.

"We'll want something that sets off your eyes as well," he says. "Your eyes are quite dark—that's unusual, and that makes them an asset we should use. A man might initially be drawn to a woman's breasts or ass or some other more obvious part of her body, but it's her eyes that will catch and keep him."

The fact that he seems to be suggesting that *my* eyes might catch and keep anyone makes me blush even harder. I still can't bring myself to move, but I glance away, trying to save some face.

"Don't look away from me," he says.

The order is so direct that my eyes snap back to his in surprise.

"I didn't mean to," I say. "I just—"

"And that's the problem." He's frowning slightly, still holding me in his hazel gaze. "You let your insecurities rule you. The more vulnerable you feel, the harder it is for you to hold someone's gaze. That won't do, Felicia. You need to learn to maintain eye contact with someone you find attractive."

I start to protest, but he cuts me off.

"Meeting someone's eyes *will* make you feel more vulnerable," he says. "But you shouldn't fight it. Because it will also help you form a deeper connection with that person. They'll find you more engaging. And have a much stronger reaction to you." His voice drops lower as he adds, "Especially with eyes as expressive as yours. They're your ticket in. They're what's ultimately going to win you what you want."

What I want? He's right—holding his gaze is making me suddenly feel incredibly exposed. I want to look away from him again, but I fight the urge.

"You want an interview," he reminds me. "And you're hoping your feminine wiles will win you one." He leans a little closer, never breaking my gaze. "Which means you shouldn't be so afraid of using them."

I can't take it anymore. I yank my hand out of his grasp and turn partially away.

"I'm not afraid of using them," I say. "I just don't know how. There's a difference."

"You have trouble looking people in the eye. You're uncomfortable speaking with men you find attractive. You—"

"None of those things make me afraid," I insist, wondering why he must point out again and again that he knows I'm attracted to him. "I'm just... out of practice."

He starts to speak, but I spin away from him and march over to the gold gown.

"Do you want me to try on some dresses or do you want to insult me some more?" I snap.

My tone seems to surprise him. Honestly, it surprises me, too—but I guess even I have a breaking point. I'm still shaking in anger—or humiliation, or whatever it is I'm feeling right now—and the salesclerk comes rushing over, probably afraid I'm going to harm the gold gown in front of me.

"Did you want to try this one?" she asks, looking less than thrilled about the idea.

I nod and tell her my size. On our way to the fitting rooms, I point out several other gowns I'd like to try— including a black one, because I don't care what Roman thinks right now. I don't bother looking at him as I make my selections, even though I'm sure he has plenty of opinions. He needs to remember that I can and will think for myself—and, frankly, I need to remind myself of that as well.

And before I know it, I'm shut in a lavish fitting room—complete with a gilded mirror and an over-stuffed armchair in the corner—with a bunch of gowns I'm afraid to touch.

I undress quickly, trying to suppress my annoyance and embarrassment. Roman's words echo in my mind, and though the truth is hard to accept, I know I can't hide forever. I need to grow a thicker skin. I need to allow myself to be vulnerable.

My hands are still shaking as I fold my work clothes and set them aside. When I'm down to my underwear, I finally turn and look at the mirror.

I don't dislike what I see. I might not look like the actresses and models that the Fontaine boys normally date—I could stand to lose some weight, get a better haircut, and learn how to apply makeup like an adult— but I'm not hopeless. At least I don't think I am—and judging by some of the things he's said over the past few days, Roman doesn't seem to either.

But he also thinks I'm afraid of my sexuality, so I'm not sure what to believe right now.

Might as well try on some of these gowns.

I almost go for the black one, just out of stubborn-ness, but I find myself reaching for the gold dress first. My fingers skim across the beading as I build my courage. There's no reason to be afraid of a dress, no matter how much it costs. I slip the straps off of the padded, silk-lined hanger.

The dress is heavier than I expected, though I'm sure the beads are to blame for that. It definitely weighs more than any dress I've ever owned, and I hope it won't require some ridiculously high heels to complete the ensemble. I'd probably tumble right over and knock myself out before I ever made it to any of the Fontaines.

For all of the beads, though, it's still a very slinky gown. The kind that doesn't have any real shape of its own—also known as the kind that requires a full set of body-molding undergarments because it clings to every single one of your curves. Its straps are delicate braids of gold ribbon that crisscross in the back. I'm afraid I'll rip them just getting it over my head—and I wonder if maybe I should have accepted the salesclerk's help when she offered it. As it is, I know she's hovering just outside, probably waiting for the telltale *rrrrip* of a seam breaking, but I can't bring myself to call her. We all know I don't belong here, don't belong in these clothes. If I'm going to look like a joke in this gown, I don't want anyone else to see it.

Just do it, I tell myself. *Just put it on.* It's only a damn dress, after all.

Two minutes later, I've managed to pull it over my head without tearing anything or causing my friend on the other side of the door to have an aneurysm. I hold my breath as I turn back toward the mirror.

And then I gasp.

I look good. Better than good—I look like a fucking movie star. The gold fabric seems to cling to me in all the right places, and the hundreds of little beads shimmer beneath the fitting room lights, making me sparkle. I twist back and forth, trying to examine myself from all angles, waiting for the illusion to break. They must have done something to the mirror in here—

there's no way I can look this flawless. I totally understand why someone might dish out a thousand dollars for a gown like this.

But I don't even want to think about the price right now. I'm not even sure I'd be able to find the tag. This is probably one of those "if you have to ask, you can't afford it" places. And anyway, I don't think I can rip my eyes away from my reflection. I look so glamorous, so beautiful—like someone who should be *in* a magazine like *Celebrity Spark*, not a writer.

There's a knock at the door. "Miss? Do you need any help?" The poor clerk's voice sounds a little strained.

"I'm fine," I call back. I'm not ready to go out just yet.

"If you need help getting something on—"

"It's okay," I tell her. But as much as I'd like to stay in here and keep looking at my reflection, I know I should probably show her that I haven't set anything on fire. Which means opening the door and letting her— and Roman—see me.

I'm suddenly nervous again. Like, butterflies-in-the-stomach, trying-not-to-vomit nervous. I wasn't exactly calm when I walked in here, but this is different. My anger is gone. I've gotten over any offense I took to Roman's bluntness. But now I've gone and fallen in love with a dress, and I'm afraid that as soon as I step out of this room, it will be over. I'll no longer be the movie star. Just an awkward girl in a dress that's way too expensive for her. If Roman doesn't like this gown, then it's proof that what I see in the mirror is just an illusion. A desperate figment of my imagination.

Don't worry about what he thinks, I tell myself. He's the one who told me to stop worrying about what other people think. But that's easier said than done. I don't care how confident you are—if you're really excited about something and other people are underwhelmed, it can be heartbreaking.

But it's time to be brave. To be vulnerable.

I open the door. The salesclerk is waiting for me, and relief flashes in her eyes when she sees that I haven't destroyed the dress. But I don't spare more than a glance for her. My eyes go past her to where Roman is sitting, waiting for me.

He rises as soon as he sees me. His eyes drift over my body. First quickly, then slowly. Taking in every inch of me in this dress. His gaze moves from the delicate braided straps down over my breasts and waist and hips—all emphasized by the clingy fabric—and then finally down to where my bare toes peek out beneath the hem.

I don't know how long he looks at me, but it feels like forever. And he hasn't said a word, or given any indication of whether he likes it or not.

"Well?" I ask him finally. "What do you think?"

Roman still doesn't say anything. Instead, he walks

slowly around me, examining me from every angle. I try not to wither under his scrutiny, reminding myself to be strong.

Finally, he's back in front of me again.

"Give us a minute," he says.

It takes me a second to realize he's talking to the salesclerk. She throws an uneasy glance in my direction, as if I might rip the dress the moment I'm out of her sight, but she must decide it's not worth arguing with Roman. He's the one with the money, after all.

She retreats back into the boutique, and then Roman and I are alone.

He still standing in front of me. Still silent. What could he possibly have to say to me that he couldn't say in front of the clerk? Whatever it is, he doesn't seem to be in a hurry to share.

"Don't you like it?" I ask, my voice little more than a whisper. I want to shout at him, *I don't care if you don't! I love it!. I never want to take it off again!* But I want to hear his honest thoughts first. Besides, he's the one with the *Celebrity Spark* credit card. What *I* think doesn't really matter in the end.

"Come," he says after a moment. "Let's look in the mirror." He takes my arm and guides me over to a large three-way mirror just past the room where I was changing. His hands brush against my bare arms as he positions me in front of it, and then he takes a step back.

"What do you see?" he asks.

"I've already looked at myself," I say, confused. "I want to know what *you* think."

He steps forward again, and now he's standing right behind me, looking over my shoulder at the mirror, meeting my gaze in the reflection.

"I'll tell you what I think," he coaxes, "after you give me your initial thoughts. How does this dress make you feel?"

For a moment, I just look at our reflections. Roman is still wearing his business suit, and it's expensive enough that it almost passes for what an actor would wear on the red carpet. And in this dress… for the first time, I don't feel so out of place next to him. We look like some fancy Hollywood couple. I can almost buy that the girl in that reflection, in that dress, would catch the eye of Roman Everet. Even with the unruly hair.

"I feel glamorous," I say softly. "Like a celebrity."

"Will feeling like a celebrity help you on Saturday?" he asks, trailing a finger down my arm.

"Maybe," I say. But this dress is so much more than that. "I feel… beautiful." The last word is almost a whisper. It's silly. I know I shouldn't need a ridiculously expensive gown to make me feel pretty. But at the same time, there's something magical about this, something so wonderfully freeing about allowing myself to put on a gorgeous dress and feel worthy of it.

But Roman's not about to let me off the hook that

easily.

"What about it makes you feel beautiful?" he asks.

It just does, I want to say. But I study my reflection all the same. What is it exactly that I love so much about this dress? The silky fabric? The shimmer? The beading or the braided straps?

I must take too long to answer, because Roman leans a little closer so that his mouth is right next to my ear.

"I'll tell you what I see," he murmurs. He reaches around me, and his fingers come to rest on the strap leading over my right shoulder. "This," he says, his fingers sliding up the strap, "shows off your shoulders and collarbone. If you wear your hair up, it will only enhance the effect." He gathers as much of my hair as he can in one hand and gently twists it up, leaving my shoulders bare. His other hand rises to my neck, and I jump a little when his fingers brush against the skin there.

"Most women want to show off their breasts or their legs when they're trying to get a man's attention," he says, his voice lower than it was a moment ago. "But there are other, less obvious parts of a woman's body that are just as erotic." Once more, his fingers graze my neck, tracing a path along my skin. A tremor moves through me.

"A woman's neck is one of the most sensual and enticing parts of her body," he says. "The skin is so soft, and so thin that a man can see and feel exactly how she is responding to him." His finger comes to rest beneath my jaw, right where I know my pulse is beating overtime. "For most people, the neck is an erogenous zone, but a lot of us forget that until someone touches or kisses it. Our subconscious minds don't forget, however. Leaving her neck bare is a subtle but very effective signal to that very animal part of a man's brain."

His fingers are moving slowly down the front of my throat now, and his warm breath continues to wash across my ear.

"Hair up," I whisper. "I-I understand."

"Some might recommend a necklace," he continues, his voice like rich, dark syrup. "Something to draw the eye from your face and neck down to your breasts." His hand moves away from my throat, but that gives me little relief because now his fingers are drifting down over my collarbone. He traces an invisible necklace across my skin, marking out a curved path down my chest to where my breasts rise from the top of the dress.

I try to calm my breathing. To focus on his words, and not the strange things his touch is doing to my heart. Both Roman and I know what he does to me, but I don't want him to think I'm not in control of my body. But something about this dress is getting to me. I can't think straight anymore.

"I don't think you need a necklace," he says. "Not in

this dress. There's already more than enough to draw the eye." His finger pauses right at the top of the valley between my breasts, and for a gut-twisting moment, I think he's going to keep going.

But he doesn't. Instead his finger lingers, as if he can't decide whether or not to test my limits. That *is* what he's doing, isn't it? Testing my limits?

"Well?" he says after a moment, his lips not an inch from my ear. "What do you think?"

I think I should get myself under control. Roman is my boss—however unconventional our current project—and I shouldn't be thinking the things I'm thinking right now. Or feeling all of the blood rush between my legs. He has me wrapped around his finger, and we both know it.

"Felicia?" he prompts.

Hearing his tongue roll around my name makes my knees weak.

"I… I think you're right," I say.

"Mm. Anything else?"

I'm not sure what he's fishing for, but I take a stab. "I… think the color is perfect."

"Yes. The gold suits you." His eyes run down my body in the reflection. "The shape as well."

When I studied myself in the fitting room, I was surprised by how much I liked the way the dress hugged my curves. Now, though, with Roman's eyes on me, I'm painfully aware of just how much this gown reveals. I might not be showing a lot of skin, but anyone who sees me can't be in any doubt of exactly what's beneath the beads and fabric.

"You don't think it's too fitted?" I ask, remembering his comments about subtlety.

"No," he says. "No, I think it's perfect."

Perfect. The word sends a frisson of pleasure through me.

"It fits exactly as it should," he elaborates. "It skims across your breasts and hips without clinging to them. This gown was designed to look sleek and expensive while making sure everyone who looks at you is fully aware of the shape of your body. Even the beading is designed to add to this effect. Look." His hand—his teasing, torturous hand, which has rested above my breasts all this time—finally moves, dropping to my waist. His fingers drift over the beads sewn onto the silky fabric, tracing the patterns.

"See how this curves through here?" he says. "It's drawing your eye inward with the curve of your waist. Emphasizing the feminine lines of your body." He's still so close to me that every word is another rush of heated breath against my skin. He's near enough that I can smell that delicious manly scent of his, but I try to focus on what he's showing me.

Not that I'm particularly successful at it. His finger is still moving across the delicate line of beads on the front of my gown, following the winding path across my stomach and over my bellybutton.

"But that's not the only place these patterns lead the eye," he goes on. "As you move higher up the dress, they have a very different objective." To illustrate, his hand follows his words, moving over the fabric until his finger is just below my left breast.

"Here," he breathes, "they aren't arranged to show how your body curves inward, but rather how it curves out."

His finger shifts, sliding across the lower slope of my breast, and my heart stops. It's only the lightest of touches, the barest of caresses, but it sends prickles across my skin. I bite down on my lip as my nipples harden in response, but I can do nothing to hide the very visible reaction of my body. The thin fabric of the dress does little to conceal the hard nubs, and they stand out against the swirling designs made by the beads. But in spite of everything, I can't seem to bring myself to move away from him.

And Roman says nothing. He must notice—*how could he not?*—but I'm afraid to meet his gaze in the reflection. My entire body feels completely out of my control, frozen in pleasure and anticipation. If I meet his gaze, I'll have nothing left.

Roman shifts behind me, making me jump, but his arm remains around me.

"Rounded shapes have always been symbolic of the female form," he says, his voice low and smooth. "It's no accident that these beads are arranged in curled, spiral lines. They echo the lines of a woman's breasts, her hips, her ass. And more intimate parts of her, too. Her mouth. Her bellybutton. Her *nipples*."

The blood rises to my cheeks. But my feet are glued to the ground, my entire body at his command. I long to lean back into him, to feel his body flush against mine. To beg him to move his hand a little higher, to tease and massage one of those hard little points that longs for the attention of his fingers.

Oh, God. I can't believe this is happening. I can't believe that I'm standing in a fitting room in an insanely expensive gown and aching for Roman Everet to touch me. I can't believe that Roman Everet *is* touching me, that it's his finger gently grazing the underside of my breast. That is certainly *not* professional, no matter the arrangement between us.

My heart is beating too hard. My breath is coming too fast, my breasts heaving within the silky confines of the gown. All of my nerves are on fire, and I'm drowning in the sensations—in the luxurious softness of the dress against my bare skin, the tantalizing touch of his hand, the overwhelming heat of him.

But he doesn't move any further. His hand continues to move softly just beyond what's appropriate, but still so far from what my body desires. I want him to grab me. To twist and squeeze and make me ache. I want him to throw me up against the mirror, up against that reflection of the beautiful Hollywood couple.

His hand moves. Not up, not toward the nipple that begs for his attention, but down, down across my belly to where a different part of me is throbbing. His fingers skim across the fabric, but even that lightest of touches affects my entire body.

He has to move closer to me to do it. His chest is right against my back now, but I don't let myself relax into him. For once, he doesn't seem completely in control—he seems as caught up in the moment as I am. I'm afraid that moving at all will make him realize exactly what he's doing, exactly how many lines he's crossed.

He's reached my waist, and his finger follows the line of beads that curves down my hip.

"And these lines," he murmurs, and this time his lips actually touch my ear. "These lines…" Down here, at my hips, the fabric pulls slightly away from my body, the skirt widening toward the floor. His touch is so light, so delicate as he moves his finger across the beads over my upper thigh that the fabric doesn't even brush against my skin, but that doesn't seem to make any difference. My body is on fire, and every touch of his hand is tortuous and delightful. I watch his progress in the mirror, watch his finger drift oh-so-slowly across my thigh toward the place where my legs meet.

"Where do these lines lead?" he rasps in my ear.

I know where I want them to lead. I know where I

want his hand to move next. But I can hardly form coherent thoughts, let alone a coherent response.

His finger pauses on the fabric, right above the crest where my legs meet. If he were to apply the slightest bit of pressure, to push down a little bit harder, he'd touch me right where I ache to be touched. But he doesn't move. He just waits. And with every second that passes, his breath comes a little quicker against my ear and his body feels a little bit warmer against my back. I'm quivering from head to toe, longing for him to move, to touch me—and at the same time, the thought that he might do so terrifies me. I keep looking at his hand in the reflection, keep wondering how far I should let this go, keep dreading and hoping for the moment when the spell breaks and I have control of myself again.

His lips touch my ear again, sending a fresh ripple of pleasure between my legs.

"Do you want it?" he murmurs.

I let out a shaky breath. *Yes. Yes, I want it.* But I can't seem to say even that. After a couple of seconds, I only manage to echo, "It."

"The dress." His voice is rough.

For a moment, I don't understand. "Hm?"

"Do you want the dress?"

Oh. When he said "it," he meant the *dress*, not… not…

I'm speechless. And still trembling, still tight and nervous and flushed from head to toe.

"Y-yes," I finally manage. "I want the dress."

"Good." The word is like a caress.

"That… that settles it, then," I say, because I can't seem to do anything but reiterate it to myself over and over again. "This is the dress." *He meant the dress, the dress, the dress…*

"Yes. This is most definitely the dress."

There's something in his voice—an appreciation, maybe—that makes me look up, to seek his eyes out in the reflection in front of us. I've spent most of the conversation watching his hand, fixated on the movements of his finger and never daring to meet his eyes in the reflection. And when our eyes lock now, I remember why. The minute our gazes meet, it's like a shock moves through my body. I'm pretty sure a gasp escapes my lips. There's something in his expression—something dangerous and arousing and exciting—and suddenly I forget the dress all over again.

His body is tense. I feel it everywhere we touch, through his arms and his chest and his thighs. His hand still rests against the fabric of the gown's skirt, though even that is forgotten as I lose myself in his eyes.

I hadn't thought his gaze could get more intense, but I was wrong. Even through the reflection, those eyes hypnotize me, tempt me to a dark place of exquisite pleasure. All I have to do is give in.

Suddenly, it's all too much. I jerk away from him— nearly tripping over the hem of the dress in the process, nearly tumbling headfirst into the mirror, but desperate to get out of his reach. I need to think. Need to breathe. Need to get my body under control and snap out of this ridiculous game of pretend.

"That's... that's settled, then," I say, my voice still shaking. "This is the dress. I... I think I should change now."

For a moment, he just looks at me. There's still something dark and thrilling in his eyes—something that makes me think for half a second that he's going to run over and grab me and push me up against the wall—but he doesn't move. He doesn't speak. Maybe he's waiting for me to do something. Or maybe, like me, something about this moment has stunned him, left him frozen.

My stomach is flip-flopping like crazy. His eyes haven't left me. In fact, they burn as bright as ever.

"Are you sure?" he says.

The invitation in his tone makes my legs nearly buckle. I'm not the sort of girl who gets invitations like that. And I'm not the sort of girl who has exhilarating sexual encounters with billionaire businessmen in fitting rooms.

"I-I need to change," I tell him again. I run into the dressing room and slam the door behind me.

This isn't happening. This... This sort of thing doesn't happen to me.

There's a knock on the dressing room door.

"Felicia?" Roman says.

His voice is soft but sure. Like he knows exactly what he wants. *What we both want.*

"I'm changing!" I say. It's more or less a squeak.

He doesn't knock again, but I can feel his presence on the other side of the door as solidly as I felt him against my back only a moment ago. Part of me wants to throw open the door and leap into his arms, and another part of me wants to hide in here forever.

For a long time, neither of us moves. Neither of us speaks. And then, just when I think I can't bear it anymore, I hear him step away. My body relaxes.

Well—not entirely. The tension of having him near me is gone, but another tension still remains. My nipples are still hard as pebbles beneath this dress, and the ache between my legs still begs for attention. Almost involuntarily, I turn toward the mirror. My hands rise to my stomach, and my fingers trace the paths that Roman's finger followed only a short time ago.

My stomach is tight. My fingers wander across the surface of the dress, but they don't stop were Roman's did, just beneath my breast. Instead, they continue on, moving over the curve of my body to where the hard shape of my nipple pokes through the fabric. My touch goes where his would not, and when the pad of my thumb presses against that sensitive nub, I let out an audible gasp.

Once I've started touching myself, I can't seem to

stop. I rub my thumb gently back and forth across my nipple, reveling in the shivers of pleasure it causes. It's a release, and yet at the same time, it's not—for with every touch, the ache between my legs only grows. I move my other hand up to my other nipple, rolling it beneath my palm.

I can't believe I'm touching myself in a fitting room. Still, my fingers move, giving me the contact I longed for. If I hadn't run away, would Roman be touching me like this right now?

I don't know whether it excites me or terrifies me to think about him in that way. A little of both. Sure, he's attractive—very, very attractive—and those eyes of his seem to see right into me. But he's apparently an expert in the art of seduction—and "pick up" masters don't exactly have a reputation for sticking with one girl for the long haul. I'm not sure how I feel about being another conquest for him. On top of all that, there's still the teensy-tiny detail that this guy holds the fate of my job in his hands. I probably shouldn't complicate things.

But *God*, do I want to complicate things.

Touching my nipples through the fabric suddenly doesn't seem like enough. I push the braided straps off of my shoulders and let the top of the dress fall away, baring my breasts to the air. Once more, my fingers move to my nipples, and I watch myself in the mirror— watch my hands move the way I wished Roman's had, watch myself ease the aching need in my body.

I might not be the sort of girl who has a wild encounter with a billionaire in a fitting room, but apparently I *am* the sort of girl who indulges in her own pleasure there. I don't know what's gotten into me.

I'm getting wetter by the minute. I know I shouldn't be doing this, not here, but it's like my body has a mind of its own, a single, pulsing urge. The ache between my thighs is almost unbearable, and I find myself backing toward the armchair in the corner of the room. When the backs of my legs hit the chair, I sink down. I yank the skirt up my legs, high enough for me to slide one of my hands beneath the hem. For me to find the ache, the wetness, the need.

The whole scene stares back at me from the mirror, making me all the more aware of my wantonness. I let one finger part my lips, let it slide all the way down the length of me. Let it move back and forth across me, then a little deeper—until the tip of my finger penetrates the core of my desire.

And that's the exact moment when the dressing room door flies open.

7

FOUR DAYS

THE GOLD GOWN hangs in my closet as a testament to my sin. I can't even look at it without feeling like I'm going to throw up—or seeing the shocked face of that poor salesclerk in my mind.

At least it wasn't Roman who opened the door, I tell myself. *If Roman had seen me...* But honestly, it doesn't matter whether or not he witnessed the incident with his own eyes. Roman *knows*. The salesclerk made it very clear why he'd have to purchase the dress. Roman knows, and I'm never going to live this down.

What's worse—in its own twisted way—is that Roman is fully aware of what happened in that fitting room but didn't say or do anything about it. He didn't utter a word to me when he paid for the dress, nor on the entire ride back to the *Celebrity Spark* offices. Something happened between us in front of that mirror. Something complicated and thrilling and... well, probably ill-advised. But after we left the boutique, he acted like it never occurred. And I was too humiliated to broach the subject myself.

Honestly, I'm so embarrassed about the whole thing that I almost called in sick to work today. But it's not like that would have changed anything. Staying home wouldn't have erased what happened last night.

In the end, my fears of facing Roman all came to nothing. He was only in the *Celebrity Spark* offices for about an hour today, and he was on his phone the whole time. He looked stressed. Pissed, even. But he never walked by my cubicle, never even glanced in my direction. In some ways, that made today a little more bearable. On the other hand, he's given me plenty of time and space to allow this incident to evolve into a big, horrible, life-ending catastrophe in my mind. I've been sitting on my bed since I got home, staring at the dress in terror.

I've relived that mortifying scene a hundred times in my head. And I'm so lost in the hundred-and-first replay that the sudden chime of my cell phone nearly makes me jump out of my skin. My stomach drops. It's Roman. I know it is. I should just ignore it.

But my eyes drop down to my cell of their own volition, and I see that it isn't my boss after all. It's my brother.

I almost ignore it anyway. The last thing I want to do is talk to Matt while I'm recovering from a certain delicate situation. But alternately... my brother might be just the thing I need to distract me. I grab the phone.

"Hey," I say, shoving the cell beneath my ear. *Please be having one of your quarter-life crisis moments.* I've had to talk Matt off a metaphorical ledge a couple of times since he moved out here to pursue his dream of working in the film biz. If I'm lucky, it might take me a couple of hours to convince him once more that he has what it takes to cut it in the industry.

The first thing I hear is noise—a *lot* of noise. Voices, music, glasses clanking—

"Sis!" Matt yells into the phone, though I can barely hear him over all the *ambiance.* "You've got to come down to Marietta's."

I laugh at the very suggestion. Matt might enjoy L.A.'s nightlife, but he knows I couldn't care less about going out to clubs and bars.

"I'm not going out," I tell him. "I have work in the morning." And considering how little I got done today, I'm going to have a lot to do.

It's his turn to laugh. "This *is* work. At least for you."

I lean back against my pillows with a smile. "Do I need to remind you what I do for a living?"

"You spy on celebrities, right?"

"I don't 'spy' on anyone. I'm not one of the paparazzi. I just write."

"So when you told me to call you if I ever ran into someone famous, that was just for shits and giggles?"

"Is there some hot celeb action going on down at Marietta's, then? Some underage starlet getting drunk?" I know of Marietta's. It's a mid-level club. Not exactly where celebs go to see and be seen. It might get a few C- and D-listers now and again, but those aren't the people who will help me keep my job.

"Actually," Matt yells over the noise, "I'm pretty sure I'm looking at Raphael Fontaine."

I sit up. "Raphael Fontaine?"

"That's what I said, isn't it?"

"Are you sure?"

"I think so. I mean, he's wearing sunglasses and a hat. He's definitely trying to pass as a regular guy. Covered up his tattoos and everything."

"Are you certain it *isn't* just a regular guy? How much have you had to drink?" I don't want to get my hopes up—or drive all the way out to Marietta's—for nothing.

"Just a couple of beers. But I was right next to him for a second at the bar and heard him talk. I'd know that voice anywhere."

And he would. A couple of years ago, Raphael was the face of an ad campaign for a designer's new luxury cologne—he appeared in both the campaign's print ads and television commercials, and in the latter, he delivered the cologne's now-famous tagline: "A life of desire. The scent of lust." And let me tell you—those words melted a thousand panties. Raphael's voice is deep, almost gravelly, and I swear, it vibrates right through you. Even my brother—who's never met a pair of breasts he didn't like—apparently noticed.

I'm off my bed.

"I'll be there in twenty minutes," I tell him. "Don't let him leave."

"I'm not sure I have any control over that."

"Just don't," I tell him. Then I throw my phone down on the bed and run into my closet.

Twenty-three minutes later, I'm at Marietta's.

Well… sort of.

As a matter of fact, I'm *outside* Marietta's, at the back of the longest line ever. I can count sixty people in front of me from where I'm standing. I can't even see the entrance to the place.

I try not to get discouraged as the minutes tick by. This might not be how I planned on spending my Tuesday night, but A, at least it's helping me keep my mind off of the thing-that-happened-last-night, and B, I figure the universe has to be throwing me a bone. I mean, getting the chance to talk to Dante Fontaine was insane on its own. But *two* Fontaines in less than a week? I guess the higher power figures I deserve a break. Or maybe my guardian angel just wants me to keep my job.

Assuming it *is* Raphael my brother saw, of course. I've called Matt three times since I got here—*he* managed to get in, so maybe he can get me past this line—but he hasn't answered. He probably can't hear his phone over the music. Even out here, I can feel the thump of the bass in my bones.

I cross my arms and glance down the length of the line again. It's a little breezy tonight, and I'm glad I grabbed a pair of black skinny jeans instead of a skirt. I almost topped it off with a sequined tank top I found in the back of my closet—a remnant from my college days—but in the end, I remembered Roman's advice about subtlety and opted for a shimmery blouse instead. Now that I'm looking at the other women in this line, though, I'm beginning to reconsider my choices. I don't care what Roman thinks—a tight little skirt and some killer heels would probably have gotten me through the door a lot faster. Even as I watch, a bouncer walks down the queue of waiting people and beckons to a couple of girls in short, sparkly dresses. They beam as he leads them around the building toward the door.

Yeah. Definitely should've gone for a more obviously sexy look tonight. I was in such a rush to get out the door that I didn't even get to do my makeup properly. At this rate, I'll be out here all night.

I shoot a text to Matt, praying that he feels the buzzing in his pocket. But knowing my brother, he's had another few drinks since we spoke. Or he's hooking up with someone in the bathroom or something. Matt was always the wild one. The one who sneaked out past curfew, the one who got caught having sex as a teenager.

The one who would always throw big parties when Mom went out of town. I was the responsible one. The good girl. Though after last night, I'm not sure *what* I am anymore.

But I push those thoughts aside. I need to focus on the task at hand, and that means figuring out how to get in this club and make a move on Raphael Fontaine. I have no idea what I'm up against or what sort of situation I'm walking into. Is it really Raphael? Have other people recognized him? Hell, things will be hard even if I somehow manage to get Raphael all to myself. He always struck me as the wild card of the Fontaine boys, and I don't know how to approach him. My lessons with Roman haven't gotten this far.

Still, it's thrilling to be out here on my own, to be doing this without my overbearing—and confusing, and oh-so-sexy—teacher. A week ago, I wouldn't have even dreamed of walking up to Raphael Fontaine, let alone trying to flirt with him. Now, I feel brave. Or reckless. And I'm enjoying it more than I want to admit.

But as the minutes creep on, I find myself growing impatient. Matt hasn't returned any of my calls or texts. I'm convinced he's forgotten all about me—which, unfortunately, isn't uncommon with my brother, especially when there are ladies around. Even as I stand here, he's probably going at it like rabbits with someone in the bathrooms—and I definitely do *not* want to think about that. Meanwhile, the line hasn't moved more than a couple of feet, and that's only because every few minutes one of the bouncers comes by and selects another couple of women from the waiting crowd. He never spares me more than a passing glance.

What am I even doing here? It's looking less and less likely that I'm going to get inside. And even if I do manage it somehow, I have no idea if I'll be able to find Raphael in the massive crowd—assuming it *is* Raphael in the first place. I'm beginning to think this night might be a bust.

As my hopes sour, so does my mood. I really wanted to prove something tonight, to show myself that I could do this on my own. The thought of walking into the *Celebrity Spark* offices tomorrow with the promise of an interview with Raphael Fontaine would show everyone that I deserved to be there. And it would show Roman... well, I'm not exactly sure *what* I want to show Roman at this point. But I'll deal with those confusing thoughts later. Right now I'm frustrated. I'm tired. I'm bored. And that 24-hour diner across the way is suddenly looking pretty damn tempting.

I glance down at my watch. I've been here for more than an hour. Maybe it's time to call it a night.

A couple of minutes later, I'm sliding onto a stool at the counter of Big Barb's Diner. It's busy in here—no doubt they get a lot of people coming out of the club— but since I'm alone, I don't have to wait for a seat. The diners on either side of me here at the counter are a little closer than I'd like, but neither of them reeks of cigarettes or booze, so I'm calling this a win.

"Know what you want?" the waitress asks me.

I take a quick glance over the menu. I felt so sick earlier over the whole fitting room incident that I didn't even attempt to eat dinner tonight. Now I'm starving.

"Double cheeseburger," I say. "And chili fries." I'm probably going to regret this an hour from now when I'm trying to fall asleep, but I don't care. It's been a rough few days.

There's a low chuckle beside me. "You must be hungry."

I suck in a breath. I know that voice. It's the same one Matt claimed he recognized. The one that's fueled so many women's sexual fantasies. I'm almost afraid to look, but I can't keep my eyes from drifting over to the man on my left.

There he is in the flesh. *Raphael Fontaine.* Third son of Charles and Giovanna Fontaine. The sexy, rugged, deep-voiced, dark horse of the family.

He's wearing his sunglasses, just as Matt said. Back home, any guy who wore sunglasses inside at night might as well have had the word "douchebag" tattooed onto his forehead, but here in L.A., no one even spares him a second glance. Half the guys in this diner are wearing them, and he might as well be any other clubgoer.

He's not, however, wearing a hat—and I can see

why he didn't bother. He's shaved his head. Not in the shiny, cue-ball kind of way, but in the close-buzzed, I-could-be-the-leader-of-a-sexy-motorcycle-gang way. Before, he had thick, dark hair like his brother Dante, but now, he's almost unrecognizable. Though I have to admit, the new look definitely suits him, especially with that layer of stubble on his chin. And the edge of that tattoo peeking out above the neck of his T-shirt. I definitely approve.

And I'm definitely staring. He said something to me, didn't he?

"Yeah. Yes—I'm starving," I say quickly. I can't believe that after standing in line for nearly an hour, I walked in here and sat down next to him without even realizing it. My guardian angel—or whoever is looking out for me—is definitely getting some major props.

"This place has the best chili fries in the city," he says. "Milkshakes, too. Though I expect more people would argue with me on that one." He glances at me as if he expects *me* to be one of those people, but I just shake my head and try not to turn into a weird giggly goofball. *Raphael Fontaine* is talking to me about milkshakes, of all things.

"I've never had one," I say, hoping I sound normal. "Never been here before."

"Ah. A Barb's virgin."

I let out a nervous laugh. "I guess you could say that."

He's got a crooked smile, and somehow that makes the whole package more enticing.

"Well, we'll have to fix that," he says. In the deep, rich tones of his voice, that comment sounds a lot more suggestive than I'm sure he intended. But then he holds out his hand to me. "I'm Rafe, by the way."

Rafe. Oh God, I can't believe he's asking me to call him by a nickname. But now I'm in a pickle—does he assume I've recognized him, or is this his way of giving me his name without revealing who he is? And if that's the case, should I play along with his bluff?

I decide to roll with it.

"I'm Felicia," I say. I shake his hand, trying not to show how flustered he's making me.

"So, Felicia," he says—and God, does my name sound sexy on his tongue—"How'd you end up here? You don't look like you came from the club." His eyes scan over my blouse and jeans.

"Well, I sort of did," I tell him. "I just never made it past the line." My eyes drop down to my outfit and I feel a blush creeping on. "I think I was a little under-dressed."

"So they let your friends in without you?"

"Oh, no. Nothing like that." I'm definitely blushing now. "I was just there to meet my brother, but he wasn't answering his phone. And then I got bored and hungry."

He's looking at me a little oddly, but there's still a

crooked smile on his lips, like he's enjoying this.

"Most women don't go to clubs to meet up with their brother," he comments. "Isn't that what Sunday brunch is for?"

I can't exactly explain the *real* reason why I showed up at Marietta's. "I just thought it would be fun to dance a little."

He gives a low, deep laugh. "Marietta's isn't exactly a *dancing* club."

"Are you kidding? I can hear the music from here."

Another laugh. "You're cute, you know that?"

I don't even get the chance to enjoy the fact that he called me *cute*, because I suddenly realize what he's saying. And how absolutely naive I must sound.

"I didn't… I mean, he just called me and asked me to meet him. I thought it might be fun," I say.

Raphael—Rafe—seems amused by this. He leans a little closer to me, his smile deepening.

"I think you and I might have different ideas of what *fun* entails," he says.

Is he… *flirting* with me? Or am I just imagining the implication in his tone? Either way, I'm having a hard time concentrating. Good God, he smells amazing. It's nothing like the way Roman smells—though why I'm thinking of him at all right now, I don't know—but rather something a little more *natural*. Like… pure man.

I need to keep this going, whatever else I do.

"And... what do you consider *fun*, then?" I hear myself ask.

He grins and sits back. "I think you know the answer to that already." His gaze drifts over my clothes again. "I have a feeling you aren't half as innocent as you look. Tell me the truth—you just didn't find anyone to your liking at Marietta's, is that it?"

"Oh, no," I say automatically. "I'm not... I didn't come here to..." I must be bright red by now.

"You didn't come here to...?"

"I'm not that kind of girl," I whisper.

"What kind of girl?"

My mind is whirling. "The kind who... who goes to a club in the hopes of meeting someone and going at it like rabbits in the bathroom."

He nearly chokes, the laughter comes up so fast. It takes him a minute to get himself under control.

"Do you have a problem with rabbits?" he asks. "Or just sex?"

"Neither," I say quickly, wanting to melt. "I just wouldn't have sex with someone in some public bathroom."

"Some people do actually leave the club before having sex. But honestly, you shouldn't knock something before you've tried it."

"Some things you don't have to try."

"And some things you should."

The rich, deep tones of the word *should* travel all the

way down my back. This whole conversation feels dangerous—but even as part of me wants to run away, another part of me is excited by his forwardness. I feel suddenly bold.

"What about you?" I say. "Why aren't you in the club?"

There's that smile again. "I didn't find what I was looking for."

"What? Or who?"

He doesn't answer, but his continued grin tells me everything I need to know. That grin could lead a girl to do some very, very wicked things—even a girl who claims she wouldn't. *Before yesterday, I wouldn't have called myself a girl who'd touch herself in a fitting room, either. I guess these things can change quickly.* Especially with a man like the one beside me.

I realize I'm staring again, but I'm saved by the arrival of food—first his, and then mine. As expected, the chili fries look amazing. But I'm no longer focused on the food. I haven't forgotten my original objective for coming out here tonight, and I'm beginning to think Rafe might be even more responsive to my advances than his brother. But I have to take control of the interaction first. I can't let him keep flustering me.

I take a bite of my cheeseburger as I think, going through all of Roman's lessons in my head. Just the thought of my boss makes my heart beat a little faster, my cheeks feel a little warmer, but I don't let myself think about any of the things that happened last night. Whatever's going on between me and Roman is… is too complicated to worry about right now. I have a job to do.

In the end, my plan is a simple one.

There's a bottle of ketchup on the counter in front of Rafe. I don't normally put extra ketchup on my burger, but tonight, I think I'll make an exception. Slowly, I lean forward and across him, making sure my arm brushes against his as I grab the bottle. And when I lean back in my seat, I settle a little closer to him than before. It's not hard—our stools were already pretty close together—but now my hip rests against his. It's not exactly subtle, but I'm not sure I need to be subtle with this one.

Out of the corner of my eye, I see him smile. I pour the ketchup on my burger, then lean slightly toward him.

"Want some?" I ask innocently.

"Of course." He takes the ketchup from my hand, brushing his fingers against mine in the process in a way that is *definitely* intentional.

My heart flutters. He's definitely flirting with me. I'm not even sure how this happened. Not even a week ago, I would've had my foot in my mouth by now. Instead, Rafe Fontaine is talking to me like a potential conquest. And honestly, not many girls would mind being invaded by him. And while in the past I would've admitted a partiality toward the dark and sexy Dante, or toward the golden demigod Luca, I'm beginning to think I might be one of those girls who drools over Rafe instead.

"So you've never had sex in a public place?" he says as he pours the ketchup on his food.

My skin heats again. I thought we were past this part of the conversation.

"It just… never appealed to me," I say quietly. I'm not ready to confess anything about last night, especially to Rafe Fontaine.

"You'd never try it?"

I take my time mulling over my response.

"Maybe… maybe under the right circumstances," I say. "With someone I trusted."

"Not a one night stand?"

My pulse thumps. "I—I don't know. I've never had one."

"You've never done a lot of things."

I don't answer. I'm losing control of the conversation again, letting him unsettle me with his personal questions and sexy smile and ridiculously tantalizing voice.

"Do you ever just want to let loose?" he asks me in that sexy rumble of his. "To push your limits a little?"

Yes, I want to say. And my body would agree. Last week, I never would have even considered the idea, but since I started my lessons with Roman, I find myself thinking and feeling and doing things I never would before.

But if I admit that, I'm playing right into him.

"And what if I'm fine the way I am?" I ask lightly.

That earns me another laugh. "I never said you weren't." But when he starts to pick at his chili fries again, I know he's leaving something unsaid.

"You don't believe me," I accuse him.

"I never said that. In fact, I'm not sure I'd believe you if you claimed otherwise. You seem pretty critical of the idea of casual sex."

It's hard to read him with his eyes hidden behind those sunglasses, so I can't tell if he's teasing me.

"I'm not being critical," I say. "Just because I'm not sure the idea appeals to me doesn't mean I'm opposed to other people having it. If it makes them happy, they should have sex with whoever they want, whenever they want, wherever they want. Within reason, of course."

That crooked smile is back. "And how exactly would you define 'reason'?"

"You know what I mean. Not in the middle of the street or something."

"But in the club?"

"If they want."

"In a diner?"

His directness knocks the breath right out of me.

"H-hopefully not *in* the diner," I say, a little too quietly. "Some customers might not appreciate that kind of entertainment while they're trying to eat."

"In the bathroom, then?"

I force myself to swallow. "That's a better alternative, yes." *Did Rafe Fontaine just invite me to have sex with him in the bathroom?* Am I going crazy?

He's gone back to eating. I do too, resisting the urge to shove three chili fries in my mouth at once. I can hardly think straight with him so close to me. The side of my thigh is still pressed against his, and if anything, it seems like he's actively returning the pressure. What am I supposed to do now? What would Roman tell me to do?

Roman. Thinking about him adds another level of complication to this. After last night, I have no idea what he'd tell me to do. But I know one thing—if Rafe had been the one with me in front of that mirror, he would have done a lot more than just teasing. And he never would've let me go home alone after the *incident.*

No, Rafe is something completely different. Something bad and dirty and thrilling. Something I think I like, in spite of all of my good sense. And I still can't believe I haven't made a fool of myself yet. Or spilled something on myself.

He's looking at me again. "Have I scared you?"

I shake my head, hoping my cheeks aren't as red as they feel. "No."

"Good." He leans a little closer, then turns his head so his mouth is right next to my ear. "I want to take you to the bathroom." His words are a hot whisper.

I've never had an invitation like that from any guy in my entire life. I don't know how to respond. Part of me is terrified. I can't possibly go have sex with someone I just met, even if that man is Rafe Fontaine. The other part of me, however, is screaming, *Yes! Yes! Yes!*

Rafe must sense my indecision. He leans back again.

"You don't have to decide anything right now," he says, apparently unperturbed by the fact that I didn't leap into his arms and beg him to bang me right here. Hell, maybe he was *expecting* me to say no.

No. I might not be good at this, but I'm not stupid. Rafe Fontaine just came on to me. If I weren't so stunned—or afraid—he might be leading me to the bathroom right now. I never thought I'd be that girl. Not just one who could capture the attention of one of the Fontaine brothers, but one who's actually considering letting things go to the next level not twenty minutes after meeting him.

Now that girl isn't just a possibility—she's a reality.

I quickly take another bite of my burger, pretending to be absorbed in my dinner. But my eyes keep drifting back over to Rafe. *Fuck, he sexy.* He makes me want to do all kinds of terrible things. Maybe he's onto something—maybe I'm dying to let loose. I've done a lot of new things this week. Things that made me uncomfortable. Things that pushed me outside of my comfort zone. But I haven't tested all of my limits yet.

I want to. God, I want to.

"Okay," I say. I'm surprised by how sure and steady I sound.

Rafe looks over at me, the question in his eyes. "Okay?"

I lean toward him, mirroring his movements of a moment ago and putting my lips right against his ear. "Okay. Take me to the bathroom."

He takes my hand in his. His eyes burn bright, his gaze filling me with heat.

"All right, then." I don't know how it's possible, but his voice seems even deeper than before. He slides off his stool and pulls me down off mine. His fingers close around mine, enveloping my hand in warmth. A thrill runs through my body.

I can't believe I'm doing this. But I want to show myself that I can.

He leads me through the crowded diner. I feel like every eye is on us, but in reality, no one spares us more than a passing glance. Maybe they don't realize what we're about to do. Or maybe, to other people, the idea of sneaking off to a bathroom to hookup isn't as strange and terrifying and exciting as it is to me. Perhaps if they realized the sexy beast of a man leading me was Raphael Fontaine, things would be a little different. Perhaps if I were a little more focused, I'd be securing an interview rather than a steamy bathroom encounter. But tonight, I don't want to be the *Celebrity Spark* writer. I'm just

Felicia, and he's just Rafe.

"Men's or women's?" he asks.

It takes me a minute to understand what he's asking.

"Men's," I say. Somehow, going into the men's restroom makes it feel that much more wicked.

He smiles and squeezes my hand as he pushes through the door and leads me inside. By some miracle, there's no one at the sinks as we step inside, no one to see Rafe lead me into the largest stall and lock the door behind us. My heart thunders.

"Are you all right?" he asks. "Your hands are shaking." He raises my fingers to his lips and presses a kiss against my knuckles.

"I'm fine," I tell him. I'm nervous, but it's the good kind of nervous. The oh-my-God-I-can't-believe-I'm-doing-this kind of nervous.

"Good." His other hand slips around my waist and pulls me toward him. I brace myself against his chest, and beneath my fingers I feel the hardness of the muscles under his shirt.

He pulls his sunglasses off and shoves them in his pocket. I lift my face, but before I even have the chance to see his eyes—or to gasp—his mouth comes down on mine. His lips are hot and demanding and… *God*, so damn delicious. The sort of lips that take exactly what they want but give you so much more in return.

My fingers curl and grip his shirt. My knees want to buckle, but his strong arm around my waist keeps me on my feet. His fingers splay against my back, pressing me closer to him, and at the same time, his tongue slips into my mouth.

Oh my God. This man is an incredible kisser. My mouth submits to his, my lips spreading to let him explore me as deeply as he likes. My hands are fists now, and the rest of my body is coming alive to this sudden explosion of sensation and pleasure. When his tongue flicks against mine, my nipples stiffen beneath my shirt. And when he suddenly twists me and pins me right against the wall of the stall—letting me feel how excited he already is beneath his pants—the lower, more sensitive parts of my body respond as well. My thighs part almost involuntarily, spreading so that he can press a little closer between my legs.

His mouth has pulled away from mine now, and it blazes a path along my jaw to my ear. He sucks my earlobe between his teeth, and I let out a moan. I release his shirt and slide my hands around to his back, pulling him closer to me. His smell is overwhelming now, all man and musk and a little bit of sweat and, and... *fuck*, it's intoxicating, whatever it is. I dig my nails into his back and I'm rewarded with a growl and another nip at my earlobe.

"I wasn't expecting you to be quite so hungry," he says, and his chuckle is a rumble. "I thought maybe you'd change your mind at the last minute."

I can't imagine changing my mind, not after I've

been kissed the way he kissed me. But I'm too numb with pleasure to say so.

His hands, meanwhile, are accomplishing their own business. His fingers slide up my sides, pressing my blouse against my skin as he moves closer and closer to my breasts. I expect him to be rough, but while his mouth is ravaging my ear and neck, his hands are gentle, exploratory. He cups my breasts, rolling them against his palms before finding my nipples with his thumbs. He rakes his thumbs back and forth across the hard nubs, making my breath come in gasps. Making me want to beg him to squeeze, to twist, to taste. Instead, he plays with me for a moment before dropping his hands. I do start to beg then, but before I can form any real words, his mouth is on mine again, his tongue silencing mine with a delicious attack. And his hands fall down to the hem of my blouse and slip beneath the fabric.

He takes his time moving his fingers up over my belly. His hands are so warm, and his touch is infuriatingly light. I squirm against the stall wall, trying to show him with my body what I want—what I *need*—since he's holding my mouth hostage.

And all the while I'm thinking, *I can't believe I'm in a bathroom stall with Rafe Fontaine...* It's unreal. I must be imagining it. But his body feels so solid and real against mine, his skin so hot and smooth, his cock so hard...

He shifts his hips, and I whimper against his lips. My hands rise to his hair—though there's not much to grab onto. It's almost hotter that way.

After what feels like forever, his fingers finally find my breasts. I let out a small cry of pleasure.

"Is that what you wanted?" he says, his low voice rumbling through his chest.

"Yes," I gasp.

His hands slip under my bra as if it isn't there at all, and my nipples pebble against the pads of his fingers. His touch is more urgent now, too—as if he's finally figured out that I want him to be rough, that I'm not as scared of this as he believed me to be. I'm not scared at all. Just, just... *riveted*. I'm being manhandled by Raphael Fontaine. In a bathroom. In a random diner in L.A.

I'm *so* not the girl I was last week.

My need is growing stronger by the second. That familiar desire is throbbing between my legs, and my hips begin to move against his. His own body mirrors my movements, pushing me rhythmically back against the stall, sliding his stiff arousal against me through our pants.

Suddenly his hands drop from my breasts. He grabs my ass—one hand on each side—and hoists me up. I hook my legs around his hips, still grinding against him, still hardly believing how wanton I'm being right now.

When he has me pinned against the stall once more,

his hands return to my shirt. This time they decide to just be done with the whole thing, and he tugs it over my head.

"You..." he says hotly, his eyes roaming over my chest, "You are exquisite." He kisses me again, his mouth attacking mine until I'm dizzy, and then his lips drop a little lower. Down my chin. Along my jaw. Over my throat.

Unbidden, I remember my lesson with Roman last night and all the things he said about a woman's throat. I didn't even put my hair up tonight, and yet Rafe is drawn to that area anyway, nipping at the skin with his teeth.

But the thought of Roman brings a number of confusing feelings as well. I try to ignore the sudden, unpleasant twinge in my stomach, but something else occurs to me too.

"Don't leave any marks," I say between ragged breaths.

He gives a laugh. "Why? You got a boyfriend who'll get jealous?"

An image of Roman flashes again in my mind, and the guilt is a little stronger this time. I don't know why—Roman's most definitely *not* my boyfriend. And if he wanted me, he had his chance last night. He's only been teasing me all this time, entertaining himself by "teaching" me and watching me fumble my way through awkward situations. He has no right to get upset over something like a hickey.

But I have another reason to want to avoid any telltale love bites. I have a job to do on Saturday, and if I show up with marks on my neck, that's most definitely *not* going to help me. Of course, I could always try to convince Rafe tonight to let me interview him... but honestly, that's not my top priority right now.

His tongue flicks against the hollow of my throat, and all thought of interviews and magazines falls out of my brain. I only have one focus right now.

"No boyfriend," I tell him. "Just don't do it."

"Mm. Demanding little cat, aren't you?" he says against my skin. Still, he respects my request, gentling his bites, though I can tell it's taking a good deal of restraint. The muscles of his neck are tense beneath my hands, and the knowledge that I—ordinary Felicia—am doing this to him is one of the most arousing feelings I've ever known.

I arch my back, trying to get more friction between us. Rafe gives another growl and moves his mouth back up to my ear. He seems to realize it's safer to play there, and his teeth come down hard on the delicate skin. A groan escapes my lips, a sound half of pain and half of pleasure. That seems to excite him even more, because his hips begin to move more urgently against mine. The stall rattles behind me, but I don't care. This is amazingly dirty, and I've never felt so free.

"Fuck, Alicia. You're amazing," he says. "You're a

filthy little cat, aren't you?"

At first my mind brushes right past the name. He called me a *filthy little cat*. God, that's so erotic. No one would ever have called the old Felicia a filthy little cat.

But then my brain registers that he's not really calling the "new" Felicia that either.

I twist my face away from him, pulling my ear from between his lips. "What did you call me?"

A smile twists across his face. *Fuck, he's hot.*

"My filthy little cat," he repeats in his velvet rumble of a voice. God, it sounds even sexier the more he says it.

But I force myself to shake my head. "I mean before that. My name."

He's still got that lusty smile on his face. "Alicia. That's your name, isn't it?"

Good God, he's forgotten it already.

Either he doesn't notice my expression or he chooses to ignore it. His mouth comes down on my neck again, and I actually consider letting it slide. There's something naughty about him not knowing my name. It sort of hammers the whole "strangers" aspect of this situation home.

Except that I know *his* name. And even a name like Fontaine—and that amazing mouth of his—can't get me past the fact that if I hook up with anyone, I at least want him to know what to call me.

I pull away again and push against his chest. "I'm

sorry. I can't do this."

He stills, but his lips still linger by my neck. I can feel his hot, ragged breath against my skin.

"Are you sure, you naughty thing?" he murmurs.

That voice almost undoes me. *Maybe a few more minutes wouldn't hurt...*

No. No—suddenly all of this feels wrong, and not just because of the whole name thing. Whatever I was trying to prove to myself, I've proved it. I can attract one of the Fontaine brothers. I can be the girl who flirts—and manages to *get*—an objectively inhumanly gorgeous guy. I can be spontaneous and sexually adventurous.

But that's it. And now that I've done it, it just feels so... hollow.

"I need to go," I say, pulling out of his grip.

My blouse is on the ground. I grab it and try not to think about what sort of germs it's now carrying as I tug it over my head. Only after I'm fully covered again do I dare look at Rafe. He's leaning against the side of the stall, looking... well, disappointed.

It's the first time I've gotten a real look at his face without the sunglasses—the first time in person, I mean. Obviously I've seen plenty of photos of him before. But as with his brother Dante, nothing compares to seeing him in the flesh. His eyes are brown like Dante's, but lighter, and they're still half-lidded with desire. For a split second, I see a flash of something in his expression that makes me pause—something that makes him look almost vulnerable.

"I'm sorry," I say, fighting back a weird mix of emotions. "I'm guessing your original impression of me was right after all."

He rubs the back of his head and gives a little regretful shake of his head. "It could've been fun."

God, I know. I need to get out of here before I do something stupid.

"For what it's worth," I say, "thank you."

That seems to surprise him. But he doesn't say anything as I unlock the stall door and step out into the bathroom.

And nearly run into the man outside.

It's just some random guy, but he's got his cell phone up, pointing toward the stall. My stomach plummets. He was *filming* this. Not that he could see anything juicy—unless he held the phone down below the stall walls, which is a terrifying thought—but I'm sure the audio was dirty enough.

But that's not the worst of it. As I'm standing there, frozen, Rafe walks out of the stall behind me. And he must not have put his sunglasses back on yet, because the eyes of the guy in front of me widen in recognition almost immediately.

"Oh, shit," he says. "You're that guy, aren't you? That Fontaine guy?"

And I've been in the celebrity entertainment industry long enough to know that I've just gotten myself into a deep pile of shit.

8

THREE DAYS

On MY FIRST day of my first internship in this industry, I was warned that this business would come back to bite me in the ass.

Of course, that advice was given to me by a woman who'd just been fired, so at the time I figured she meant something else entirely. Now, however, I'm beginning to understand. And I'm sure there are many out there who think I'm getting exactly what I deserve, that since I work in the "gossip" industry, I don't have the right to get upset about this at all. It's karma. I had it coming.

And maybe I did. But to be fair, the entertainment industry runs on this stuff, and the business-savvy celebrities use it to their advantage. Got a movie coming out? Time to start hooking up with your costar. Or get pregnant. Or get trashed at a club and cause a scene. People like me, on the other hand? Even though I know how this industry works, I'm not quite prepared to be on the other side of things.

I have to give Rafe some credit, at least. The minute he realized what was going on last night, he grabbed the amateur photographer by the shirt and shoved him up against the wall. Snatched his phone. Deleted the video. But as I learned this morning via some paranoid internet searches, "delete" doesn't just make everything go away. The guy's phone must have automatically backed up the file to his email or something, because sure enough, I find the footage online.

It's bad. The video quality is poor, and—by some miracle—the guy with the phone didn't think to bend over and shoot beneath the stall. All you see is the door. The sound, on the other hand, comes through loud and clear.

It's absolutely horrific to hear my own moans and whimpers on camera. I thought that if I ever built up the guts to let a guy film me during sex, the results might be... well, a little sexier. This just makes my stomach turn. Last night, while it was happening, I thought the whole encounter was thrilling and erotic— even if it was a mistake. Now, I just feel dirty. And not in the good way. And hearing the short but embarrassing exchange after I pushed him away isn't much better.

Honestly, the video is so poor that, under different circumstances, it would never have made it past the guy's cell. Yeah, you'll always have pervs who hit "record" the minute they see (or hear) people going at it somewhere relatively public, but let's get real—anyone who's scouring the internet for video of people having sex has plenty of porn to choose from. Videos where they can actually *see* the action, so to speak.

What makes this video different is the last ten seconds, when first I and then Rafe walk out of the stall. As a bonus, it even captures the moment when Rafe lunges at the guy.

The video has been titled, "Raphael Fontaine attacks man after getting blue-balled by chick." Whoever came up with that isn't going to be winning any awards for snappy headlines anytime soon, and under different circumstances, I'd probably find it funny. I guess I should be grateful no one knows who I am—as long as I'm just a "chick," these three minutes of shame won't pop up in an internet search of my name—but if anyone who knows me sees this footage, I'm screwed. As awful as the quality is, there's a dead-on shot of my face right before Rafe leaps into action.

The question, then, is *who* will see this? Is this juicy enough for any of the celebrity gossip blogs to pick up? Or for people who work in this industry to seek out? Rafe has a reputation for being a player. And as far as I know, he isn't cheating on anyone. He probably shouldn't have grabbed the guy with the cell phone, but it's not like he was arrested for assault. I'm thinking— *hoping*—that this is just ordinary enough to pass under the radar. Everyone is focused on Luca and Dante right now because of *Cataclysm: Earth.*

Still, there's a knot in my stomach as I sit at my desk. I didn't think I could dread seeing Roman anymore than I did yesterday, but I was wrong. I've hit an all new low.

And, oh yeah—in spite of my efforts last night, I still managed to get a hickey. It's been so long since I fooled around with anyone that I forgot how easily I bruise. I spent an hour this morning caking layer after layer of makeup over it, but that only helped a little. I'm wearing my hair down today, but things might get tricky if the love bite is still visible on Saturday. I do *not* want to have to explain to Roman why I'm ignoring his advice to show off my neck.

If Roman finds out what happened last night...

I don't want to think about that. The purpose of seducing the Fontaine brothers was never about actually getting in their pants. It's to get interviews—something I completely forgot about in my inability to control my urges last night. And not only that, but now I've put the whole plan at risk—it's going to be impossible for me to convince Rafe to chat with me now, even if I ever muster the courage to approach him again. And if any of his family members watch this video and then recognize me at *Hollywood Saves!*, they're not going to see me as a serious, respectable reporter.

Roman's going to kill me. Or fire me, at the very least.

But for the second day in a row, he's absent from

the office for most of the morning. I still haven't exchanged a word with him since the whole fitting room incident. When he finally does arrive, he heads straight for my desk. I bury myself in my work, trying to ignore the sound of his footsteps coming closer and closer. But when he stops right next to my chair, I know I can't just pretend he isn't there.

"Felicia," he says. "I need to speak with you before you leave today."

This is it. I'm officially getting fired.

I spend the rest of the day trying to distract myself, but it's hard to convince yourself to work when you know the end is nigh. The minutes drag on forever, but the seemingly endless wait still isn't long enough for me to come up with a reasonable excuse for my behavior of the past few days. There *is* no excuse.

I wait until most of my coworkers have left for the day before I drag myself to my feet and march toward the conference room. I don't want anyone witnessing this. No doubt word will spread quickly, but I hope I'm gone by the time people start emailing the video to each other.

When I enter the conference room, Roman is, as usual, bent over his laptop. His phone buzzes, but he doesn't answer it. He doesn't look up at me, but he gestures to the chair across from him.

"I'll be with you in a minute," he says.

I don't answer. I just sink into the chair and try to

gauge his mood. As usual, his stoic exterior gives nothing away. This is just another meeting for him. He'll let me go like he did the others, and by next week I'll just be that girl who couldn't cut it. Or maybe the girl who cost *Celebrity Spark* $1300 because she touched herself in a designer gown and then had an almost-sex tape with Raphael Fontaine.

My eyes linger on his face. His jaw is tense, his brows drawn slightly together in concentration. He looks tired—but I guess I shouldn't be surprised by that. The man never seems to stop working, except when he's with me.

Tired or not, something about him still makes my heart flutter. I can't look at him without remembering the way he touched me in that fitting room, or the things I saw in his eyes in that mirror. Maybe it's best that he's firing me. I'm not sure I can survive another week as his distraction. My feelings are already too jumbled, my body on edge just from sitting across the table from him.

Finally, he looks up, and the intensity in his eyes sends a jolt through me.

"Thank you for agreeing to meet with me, Felicia," he says. "Let me send off this email, and then we can talk. I've spent all day meeting with potential managing editors."

I don't know why he thinks that matters to me anymore. But I just smile and nod. Hopefully we can get this over with quickly.

"We didn't get a chance to chat yesterday," he says. "I thought we should discuss where you are in your lessons. We only have three more days until the big event."

I blink at him. Is he serious? Is it possible he doesn't know about the video yet?

"I'd hoped we might meet tonight," he continues. "But unfortunately, I have a dinner engagement. But I thought a chat might be in order."

"Okay," I say. Relief rushes through me. He definitely hasn't seen the video. Maybe I'll survive this disaster after all. But my stomach twists at the words "dinner engagement"—is that a polite way of saying he has a date?

"I took the liberty of booking a salon appointment for you on Saturday," he says. "It will be on the company's dime, of course. But I thought that would make things a little easier on you."

I nod. Now that the initial relief has set in, I've realized that I'm not in the clear yet. There's still a possibility he could see the video before Saturday, and even if he doesn't, chances are that I still won't be able to pull off our plan.

"Do you have plans tonight?" he asks.

I sit up a little straighter. "No."

"Good. I want you to continue practicing. Find a bar, make some small talk, try integrating some of the things I've shown you. You need to get comfortable talking to men."

He's sending me off on my own. Little does he know that I got more than my fair share of practice last night. If that video didn't exist, I might have told him about what happened, how I managed to use everything I've learned to attract Rafe Fontaine—but that's not possible, not now.

So I just give another smile and a nod. "Okay. I'll try."

"If you're free tomorrow, we can have another lesson then," he says. "It will be good to go over your progress and come up with a specific plan for Saturday."

"Okay." It's still so strange for him to talk about all of this as if he's discussing a marketing plan or business campaign. But at the end of the day, I need to remember that that's what this is, after all. And be grateful that I still have a job.

He's silent for a long moment, studying me, and it takes all of my willpower to continue to meet his gaze.

"You look worried, Felicia," he says. "Have you been practicing relaxing as I showed you?"

I'm not sure how he could ever expect me to be relaxed this week—I mean, I thought I was going to be fired when I walked in here just now—but I smile and nod.

I'm not sure whether or not he buys it, but his hazel eyes continue to bore into mine. My heart speeds up, and I find myself gripping the arms of my chair as my mind continues to flood with images of the last time we were together. I'd almost swear I can still feel his touch against my throat, or the brush of the gold gown's silky fabric against my body. How can I ever be relaxed around this man? He makes my entire body come to life, makes it shiver with a glorious energy.

"There's something I need to ask you," he says, his voice a little lower than it was a moment ago.

I stiffen. Maybe I'm *not* escaping this meeting without an awkward conversation after all.

Roman leans his elbows on the table. He's not wearing his jacket today, and I try not to notice the way the sleeves of his shirt pull over the muscles of his arms. His mouth purses slightly as he studies me—as if I'm some sort of puzzle he's trying to figure out so he can toy with me some more—and the expression makes that little indentation in his chin stand out all the more. I try to keep calm.

"What do you want, Felicia?" he says.

He knows what I want. He's read it in my face a dozen times since we met last week. I dig my nails a little deeper into the arms of my chair and try to keep my face blank, but no doubt I do a very poor job of it. After a moment, he gives a low chuckle and rises.

"We should probably discuss what happened on Monday," he says.

I feel my skin start to flush. I knew this was coming,

but I'm still not prepared.

"I—I know I shouldn't have…" *Touched myself.* I can't even bring myself to say it in front of him.

He comes around the table, and then he's standing right next to me, towering over me.

"Such things can do wonders for your nerves," he says. "No doubt relieving such tensions will help you with your task this weekend. Perhaps, though, the venue was a little inappropriate."

A nervous laugh escapes me. Is he seriously just going to brush off the entire thing?

"I don't mean to suggest that such behavior isn't unprofessional," he continues. "I am partially to blame for that."

His confession startles me, and I glance up in surprise—and regret it immediately. He's looking at me the way he looked at me in the mirror that night, the way that made my insides flip-flop and my thoughts go jumbled. I try to look away again, but he reaches out and catches me by the chin.

"I want you, Felicia," he says.

"You do?"

He smiles. "I don't think I've exactly made a secret of that fact, my little seductress. You know that quite well."

I have no response for that. My heart is beating so loudly in my ears that I'm not sure I've even heard him right. *But you knew*, a little voice in my head tells me.

You knew all this time, you just didn't buy it.

Roman is watching my response carefully. "Does that frighten you?"

Yes. No. Honestly, I have no clue. But at the same time, the longer I stare in his eyes, the more I feel like my body's reaction is beyond my control.

"It… confuses me," I admit finally.

"Because you don't know how you feel." It's not a question.

"Because I don't believe you."

His thumb brushes across my jaw and up to the soft valley between my chin and my bottom lip. "Why not?"

"I'm not…" How do I even begin to explain? "You… you could have any girl you wanted."

"And?"

"And I don't understand why you'd want me. You're rich and successful. And insanely attractive. This town is full of women who'd suit you much better."

His thumb pauses just below my lip. "And what makes you think you get to decide what suits me best?"

I try to look away, but he maintains his hold on my chin.

"You have so little faith in your own allure," he continues. "You seem shocked by the idea that a man might find you attractive."

Is he really surprised by that? He saw me in the bar that night. He saw me make a fool of myself and get shot down multiple times.

"If you could see yourself the way I see you," he says, sliding his thumb fully across my lips now, "you wouldn't need a single lesson from me. You'd already know the power you hold. I'm still waiting for the moment you discover it for yourself."

I have no words. I'm still trying to wrap my brain around the idea that he wants me. *Roman Everet wants me.*

"Are you sure I'm not frightening you?" he asks again.

I somehow find the strength to shake my head. "You're not."

"Good."

Before I have the chance to say anything else, he grabs me and pulls me to my feet. He twists and pins me between him and the conference table, his face mere inches from mine.

"If you aren't afraid," he says, his voice rough, "then why did you run from me the other night? Why did you lock yourself in your fitting room?"

"I don't know," I whisper.

He leans a little closer, his eyelids dropping slightly. "Were you worried about crossing professional lines?"

I'd be lying if I said the thought hadn't crossed my mind, but I'd also be lying if I said that was my main concern.

"No," I breathe.

"Then what? Were you afraid of what you felt?

What I made you feel?"

His breath rushes across my cheek, and my pulse continues to race. Yes, I'm afraid of the things he makes me feel, but I'm also excited by them.

"No," I tell him softly.

His hips are right against mine, and one of his arms is still wrapped around my waist, keeping me close to him and preventing me from falling back against the table.

He turns his head, and his lips brush against my cheek. "Then what?"

I don't have an answer for him.

"What would you do if I picked things up right here?" he murmurs against my skin. "If I bent you back across this table right now?"

I'd fall apart. Completely. My body is trembling in his arms, my breath coming short, my fingers opening and closing, looking for *something* to grab onto.

Roman pulls back slightly, just enough for me to see his eyes again, and his gaze is dark and direct. There's no mistaking his expression right now, no misinterpreting what he wants. What *I* want.

And then he leans close again, his lips nearly upon mine, and when he speaks his voice is a rasp.

"What would you do, Felicia?"

I open my lips to respond, to tell him what he's doing to my body, to beg him to go on. But before I can get a word out, something begins to vibrate between us.

BrrrrrRING!

The cell tone tears through the heavy silence. I jump in his arms, and Roman jerks back, apparently as startled as I am.

BrrrrrrRING!

His phone is buzzing like mad in his front pocket, and I can't decide whether I'm disappointed or relieved that the moment is broken. I run my hands down the front of me, smoothing out my blouse and skirt, while Roman fishes in his pocket. My eyes drift past him to the window behind him overlooking the rest of the office, and I realize for the first time that the blinds are wide open. Anyone could have seen us. For all I know, half of my coworkers *did.* My face burns as I run my hands across my skirt a second time.

Roman lets out a curse as he looks down at the screen of his phone.

"Forgive me," he says. "I need to take this."

"Should I—"

"Stay."

I nod, then glance around, unsure of what to do with myself. Does he intend to pick up where we left off when he's done with his call? I glance at the blinds again. Maybe I should close them. Or maybe I should point out that this isn't the time or the place to do this.

But then I imagine what it would be like to have him bend me over the conference table like he suggested, how it would feel to have him push my skirt up my thighs and pull down my panties with half the office looking on…

I shake my head, cheeks flaming. I shouldn't be thinking these things. This isn't me. This is some wild, sex-starved maniac. The same girl who does unspeakable things in fitting rooms and goes into public bathrooms to fool around with Rafe Fontaine.

Rafe. Oh, God. For a moment I'd managed to forget about that whole mess.

I glance over at Roman. He's walked to the far end of the room and is speaking sternly into his phone, clearly frustrated. I'm not sure whether I should be here for this—though the snippets of conversation I hear aren't particularly juicy. He appears to be arguing about some sort of contract terms. I try not to listen. Try not to notice the way his arms tense beneath his shirt, or how rigid his back has gone. In his frustration, it's easy to see the true power of his body, and I find myself imagining what he might look like beneath his suit, what strong, hard planes his clothes are hiding. I've felt them against me—but how would they feel beneath my fingers? Against my bare skin?

I turn away. I shouldn't be thinking about this. He might want me. He might do all sorts of wonderful things to my body, but we still hardly know each other. It's lust, pure and simple. And listening to his terse conversation, it's no wonder he offered to take me on as a "pupil," or why he wants to bend me over the conference table. I don't blame him for wanting a little release, a little sexual fling to take the edge off his long, stressful days. I accept that he's attracted to me, but I also know that it ends there. We've know each other a week. This won't be a relationship. This won't be love. Can I live with that?

I rub my arms and wander over to the window, trying to sift through my feelings. My body knows what it wants. And it's been a long time since I've had any sort of sex—maybe I should allow myself to have some fun. After all, I almost hooked up with a celebrity in the bathroom of a diner last night. Maybe I'm at the beginning of a new, sexually adventurous stage of my life—shouldn't I explore it a little more before writing it off?

But when I glance back at Roman and feel the butterflies flutter in my stomach, I'm not so sure. That incident with Rafe was sexy and exciting—at the time. Today, it feels a lot more like a mistake. Something I'd rather forget about. And Rafe, attractive as he is, doesn't have half the effect on me as the man at the other end of this room. I'm already in over my head. If I allow myself to start something with this man, even knowing that it will just be a fling, I'm only going to end up getting hurt.

There. I've made my decision. But as Roman ends his call and turns toward me again, I know I'm going to have a hard time keeping my resolve. One look in his eyes and I know that even his stressful call hasn't made him forget about what almost happened between us a moment ago.

"Forgive the interruption," he says.

I try to smile. "It's all right."

There's a hunger in his expression, and for a second I think he's going to stride across the room and grab me and throw me back down on the table. If he does, I won't have the strength of will to refuse him. The effect he has on me is too strong. I look away, trying to regain what little composure I have left.

He doesn't approach me. And he doesn't say anything, either. After a moment, my curiosity gets the better of me, and I peek back at him. The hungry, lust-driven Roman is gone, and in his place is the tired, angry Roman I saw when I entered the conference room. He rubs the side of his face, and when his eyes meet mine again, there's something in them that I can't read.

"What is it about this job?" he asks.

Is that a rhetorical question? "What do you mean?"

"Why do you care about this so much? Your position here, I mean. Why are you fighting so hard for it?"

I'm not prepared for this sudden shift in subject, and I'm confused by the seriousness of his tone.

"I love this job," I say. "It's what I always wanted to do."

"A lot of people want to work in the entertainment

industry," he says. "Most of them are in it for the money or the fame. This job offers neither of those things." He marches over to the window overlooking the street and stares out, clasping his hands behind his back. "But maybe you don't consider this an entertainment job. Maybe you consider yourself to be pursuing a journalism career." He glances over at me. "Most journalists are fighting tooth and nail for positions at prestigious news magazines. They want literary awards and Pulitzer Prizes. They want to change the world with their words. *Celebrity Spark* doesn't offer you that opportunity, either. Most people use jobs like yours as a stepping stone to what they actually want to do. But you turned down my offer of a recommendation for another position. You're spending most of your free time fighting to keep this job. You're not looking for something bigger and better. Why?"

This conversation is getting more and more intense, but not at all in the way I expected.

"You're talking like this magazine isn't important," I say finally.

He gives a short laugh. "I think, objectively speaking, most people would agree with me. When was the last time someone at *Celebrity Spark* won a journalism prize?"

"I don't want a journalism prize."

"When was the last time we chose to run a story about war crimes, or food deserts, or anything of actual substance?"

I'm a little stunned, and a horrifying thought occurs to me. "Are you thinking of changing the magazine? Or shutting it down?"

"No. Of course not." He straightens. "As long as this magazine makes money, it will persist. And in spite of everything, *Celebrity Spark* gets a lot of attention, and that brings in the advertisers."

"That's your answer right there," I say.

He frowns. "I'm not sure I follow."

"*Celebrity Spark* has a lot of readers."

"And you want your work in front of all those eyes."

I shake my head. "No. I mean, yeah—that part's exciting. But I'm talking about why the magazine's important."

Roman doesn't respond. It feels weird to be on this end of the exchange—not only to be the one justifying the existence of this magazine to someone who helps run this industry, but also to have him looking at me like he's genuinely interested in what I'm about to say. Roman Everet, media mogul, is actively listening to a girl who's only had a real, paying job in this field for about six months.

No pressure or anything.

"There's a reason so many people read these magazines," I continue. "At the end of the day, when you're tired and stressed and running through the supermarket to grab stuff for dinner, you don't want to read about wars or any of the other horrible things going on in this world. Or if you're surfing the internet before bed, you don't always want to click onto a news site and read some intense political debate."

"I get it. Escapism is important."

"But it's not just escapism. It's… I mean, think about it. For as long as mankind has existed, we've had stories. Adventures told around fires. Fairy tales. These are the modern version. They're larger than life. The people in these magazines or on these gossip sites are modern American royalty. And reading about them puts things in perspective."

Roman's frown has deepened. He walks over to the coffee machine at the table at the far end of the room and says, "Go on."

"I mean… I think there are a lot of people who think of celebrities as some other species. Or at least as people who are part of some other world. Not our world. Not the real world. Celebrities have looks and money and opportunities that most of us will only ever dream about. The rest of us are, well, ordinary. Just normal people with hundreds of little problems that celebrities will never have because they got lucky and we didn't."

Roman seems to be absorbing every single word I say. He nods for me to go on.

"Except these magazines, these gossip sites… well, in their own twisted way, they give us hope," I say.

"Celebrities have everything going for them, and yet they're still making mistakes. They're still getting dumped. They still have all these issues in spite of everything. These larger-than-life people are still having some of the same problems that everyone has, and that makes us ordinary folk feel less alone. Feel like maybe we're not the screw-ups we thought we were. Because if these people who have everything are still dealing with the same things, then maybe we're managing better that we thought."

"Maybe we just enjoy other people's misery," Roman muses. "Schadenfreude is part of human nature."

His pessimism grates on me. "I don't think it has anything to do with enjoyment. I mean, at least not something as malicious as you're making it sound. It's about…"

"Insecurity."

Something about his tone makes me pause.

"Is that really what you think?" I say finally. "That everyone who reads celebrity entertainment magazines is either mean-spirited or insecure?"

"Everyone is mean-spirited or insecure. Some just more so than others."

"And what are your opinions, then, on the people who put these magazines together? The ones who perpetuate all of this?" I hate that I sound as emotional as I do, but his condescension is getting to me. Is this how he sees me?

Roman seems to realize how his words are coming across, because his face softens a little and he walks over to me.

"Why is this important to *you*, Felicia? Why are you here? Why are you busting your ass to keep *this* job?"

It's hard to think with him looking at me like that, but I want to explain myself. *No—I want him to know me. To see something beyond the girl who bumbles through flirtation and makes questionable sexual decisions.*

"I was one of those silly, insecure people who inhaled these magazines growing up," I say softly. "I always found them entertaining, but after my parents divorced, it became more than that. I was… I was hurt and confused and I felt like my family was gone."

"How old were you?"

"Eleven." I find myself looking at the ground. "Which was probably too young to be reading celebrity magazines, but they were… a distraction. And I used to imagine I'd run off to Hollywood and marry a movie star and never have to see either of my parents again. I'd go to glamorous parties and live in a huge mansion and walk the red carpets." A small smile tugs at my lips. "I used to love reading about Charles and Giovanna. And all the Fontaines, really. Sometimes I'd imagine I was a long-lost cousin of the family. Or that I married one of them. Really, it didn't matter. I just wanted to be part of a big, happy family. Even if they did have their occasional scandals."

Roman is silent. I steal a peek up at him, then look quickly away again. I don't want him looking at me like that, like he pities me.

"Then I got older and started studying journalism," I say quickly, "and I realized how much of celebrity news media is artfully crafted by PR firms. How many of the breakups and scandals are pure fiction, created to promote a particular project or keep someone in the spotlight. At first I was disappointed, but then... well, I realized that it opened up an entire new world of possibilities. It's all a big story, one ongoing narrative of fame and fortune and... *life*. A weird mishmash of fact and fiction, like a living, breathing, ever evolving movie. One that keeps the entire entertainment industry in motion. And I wanted to help write it. Not just for the good of the industry, but for everyone who ever picks up an issue of *Celebrity Spark*." I close my eyes. "God, it sounds so cheesy when I say it out loud, but—"

"No. I understand."

I risk a glance at him. He sounds earnest, but I'm suddenly feeling very exposed. *It's okay to be vulnerable*, I remind myself, but it's hard to hold his gaze, to stare into those hazel eyes after laying out my admittedly childish reasons for pursuing this particular career path. It's a very naive, admittedly idealistic view of this industry—I know as well as anyone the sort of ruthless-ness displayed by some of the paparazzi, or the way gossip sites or tabloids will twist or even create rumors about people with little concern for how they might affect the living, breathing people they name. I've never wanted any part of that sort of reporting—but does it make Roman think less of me if I even suggest that's possible?

He's watching me carefully, and I can't tell whether the fluttering sensations in my gut are a result of embarrassment or his continued nearness. He looks like he wants to say something, but it's still a moment before he speaks.

"Well," he says, "then I suppose it's important that we continue your lessons, isn't it? Saturday is only a few days away. We said tomorrow, right?"

After our moment on the conference table, I'm almost surprised to hear him bring up the lessons again. But there was a flicker in his eyes when he said the word *lessons*, and the echoing response between my legs gives me my answer.

"I'd like that," I say softly.

"Good." There's a hint of a smile on his face now. "Because there are still a number of things I want to teach you."

My breath hitches in my throat. "Such as?"

"Such as the proper way for dealing with… shall we say, *tensions.*" His finger comes up and hooks beneath my chin, even though I'm already looking him in the eyes. He holds me in place, as if now that I've consented to this—whatever "this" is—he's not about to let me go.

"You've been working very hard this week," he says. "I'm proud of you."

"Thank you," I whisper.

"Don't thank me yet. Not until you've got one of the Fontaine boys wrapped around your finger."

That's an unexpected kick in the stomach. Even after everything that's happened, he still wants me to seduce someone else. Even if it's purely for professional advancement—though I'm not sure I trust the word "professional" anymore—it still feels wrong. But that was the purpose of the lessons in the first place, wasn't it? I have no reason to be upset. If anything, this answers my question about Roman's intentions—he's looking for a purely physical diversion, a little sexual fun as he trains me in a valuable skill. I should be grateful for the time and assistance—and enjoy myself while it lasts. At the end of the day, I'm not losing anything.

But as I look up into those green-flecked eyes, I know that's a lie.

9

TWO DAYS

FOR OUR NEXT lesson, Roman wants to take me to a bar across town. It's right next to one of the big studios, so he says they sometimes get actors popping in after filming. Television actors, for the most part, not any major A-listers—but he claims he wants me to get more comfortable talking to famous men, and this seems like the easiest way to do it.

This is the point where I know I should probably tell him about the incident with Rafe, to tell him that I somehow managed to be flirtatious and interesting when it really mattered. That I managed to control my awkward, nervous impulses and capture the interest of one of the Fontaines. But there's no way to mention the progress I've made without also confessing that Rafe and I almost hooked up in the bathroom, or that even now there's a video of the incident making its way around the internet. If I'd managed to score an interview, that would have been one thing. But all I have to show for that night is the hickey I'm still hiding beneath three layers of concealer. So I decide to bite my tongue. I'll just work extra hard tonight to show him what I can do.

When work is done for the day, I run into the bathroom and change into a dress and heels. The dress is black, so it's not ideal if I want to stand out, but my wardrobe is limited right now. Maybe one day I'll have a closet full of gold cocktail dresses, but tonight, I have to work with what I've already got. And hey, I managed to catch Rafe Fontaine's attention in skinny jeans and a basic blouse, so maybe I've reached the point where the clothes are just a bonus tool.

I debate about whether to tie up my hair. The hickey has faded since yesterday, but it's definitely still there, and in spite of the extra layers of makeup, I don't want to take any chances. I leave my hair down.

When I'm ready, I go to meet Roman in the conference room. He's been in and out of the office all day, and every time I've peeked at him through the glass he's been on his phone. In fact, he's on a call now, and he lifts a finger when I enter the room, signaling that he'll be another minute.

I try not to watch him as I wait. The butterflies have been out in full force today, and I'm not sure whether I'm dreading or looking forward to our lesson. I'm thrilled by the chance to be close to him again—I find myself growing warm just thinking about the way he almost kissed me yesterday—but I'm still hurt and confused by his willingness to continue to encourage me to seduce other men.

What did you expect? I ask myself. *He's only doing what you both agreed he would do from the start. Don't think too much. Just enjoy yourself.*

But I can't keep myself from wondering what happens when all of this is over. If I succeed in securing an interview on Saturday, then Roman will be my boss for the foreseeable future. If I don't, then he'll be the man who fired me. Neither situation is an ideal environment for budding feelings, sexual or otherwise.

Fortunately, I don't have to torture myself with hypotheticals for very long. Romans call ends, and he comes to the conference room door. His eyes roam over my body.

"Very nice," he says, his appreciation clear on his face. "You won't be able to keep them away from you tonight."

My face grows warmer. Am I just imagining it, or did he purposefully brush his fingers against my arm when he reached for his suit jacket just now?

"Are you ready?" he asks.

I nod.

"Good. I'll drive."

He walks close to me as we head to the elevator, far closer than someone should stand to his employee. When we step into the elevator, his fingers brush against the small of my back, and even through the fabric of my dress, that touch sends a shiver up my spine. No one who saw us together would believe he's taking me out to pick up *other* men.

Neither of us speaks the entire way down to his car, but he takes every opportunity he can to touch me—to lightly graze my arm as he leads me through a door, to touch my waist as he ushers me around a corner. Once or twice I steal a glance at him, and he seems perfectly calm and collected, absolutely sure of himself. My feelings might be a jumble, but he appears to know exactly what he's doing. Exactly what he wants.

By the time we get to his car, he's touched me a dozen different times, a dozen different places, and my body seems to be aware of every move he makes. He opens the door to his car for me, and his hands linger on me a touch longer than necessary as he helps me inside. When I look back up at him, I see what I saw in the conference room yesterday, and before that in front of the mirror—*desire.* He makes no attempt to hide it.

He doesn't shut the door. Instead, he puts a finger beneath my chin and leans down so that his lips are right by my ear.

"You've been a very promising pupil," he says. "Very eager. I've been very impressed by your willingness to learn."

My body has come even more alive, more alert at his nearness, and my words are a whisper. "Thank you."

"Very impressed." This time he lets his mouth brush

my ear, and there's something in his voice—a promise, a need, a taunt—that makes my stomach tighten.

He pulls back, but before he releases me, he lets his finger slip from my chin down my throat. My breath stills at that delicate caress, but all too soon he pulls away. He closes the door and walks around to the driver's side.

He's teasing me. He knows the effect he has on me. This isn't the first time I've felt like a mouse at the mercy of a devilish cat, but being painfully aware of my disadvantage does little to help the situation. I'm a toy, completely subject to his whims. As long as he finds me an entertaining diversion, I'm his to control. My mind might be confused, but my body gave up the fight long ago.

We've just pulled out of the parking lot when his phone goes off. I'm past the point of being surprised by how often it rings, but that doesn't keep me from being disappointed when I realize he still has his headset clipped to his ear. Roman, at least, seems just as annoyed. He lets out a sigh before answering.

"Roman Everet."

There's a short pause as he listens to the person on the other end of the line, and then he lets out a curse.

"Are you sure you need it tonight? Have you tried Daniels?" Pause. "I don't have it on me. I'm in my car. Are you sure it can't wait?" Pause. Sigh. "Fine. Fine, I'll get it to you. But it'll take half an hour at least. It's back at my house." And with that, he hangs up.

"Do we need to postpone our lesson?" I ask.

He lets out a long, exasperated breath. "Unfortunately. I really need to send over this contract tonight. Do you mind if we swing by my house? The bar won't even be busy for another hour."

I was assuming, when I asked about postponing, that he'd drive me back to my car and we'd just pick this up tomorrow. But going to his house... that's something else entirely.

"That's fine," I tell him.

He must hear something in my voice, because he glances over at me, and I don't miss the wicked gleam in his eyes before I quickly turn my gaze back to the road. I know what things can happen when you go home with someone—even for *professional*, work-related reasons. Heck, *especially*, for work-related reasons, if my past week is any indication.

He doesn't say anything, but out of the corner of my eye, I see him smile.

A short while later, we're driving through one of the swankiest parts of Beverly Hills. I try not to gape at the elaborate gates and mansions on either side of the road. I should have seen this coming—I mean, the guy's a billionaire—but that doesn't keep me from freaking out a little. I can't believe I get to see where Roman Everet lives. That silly fantasy about being his girlfriend and experiencing all of the corresponding luxuries is getting easier and easier to imagine.

Calm down, Felicia, I remind myself. *You know what he wants, and it isn't to introduce you to his parents or anything.*

I bite down on my lip as he finally pulls into a driveway. There's a huge metal gate in front of us with a giant "E" etched on the front. He hits a button in the car, and the gate swings slowly open.

As he pulls down the driveway, there's just enough light from the setting sun to cast the grounds in a dark bronze hue. But my eyes go straight to the house— which is a huge, modern stucco with a roof of terracotta tile. The perfect California dream home.

"It's gorgeous." I don't mean to say that out loud, but the words just slip out.

He chuckles. "I'm glad you approve."

And the inside is just as beautiful. It's exactly how you'd expect a media mogul's mansion to look: clean and contemporary, decorated with modern art and—of course—all the latest in technology.

"This might take a few minutes," he tells me. "Can I get you something to drink in the meantime? A glass of wine, maybe?"

"Sure." What I really want is a tour of this place, but I can't exactly ask for that.

Next thing I know, he's ushering me out back with an entire bottle of red. I gasp when I see his backyard. Of course, no California mansion is complete without a pool, and this is a particularly amazing one. There's also a hot tub—and I resist the urge to ask how many of his girlfriends he's had in there.

"Make yourself comfortable," he says, his hand pressing gently against the base of my spine as he leads me toward a lounge chair. He slides the bottle into my hand, and his fingers linger on mine as I sink down onto the cushions. "I'll be quick."

I do as he says, settling back in the chair and pouring myself a glass of wine. I slip off my shoes and prop up my feet, staring out across the pool and grounds.

It's so beautiful here. A light breeze rustles the leaves of the palm trees on the far side of the pool, and the last rays of the sunset paint the sky crimson. Directly overhead, some stars have already started twinkling awake, and I watch them for a little while as I sip at my wine.

Who'd have thought that I'd end up at Roman Everet's mansion, sipping wine next to his pool? Two days after fooling around with Rafe Fontaine, and four days after falling into Dante Fontaine's lap? It's like I'm living someone else's life.

No—for better or worse, this is *my* life. At least this week. Next week I might be ordinary Felicia again, but this week, I can dream. I can enjoy being New Felicia while it lasts. The adventurous Felicia. The brave Felicia. The Felicia who somehow had a man like Roman Everet pushing her back against a conference table as if he would take her right there.

And that same man will watch you try and seduce another man on Saturday, I remind myself. I can lie here all night pretending that my life has changed, that a week of lust and lessons has transformed me into a new person. I can pretend for an evening or two that I'm the girlfriend of a billionaire, but it will all disappear in the morning. It's like my very own Cinderella story, and yet I know Roman won't come after me if I forget one of my discount-rack shoes. There will be another magazine to buy, another phone call to answer, another girl to serve as a distraction.

He was supposed to be hiring another managing editor today, I remember. *There's no reason for him to be at the office anymore, not once the new management system is in place.* Maybe that will make things easier—if I manage to keep my job, that is.

Those thoughts circle around and around in my head as I sit staring up at the sky. After a little while, my eyes fall closed, and I must drift off because I don't realize Roman is back until he says, "Felicia?"

I jerk back into full consciousness, and the wineglass falls out of my hand. It shatters against the ground.

"Shit," I say, sitting up. "Shit, I'm sorry."

"Don't be," he says, kneeling down. "It's just a glass."

I lean down and try to help him pick up the pieces, but he puts a hand on my shoulder, stopping me.

"I've got this," he says. "You just sit back."

And since it's his house, I let him call the shots. Still, I hate watching him having to clean up a mess I made.

"How much did that glass cost?" I ask.

"Does it matter?"

I frown. *That means it was probably expensive.*

"Don't look so distressed," he tells me. "I have many more." His eyes linger on my face. "I mean it, Felicia. There's nothing to worry about. I thought I told you to relax."

"How am I supposed to relax while you're cleaning?"

"Try. It'll be good for you."

I let out a short laugh. "Me? You're the one glued to your phone all day. Big deal going on?"

He gives a little half smile. "There's always a big deal going on."

"Don't you ever stop and take a break?"

"'Breaks' don't exist. Not in this town."

I frown and tug at the corner of the nearest cushion. I suddenly find myself wanting to understand, wanting to know so much more about this man in front of me.

"Why do you do it?" I ask softly.

He glances up at me. "I worked very hard to get where I am, Felicia. I do what I need to do to maintain the business I've built and the life I've created for myself."

I knew Roman was a self-made man, but otherwise I

know very little about his background.

"Did you always want to work in the entertainment industry?" I ask.

"Business is business, no matter what the industry," he says. "The basic principles are the same, and I'm damn good at those. The finer details were easy enough to figure out as I went along."

That didn't exactly answer my question. "But what was your dream? Or was your end goal just to take over the world?"

I mean it as a joke, but his expression is serious as he sits up.

"There's no end point. The business is always evolving, and there's always another chance to grow and evolve with it." He glances out across the pool. "What would I do otherwise—spend my days sitting on a beach somewhere? What kind of life is that? I'd be bored out of my mind after a week."

"That doesn't mean you can't have fun sometimes," I say.

His eyes flash.

"I promise you, Felicia, I have plenty of fun," he says. "Just probably not in the way you imagine."

Before I can respond, he stands, carrying the broken bits of glass back into the kitchen. What little remained of my wine has already soaked into the stones, and I suspect the California sun will fade the stain to nothing within days. Shamefully, I'm a little saddened by that thought—a part of me would have liked to think that whenever he saw that dark spot on the stones, he might think of the awkward, clumsy girl who left it there during that brief but intense week he used her as a distraction.

His words echo in my mind: *There is no end point.* Is this really how he sees the rest of his life—just one business call after another? One more meeting, one more deal, one more buyout, and on and on until the day he collapses from exhaustion?

Before I can come up with an answer, he returns from the kitchen with two glasses in his hand. He pours each of us some wine and hands me one before sitting down on the lounge chair beside mine.

"Are we pregaming for the bar?" I ask.

"Change of plans for tonight," he says. "I thought we'd do our lesson here instead."

My heart leaps into my throat. "Here?"

He gives a dark chuckle. "You've already kicked off your shoes. Besides, there are certain lessons that are better to do in private, where there's no one to disturb us."

I take a long sip of my wine. He wants us to be alone. To do this lesson *in private.* Was this his plan all along, to get me to come back to his house? *No,* I tell myself. *He knows what he does to me. He knows that all he had to do was ask.* That call back in the car was legitimate—why is he suddenly changing our plans for the evening? But "why" isn't the most important question—that distinction belongs to the *what*.

"What are we going to do?" I ask, trying to keep my voice from revealing how much my body is already responding to the suggestion.

Roman is sitting on the lounge chair with his knees facing me. I'm looking out across the pool, but out of the corner of my eye I see him smile.

"Not *we*," he says, amusement in his voice. "*You*."

Oh. I'm almost afraid to ask, but my curiosity gets the better of me. "Then what am I going to do?"

"You're going to close your eyes."

I'm almost afraid to, but I find that I can't disobey. My eyes fall closed. When he speaks again, his tone is calm and sure and dripping with honey.

"I want you to imagine yourself walking into a bar," he says.

A nervous laugh bubbles up out of my throat. "Are we telling jokes? Or is this just some weird business visualization exercise?"

"I think this will help," he says. I hear him take a sip of his wine. "And don't speak. Just imagine."

I nod. I have no idea where he's going with this, but I'll play along.

"This isn't just any bar," he says. "You'd probably call it a lounge. Everything is polished and expensive. The lights are low and there's soft music playing— maybe even a pianist in the corner. You're here alone, but you're wearing your gold gown, and it makes you feel brave."

Actually, I feel a little ridiculous. But his voice is soft and soothing, so I decide to focus on those mellow, intoxicating tones and imagine the scene he's describing.

"You walk across the room to the bar," he says. "You feel eyes on you as you pass, but you ignore them. You're heading straight for a man at the bar. A man you recognize."

My pulse quickens, and in the scene in my mind, I picture Roman turning toward me in that lounge, Roman's eyes darkening as he takes in my gold dress, Roman beckoning me toward the bar. I imagine myself walking faster, my feet trying to catch up with the beating of my heart. But then Roman surprises me.

"It's Luca Fontaine," he says. "The man you've come to see. The man for whom you've put on that gold dress. The man you've spent a week preparing to meet."

The image in my head dissipates. I wasn't expecting him to lead things in this direction—and I'm grateful he can't read my mind. I try to do as he says, try to re-imagine the scene he's describing, this time with Luca Fontaine.

"You slide in next to him at the bar," Roman says. "You're close enough to touch him, if you wanted to. And you're close enough to smell him. What does he smell like?"

It takes me a second to register that he's asked me a

THE SECRET TO SEDUCTION

question, and even then, I struggle to find an answer. How the heck am I supposed to know what Luca Fontaine smells like?

"I don't know," I say. "Like a man."

"Is he wearing a scent?"

"I don't know. Maybe. Probably." I open my eyes a sliver. "I'm not very good at this game."

"It's not a game. It's an exercise," he says. "This is to help you get over your nerves when you're talking to Luca or Dante or one of the others on Saturday.

"Oh."

"It's normal to get starstruck when you're new to this industry," he continues. "And your situation is particularly unique. Am I correct in assuming that you find Luca Fontaine attractive?"

"Y-yes. I guess. But—"

"And I think you know that you can't just accidentally fall into someone's lap every time you want to get his attention."

He doesn't need to remind me. But he also must realize by this point that *he* has a much bigger effect on me than any of the Fontaines.

"I think we should continue," he says, setting his wine on the patio table next to him. "Close your eyes again."

I do.

"What does he smell like?" he asks once more.

My imagination isn't quite that good—especially

with Roman sitting so close, with *his* scent reaching my nose. I take a deep breath, letting it invade my senses.

"He's wearing something," I say. "Cologne or after-shave, maybe. But it's very subtle. I only smell it because he's so close."

It might just be my imagination, but I swear I hear Roman lean a little closer to me.

"Do you like the smell?" he says.

"I… yes."

"And how does he look? What's he wearing?"

I try to imagine Luca, but my mind keeps coming back to the man in front of me.

"A suit," I say after a moment. "An expensive suit. With a dark shirt." It's something I've seen Roman wear a few times this week—though today his shirt is white. But it's also something Luca Fontaine would wear out to a nice lounge, so I'm not completely giving myself away. I try to refocus the image in my head, try to visualize the famous actor instead of Roman next to me at the bar, as I'm supposed to.

"You catch him stealing a glance at you as you order a drink," comes Roman's voice beside me. "What do you do?"

Maybe he's onto something with this exercise, be-cause even *imagining* that sort of attention makes me a little anxious. "I-I don't know."

"Don't overthink it. Just trust your instincts."

My instincts don't have a very good track record,

but I try to take his advice.

"I don't talk to him at all," I say. "I wait for him to speak first."

Roman is silent for a moment, and I can't tell if that means that I said the wrong thing.

"How do you know he'll speak to you?" he asks me after a moment.

I want to remind him that we're talking about an imaginary scene with an imaginary form of Luca Fontaine, but that answer isn't good enough.

"I'm wearing the gold dress," I say finally. "He won't be able to resist."

That gets a chuckle from Roman. "Nice try." I hear him lift his glass and take another sip. "Maybe it will be easier if you pretend I'm him. Talk to me like I'm Luca. I'll play his role."

My stomach flip-flops. "This is silly."

"Try," he says, as if he were urging me to eat my vegetables or something equally mundane.

But as strange as the request might be, as nervous as it makes me, I find myself wanting to rise to the challenge. To prove to myself—and to him—that I can take the initiative, that I can lead the course of a seduction.

"I look at his drink," I say. "And then I order the same thing."

"That could be dangerous," Roman says. "If you do that, he might want to start a conversation with you about his drink of choice. He'll notice if you don't know what you're talking about. You'll lose his trust right from the start."

"I'll order my own drink, then," I say. "A Long Island." Historically, Long Island Iced Teas aren't exactly my friend, but in this imaginary lounge, I'm willing to take the chance.

"Good choice," he says. I'm not sure whether that's coming from Roman or "Luca," so I keep going.

"When it gets here," I say softly, still unsure, "I make sure to brush my arm against his as I pull it across the bar toward me."

"Mmhm," he says in apparent approval. When he doesn't go on, I know he's waiting for me to continue the scene.

"I shift my weight so that I'm a little closer to him," I say. "Not quite touching him, but close enough that he should notice."

For a long moment, Roman doesn't say anything. And then I hear him reposition himself on his lounge chair.

"After a few minutes," he says, "you notice that he seems to be leaning a little closer to you as well."

My heart flutters, even though this is only pretend. "I… I reach across the bar for a napkin, and my arm brushes his again."

When he speaks, Roman's voice is soft and velvety. "This time, you notice that he turns his head toward you. Smiles at you."

I'm starting to get more flustered by the minute—which is ridiculous because this is just pretend.

"I smile back," I say softly.

"He takes another drink."—I hear Roman take another sip of his—"And then uses the opportunity to lean a bit closer to you."

I find myself gulping my own wine, trying to fight the fresh wave of anxiety and anticipation coursing through me. Suddenly, I feel the heat of a face next to my own.

"What's your name?" Roman asks.

He sounds different. I don't think he's consciously mimicking Luca—he sounds nothing like him, either way—but something about the way he speaks somehow completes this strange little exercise. It's not Luca whispering in my ear—but it isn't Roman, either. It's a stranger, someone who falls between the two. A man of my imagination, familiar and unfamiliar, mysterious and intoxicating.

Oh, and he asked me a question.

"I'm Felicia," I whisper.

Something brushes against my hand—first lightly, and then again. And suddenly Roman's fingers slip into my own.

But again—they aren't *Roman*'s fingers. Not right now. They belong to this Stranger, and now he's lifting my hand, bringing it to his lips. His mouth is soft and warm and firm, and when he brushes his lips against my knuckles, a tremor shoots up my arm.

"That's a beautiful name," the Stranger says. "I'm Luca."

The way he says that suddenly makes this little game feel quite serious. I know it's my turn to say something, to continue the conversation, but my tongue refuses to move. He's still holding my hand, and now his thumb brushes against the backs of my knuckles.

"I've never seen you in here before, Felicia."

This time one of those nervous giggles actually escapes. "Is that your best line, Luca?"

He answers with a low chuckle of his own. "Do I need a better one? It looks like it's working to me."

Once more, I feel the touch of his lips against the delicate skin on the back of my hand. I suck in a breath as this time the tip of his tongue flicks against my skin.

"Do I make you nervous?" he asks me.

"A little," I admit.

"More than a little, I'd venture."

My hand is still dangerously close to his mouth, but I don't pull it away. I'm enjoying the feeling of his breath on the back of my fingers.

"Nerves aren't a bad thing," I whisper.

"Not in the right situations, no. In some cases, I suppose, they can be quite stimulating." He kisses my hand again, and this time he goes even further, sliding his tongue all the way between two of my fingers.

I gasp in surprise and pull my hand away out of reflex. And Roman—or Luca, or the Stranger—lets out a low rumble of a laugh.

"You're easily shaken, Felicia."

"I'm sorry."

"Don't be. I'm rather enjoying it." I feel a feather-light touch against my cheek. His fingers drift across my skin, sliding a loose bit of hair behind my ear and lingering right at my temple.

"You're a very beautiful woman, Felicia," he murmurs.

I don't know why he keeps using my name, but something in his tone makes it sound like an endearment all on its own.

"Very beautiful," he says again, and there's a roughness, a rawness to his tone now. That familiar fluttery feeling in my stomach has risen all the way to my throat, making it hard to speak.

"You, too," I blurt, desperate to say anything, to deflect the attention away from me for a couple of seconds.

He laughs again, and the sound is even deeper than before. "You think I'm beautiful?"

My neck prickles with heat. "You know what I mean."

"Maybe I don't." He leans his face close to my ear again. "Tell me what you think of me, Felicia."

He's still supposed to be Luca, right? I don't even

know anymore. "I—I just met you."

"And yet I knew I wanted you the moment I laid eyes on you, before we ever spoke a word to each other."

I'm trembling now, no less because his fingers are still in my hair, still brushing against my ear, still toying with me.

"You're very quiet, Felicia," he says. "Have I frightened you?"

Rafe Fontaine asked me almost the exact same thing in the diner, and Roman himself posed a similar question in the conference room yesterday, but it feels different tonight. So much more intimate.

"No," I tell him, just as I told him before. "You haven't."

"You're just nervous?" he says.

"Yes."

"And a little uncertain." It's no longer a question.

"Yes."

"And aroused."

"Y—" I cut off the word abruptly. Are we still playing? Is he still supposed to be Luca, or has he slipped back into his old self?

His hand falls from my ear and he pulls back, letting out a sigh. "Felicia, he has you twisted around his finger."

He used the word *he*. Does that mean everything he said was just part of the exercise?

I peel open my eyes, almost afraid to look at him.

He's watching me closely, but in the dim light I can't tell what he's thinking.

"You weren't in control of that conversation," he says bluntly. The deep, seductive tones he was using a moment ago are completely gone, and he's back to talking to me as if we're just discussing business. "If you're going to do this, you need to take charge of yourself first. You were shaking, Felicia."

I have no response for that, so I just raise my wine-glass to my lips.

"I know this isn't something you can change over-night," he says. "But if we can't calm your nerves, then we need to come up with some sort of actionable plan for you for Saturday. You have to stay focused. This isn't about letting Luca Fontaine into your pants. It's about securing an interview. Did you even remember that's what you were trying to accomplish?"

Honestly? I didn't even realize that was the objective of this little exercise. But I'm not sure I would have remembered that either way.

"The only way to overcome certain social anxieties is to practice," he says. "Perhaps tomorrow we'll go out somewhere and work on that some more. But I think your problem runs a little deeper. You need to relax, Felicia."

"You keep saying that," I mumble into my glass, my ears blazing at his harsh critique.

"I don't think it's just the nerves." He sits a little

straighter. "When was the last time you had sex?"

I jerk, nearly spilling my wine again. "That's a very personal question."

"I think it's important in your situation."

"My situation? I don't think—"

"But maybe I'm asking the wrong question. Tell me, when was the last time you had an orgasm?"

I let out a little gasp.

"That's none of your business!" I say. I'm going to need a lot more wine before we have this conversation.

"I'm not trying to make you uncomfortable," he says. "But there *is* a difference in the way people conduct themselves when they're sexually fulfilled, especially around those they find attractive. You'd be amazed how many issues could be cured with the proper... satisfaction."

I can't look at him, not when he speaks like that. Not when he's gazing at me that way. I reach for the bottle of wine and top off my glass.

"I think," he says slowly, "a little release would do you wonders, Felicia. Ask any man you know if he takes the edge off before a date. You'll find all of this a little more enjoyable when you aren't sexually frustrated."

"I'm *not* sexually frustrated!" I say, but the words are more of a knee-jerk reaction than anything else.

Roman still hasn't taken his eyes off of me. "I don't hear you claiming to be sexually satisfied, either. Unless there's a boyfriend I don't know about?"

"I don't see how that's any of your business."

He still doesn't look away. "Is it not?"

I bury my nose in my glass. But Roman isn't even done.

"This isn't to say, of course, that you can't satisfy yourself," he says. "Everyone does."

And he knows perfectly well that *I* do after the incident in the fitting room, so I don't know why we're having this conversation.

"I touch myself," I say, and admitting it out loud is more freeing than I expect. "You know that already. I'm not ashamed of it."

"Then let's have an objective, adult conversation about it," he says. "On Monday night, you decided to pleasure yourself in a fitting room. I suspect, because of how things played out, that you didn't bring yourself to satisfaction."

Kill me now. I shake my head and drown myself in wine again.

"What happened when you went home? Did you finish the job?"

I can't believe I'm talking about this with Roman Everet. One minute he's telling me he wants me, the next he's asking me to pretend he's someone else, and the next he's asking about *this*.

"No," I whisper. No, I never *finished* on Monday. The moment had most definitely been ruined.

"Understandable," he says. "But while mentally, you

had no interest in completing what you started, your body never got the release it needed. Have you touched yourself since?"

Honestly, I haven't—even though I've had a couple of encounters since that night that left me aching for sexual pleasure. But this whole week has been so overwhelming and confusing that I never actually followed through.

I don't say any of that out loud, but apparently Roman reads the answer on my face.

"Well," he says, "I think we have your assignment for the night."

My chest tightens. "Assignment?"

"Yes," he says. "I think you need the release."

This is insane. "Are you… are you telling me to pleasure myself?"

"That's one way to accomplish it."

In my mind, I hear what he leaves unsaid, and my entire body reacts. Feeling brave, I finally sneak a peek at him over the rim of my glass. The hand that lifts his wine to his lips is perfectly controlled. As usual, he maintains complete power over his body and expression.

And I find myself suddenly aching to be bold again. "When was the last time you got off?"

My question startles him, and I'm pleased to see the surprise register on his face before he gets control of himself again.

But when he answers me, he's as calm as ever. "This

morning."

"By yourself? Or with someone else?"

He gives a little smile. "By myself."

Ah, so even the rich and attractive Roman Everet sleeps alone sometimes. I take another drink, feeling bolder and bolder by the second.

"Is that a daily habit?" I ask.

"Yes. A very important one, in my experience."

Silence falls between us, and there's not enough wine left in my glass to keep me from feeling sheepish and awkward again. What are we doing? What is this *thing* going on between us? It isn't just business. His desire is plain on his face, and I'm sure my own is just as obvious.

"Do you really think it would help?" I ask after a moment.

"What?"

"Letting myself go."

He sets his glass on the table. "I think only you can answer that."

I let out a breath and set my own glass down next to his. He watches my every movement like a hunter watches its prey, and yet he doesn't lean toward me, doesn't grab me like he did back in the conference room. Maybe he's waiting for me to admit what I want, what I need.

I'm not that brave. Not yet. But there's one thing I *do* have the courage to do.

"Will you close your eyes while I do this?" I ask, my heart in my throat. "While I touch myself?"

He opens his mouth to say something, then seems to think better of it. My skin is already tingling with sensation, my body already starting to ache. I can't believe I'm going to do this—but I've already pushed my limits so many times this week. What's once more?

"Close your eyes," I say again, though it sounds more like a plea than an order.

He nods and leans back in his lounge chair. I wait until I see his eyes fall closed before my hands move.

At first, my movements are slow and careful. I let my palms slide up over my sides and across my belly as I try to come to terms with what I'm about to do. But I'm feeling brazen, and though I'm nervous, I'm not afraid. I can already hear my breath coming faster. I can hear Roman's breath, too, slow and steady in the chair beside mine.

My hands dance across my belly for a moment before moving lower. I'm glad I decided to wear a dress tonight. It makes things easier. Slowly, my fingers tug up the fabric of the skirt, exposing my bare thighs to the night. The summer air is balmy against my skin, and it makes it that much easier to let my legs fall apart. When the fabric is up past my hips, I release it and let my fingers come to rest just above the lacy panties that I know do little to cover the carefully-trimmed patch of hair beneath.

I take a deep breath. Two. My knees bend, my thighs fall a little farther apart. I'm surprised at how ready I am. I can smell my own arousal, and I suspect Roman can, too. Did I just hear his breath hitch a little?

One hand slides down across my skin and beneath my panties, moving through my little patch of hair and on to the delicate flesh beyond. I shiver as the tip of one of my fingers grazes the delicate, swollen nub at my crest, but I don't linger there. Instead, I trace myself down and up with my finger, marveling at how such a familiar touch can cause so many new sensations. I've pleasured myself before, but this is different. My entire body is on edge, and parts of me seem to be truly awakening for the first time.

The whole night seems to pulse with the rhythm of my blood, with the rhythm of my exploratory touches below. Maybe Roman was right—I needed this more than I thought. My body has been craving release for a long time, and I've been so preoccupied that I never realized what I was denying it. The fact that Roman is beside me and experiencing every moment of it with me is a different sort of thrill. I still don't know quite what's come over me, but this doesn't feel as awkward as I thought it would. If anything, it feels right that he's here with me, like his presence completes the buzz that surrounds me right now.

I'm not sure how long I lie beneath the stars, reveling in the strange new pleasures at my own hand. But though the sensations swell and build within my body, release continues to feel just out of reach. I arch my hips, trying to create more friction, but that's not the problem. I've brought myself over the edge a hundred times before, and though every aspect of this feels more heightened tonight, orgasm feels that much further away. Like the buildup has been so long, so great, that I'll never reach the peak.

I let out a frustrated whimper. Beside me, I hear Roman move on his lounge chair.

Roman.

I don't want to cross that line. Even now, with so many lines already crossed, it feels like a mistake. A sure way to get hurt. The minute he touches me, it's done. There's no going back.

But my body aches with need, and between that and the lesson and the wine I'm not thinking very clearly.

"Roman..." The word is a croak.

And I feel his presence next to me—right over me—in the space of half a breath.

"I'm here," he says, and the controlled, matter-of-fact Roman is gone. His voice is rough. "I'm here."

His hand slips inside my panties and slides on top of mine, joining my fingers in their mad dance between my legs. I moan as he guides me—down one side of me, back up the other, lingering for a brief moment at my crest before moving down again. His touch is fire and exquisite joy, and the skin on his fingers feels so rough against my flesh.

He continues to lead my hand along with his, as if showing me new ways I might touch my body. I lift my hips, pressing against the tangle of our fingers, aching for more. Aching for that release he promised, the release I need.

I hear him shift beside me, and his hand moves away from mine. I let out another whimper.

"Trust me," he murmurs. "I'll get you there, I promise." He yanks the crotch of my panties aside, exposing me completely to the night air, but before I can fully appreciate that sensation, it's replaced by another one—the feeling of his hot mouth coming down on me.

I gasp at the first touch of his lips. The first flick of his tongue is even better. I writhe on the lounge chair, nearly delirious with the building pressure, desperate to feel anything and everything he can give me. He attacks me with a hunger, and I find myself grasping for his shoulders, needing something to anchor me as his mouth multiplies the sensations running through my body. His tongue presses against me—presses *into* me—and suddenly, it's as if everything has come together. Pleasure explodes inside of me, and I throw my head back as a wave of release crashes through my body.

It takes a moment for my vision to clear. When I can think and see and hear again, Roman is still kneeling between my legs. When our eyes meet, he smiles and then turns his head, planting a rough kiss on my inner thigh.

"That was just as beautiful as I thought it would be," he says, his voice thick. "How do you feel?"

I can't even begin to describe it. In fact, I don't think I can speak at all. I let out a laugh and let my head fall back against the cushions.

"I've been wanting to do that since the first time you walked into the conference room," he says. "You were so wound up, so anxious. I wanted to throw you down and bury my face between your legs and lick all of the tension out of you."

I smile as I remember the girl that walked into the conference room that day. She feels like someone else. A stranger.

"I wanted to watch you come undone," he says. "Watch you fall apart. Watch you succumb to the desire you tried so hard to fight." He kisses my thigh again, and this one's even less controlled than the last. His teeth graze my tender, sensitive skin, and I whimper.

He spends a few minutes nibbling at my skin, kissing and nipping until I begin to tremble again. But eventually his lips become gentle, his kisses against my thighs longer and softer. Finally, he lifts his head once more.

"How do you feel?" he asks.

"Wonderful," I say. The word is half a sigh. My whole body seems different. It feels languid and satisfied and… powerful.

He seems to like that answer. He leans forward and kisses the skin right above the waistband of my panties, and I find myself reaching for him again, letting my fingers glide into his hair.

"Thank you," I whisper.

He gives one of those dark chuckles, and I feel this one all the way to my core.

"Don't thank me yet," he says against my skin. "There's still a lot of tension to work out of you."

10

ONE DAY

WHEN I WAKE up, I feel like a different person.

I roll over in bed, rubbing my eyes and wondering why I feel so rested, so… *calm.* Like every worry, every bit of stress, is gone from my body. It's not until I reach for my cell on the nightstand that I realize that the nightstand is all wrong. There's a lamp where there shouldn't be.

And then I remember.

I jerk upright. I'm not in my bedroom. I'm in Roman's. *I spent the night here.*

The bed next to me is empty. And—a quick touch tells me—cold. As my fingers skim over the rumpled sheets, last night comes rushing back.

He made me come twice more next to the pool. Once again with his tongue, and then with his fingers. My body aches at the memory of it, and I wonder how I could have gone my whole life without experiencing pleasure like *that.* The few partners I've had in the past never gave me anything close. I'm not sure I could even replicate the experience with my own fingers—it's like Roman knew how to wake sensations in me that I didn't even realize were possible.

I remember, through the haze of my pleasure, asking to return the favor. I even got as far as reaching for his pants—and believe me, he was more than ready for a little release of his own—but he pulled my hands away and insisted that this was about *my* experience, *my* release.

I think I must have drifted off sometime in the wake of that third climax, because sometime later I became aware of him carrying me up the stairs.

"I can drive you home, if you like," he said when he realized I was awake. "I just thought I'd take you somewhere more comfortable."

I don't think I responded. I'm pretty sure I just snuggled closer to him. He smelled so good, and his chest was so warm and solid beneath my cheek.

I remember him tucking me beneath the covers of a bed, and then I remember myself grabbing his hand and asking him to stay. He did.

My next bit of memory is a little hazy—and part of me wonders if it might have been a dream. But I remember waking in the night, remember feeling his heat next to me, remember that familiar need coming to life in my body. I just meant to snuggle against him, to let my body melt against his, but he must have been awake—or, as I was, aching with desire even in a state of half-sleep. We moved against each other—first, just trying to reposition our arms and legs so we fit more closely together, but soon our movements became more than that. Our limbs twisted around each other and our hips ground together, and I have a very vivid memory of all the hard planes and parts of his body. I gasped and clutched at him, and he groaned into my hair. We writhed together in madness and agony, and his hardness slid against me again and again through our clothes until I fell over the peak for the fourth time in only a matter of hours. I don't know if he reached a similar point of pleasure. I only know that after my shudders of sensation stopped, he moved away from me, and then I must have fallen asleep once more.

And now it's morning. I spent the whole night next to Roman in bed—at least, I assume it was the whole night. I hope he hasn't gone too far—my car's still at work.

Shit. Work. It's only Friday, and that means I'm supposed to go in today. Roman, too—considering he's in charge and all.

I look at my cell. It's only 7:30 AM, so we're not late yet, thank goodness. I'd prefer to get to the office before everyone else shows up. I know how it'll look if Roman and I walk in together, and I don't want to make this any more complicated than it already is.

It's too late to avoid complications, I remind myself. It

was simple enough to pretend I was only imagining the way he's been looking at me all week, or reading too much into the things he said in some of our lessons, or even misremembering the hunger with which he touched me in the fitting room. But there's no pretending last night didn't happen. We might not have had *actual* sex—heck, we never even *kissed*—but something happened between us. Something physical and real. And there's no imagining that away.

I'm still wearing the dress from last night. My shoes are nowhere to be seen—they're probably still next to the pool—so I pad barefoot out of the room in search of Roman.

I find him in the kitchen. The kitchen itself is impressive—it's huge and modern, with the fanciest stainless appliances I've ever seen—but my eyes go straight to him. He has one hand on a pan of crackling bacon and the other on his laptop, which he's set up on the massive granite-topped island in the center of the room. He doesn't notice me right away, so I stand in the doorway and just watch him.

He looks so *normal*. Roman is usually so polished, perfect from head to toe. I've never seen him without some sort of business attire—or with even a hair out of place. Yeah, he's already wearing a pair of suit pants this morning, but his white button-down hangs open, and he's left his undershirt untucked. Even his hair looks a little mussed. The whole picture is unbelievably sexy.

As I watch, he finishes whatever he's typing and turns his full attention to the stove. He pushes his sleeves up to his elbows before flipping the bacon in the pan, and I can't help but smile. I can't believe Roman is cooking. He's always been the quintessential picture of the businessman, the boss, the billionaire, and seeing him like this—doing something so ordinary—stirs something warm in my belly. Somehow that makes all of this more real, like we've broken through the act to the truth underneath.

"I was just about to come wake you," he says without turning around.

I jump. How long has he known I was here?

"That smells delicious," I say, trying to take the attention off of me.

"No one can resist the call of bacon," he replies. "At least no one who's worth having over for breakfast."

I smile and move slowly toward him. The tiles are cold against my bare feet, and they're a stark contrast against the heat that seems to have enveloped my entire body. I'm not as nervous as I was last night, but I'm full of a warm, shivery energy. I want to be closer to him, and at the same time, I'm afraid. What happened between us was both strange and intense, and I'm still trying to figure out what it means.

It's not until I get closer to him that I realize I never bothered to glance in the mirror after rolling out of bed, let alone freshen up or anything. My hair is probably a rat's nest, and I bet he can smell my breath even from where he is. I should probably excuse myself and make sure I'm presentable... but I can't. Not when he's smiling at me like that, like I'm the greatest thing to ever walk into his kitchen. God, how have I never noticed just how stunning that smile is?

Because he's never smiled this way. I've seen plenty of Roman's smiles this week—smiles of amusement, smiles of arrogance, smiles of satisfaction. But even at those times, he always seemed... guarded. Always held back. This is something else—something open, something genuine. It makes my heart swell, and I'm afraid to think about what it means.

Not once last night did he kiss me. He spoke tender words to me, he touched me like some precious thing. But he wouldn't let me touch him, and though he pressed his lips against my thighs, my belly, and other more intimate places, his mouth never touched mine. But now he's smiling at me like *that*, making my stomach flutter with just the curl of his lips.

"Come here," he says.

I realize I've stopped halfway across the kitchen. I force my feet to keep moving, to keep marching toward the man who has a little more of my heart in his grip with every word.

"I trust you slept well?" he says.

I give a shy laugh. "I think you know how I slept."

"And how are you feeling this morning?"

Ridiculously amazing. Confused. Scared. Honestly, I'm feeling a lot of things, but I know what he wants to hear.

"Like I could do anything," I say.

His smile widens, and I feel as if I could fly away.

"Well, I hope you're hungry as well," he says. "Because I've got some eggs in that dish over there and some toast coming up."

"I'm starved."

He motions to a stool next to the island, and I sit while he turns back to the bacon. A minute later, he puts a plate down in front of me and slides onto the stool next to mine.

We're sitting a respectable distance away from each other, but you'd think I was sitting in his lap, the way my senses are responding to him. He wouldn't let me please him last night—at least not in the way I wanted to—but our desperate movements in the darkness gave me a new understanding of his body, of the shape and feel of every last inch of him beneath those clothes, of the smell of his sweat and arousal, of the low, growling sound he makes when he's reached the edges of his restraint. I can still hear that sound in my ear, still smell that rich, musky scent of him lingering beneath the subtle aroma of his aftershave, still feel the heat of his muscles. My senses absorb all of it, and my body's reaction is immediate and intense.

For a few moments, we eat in silence. Occasionally,

Roman leans over to his laptop and shoots off an email. Once, his phone buzzes, and he spends a few moments responding to the message.

I, meanwhile, am trying to figure out—without asking him outright—where we stand. Last night was… *incredible*. But there are still too many question marks, too many things we have yet to discuss. Last night began as just another lesson. Maybe, in his eyes, that's all it ever was—one more step toward my goal. A night of release to prepare me for Saturday.

That thought terrifies me. I'm an idiot, I know—if I wanted a relationship, I never should have looked twice at Roman Everet, never should have let myself feel anything for the man teaching me to seduce someone else.

I swallow my last bite of bacon and slide off my stool.

"I'll go freshen up," I say. "We probably should leave for work soon." We haven't even finished breakfast and he's already working.

"Actually," he says, closing his laptop and pushing it away, "we're not going in today."

"What?"

"I thought maybe we'd do something else today. Something fun."

Fun? I'm still not sure I believe that word is even in Roman's vocabulary. "What do you mean?"

"We can do whatever you want. Go down to the

beach. Go for a long drive outside of the city. Find a cozy little bakery and try every dessert on the menu. It's your choice."

I can hardly believe my ears. "That sounds like a date."

He laughs. "You say that like you're surprised."

"I just… I didn't know how…" I gesture between the two of us, unsure of how to voice it without sounding insecure. "I didn't know where we stood."

His hazel eyes search mine, and there's a tenderness there that he hasn't let me see before. He reaches out and touches my cheek.

"From our very first meeting, you intrigued me," he says. "You were clearly out of your depth, but you fought quite passionately for your job. And when you claimed that you'd seduce Luca Fontaine, I saw a drive, a fire, that I couldn't let slip through my fingers." His thumb sweeps along my jaw. "As I said, for all your determination, you seemed a little lost. And I wanted to be the one who found you."

His words are quickly undoing the last of my meager defenses, and his soft caresses aren't helping.

"I… I thought you just found me entertaining," I said.

He smiles. "I did. I do." He leans closer, and his voice drops as his lips brush against my cheek. "But I also find you charming…" He kisses my temple. "And beautiful…" Kisses my eyelid. "And irresistible…"

Kisses the corner of my mouth.

My breath comes out in a little gasp, and he seems to enjoy my reaction.

"You were even more talented a pupil than I anticipated," he continues, his mouth still dangerously close to mine. "And even when you didn't quite take to the lessons, there was an earnestness, an enthusiasm, that fascinated me. Even when you were doing everything wrong, I found myself drawn to you. Your mistakes were as delightful as your successes."

He must be joking. All those times I was tripping over my words, or hitting on married men, or hiding in bathrooms—he found that *delightful?*

"You've already gotten me into bed," I say. "You don't have to flatter me."

"It's not flattery," he says. "I know that what I'm saying now is at odds with some of the things I've been teaching you, but it's the truth." He leans closer still.

And I pull back.

"What is it?" he asks.

"I haven't had a chance to brush my teeth yet," I say. "And I'm pretty sure the first rule of kissing is that—"

"Fuck the rules. Fuck the lessons." And then he grabs me and brings his mouth down on mine.

The minute our lips meet, my heart stops. My breath catches in my chest. There's an explosion of sensation, of heat, and everything else is gone—there's only me and his mouth and his hands twining in my hair. My lips open beneath his, silently begging him to deepen the kiss, to come closer to me, and he needs no further encouragement. He yanks me off my stool, drawing me into his lap. In a handful of seconds, we've gone from our first kiss to me straddling him—but after last night, maybe this isn't so odd. I wrap my arms around his neck and hold myself against him, and his hands run from my hair down my back, and then finally curving around my ass.

"God, Felicia," he moans. "I wanted to do this the moment I laid eyes on you."

A couple of days ago, I would have deflected the comment, expressed my disbelief. Instead, I find myself asking him, "Why didn't you?"

He flashes that handsome, devilish smile.

"Because I'm not a fool," he says roughly. "What was one of the very first things I taught you?"

My brain is too muddled with desire to know the answer right now, so I shrug and shake my head.

"I told you to study your target," he says, letting his mouth brush along the length of my jaw. "To adapt your approach based on what you discover."

He reaches my ear, but he only gives it a quick flick of his tongue before retracing his path back along my jaw.

"If I'd said anything then, if I'd told you exactly what I wanted to do to you, I would have scared you away," he says. "Your desire was clear from the start, but you were afraid. Skittish. I knew I would have to take my time with you, have to peel back the layers one by one until you allowed yourself to let go." His mouth is just above mine again. "And I knew from the very beginning that you would be worth every bit of the trouble."

His lips come down on mine again, even more demanding this time, and I melt against him, responding to his need with my own. His hands tighten on my ass, holding me more firmly against his lap, and I can feel how hard he already is beneath his pants. I grind my hips against him, looking for a reprise of our frenetic encounter in the bed last night.

But it's not enough. I want more.

I grab his shirt and push it off of his shoulders. It falls to the floor. Next I grab his undershirt and yank it over his head.

He's pulling my dress up over my hips. And then he's standing—still holding me against him—and setting me on top of the island. I gasp as the cool granite hits my bare skin, but he smothers the sound with his lips. His tongue invades my mouth, and he pushes me halfway down against the countertop. I grab his pants and fumble for the zipper. My fingers brush against the hardness beneath, and all of my need and hunger from this past week bubbles to the surface.

"Fuck me." The words fall out of my mouth.

He chuckles. "Oh, I intend to. Many, many times."

He pushes me back completely against the island, and his mouth assaults mine. I hear his pants hit the floor.

"Why... didn't you... do this... last night?" I ask him between his attacks on my mouth.

"Last night was about you," he says breathlessly.

"And now?"

The look in his eyes is absolutely wicked. "Now, it's my turn."

He kisses me again, and my legs come up and wrap around his hips. We're pressed together now, bare skin against bare skin, and he groans.

"Change of plans," he growls. "We're staying here today. And I'm going to fuck you over and over again until you can't walk."

"Is that a promise?"

He sucks my bottom lip between his teeth in response, and I grab his hair and tighten my legs around him.

"Pleasthh," I beg him as he continues to suck on my lip. It's torture, being pressed against him without joining.

He releases my lip. "Patience, my little seductress."

I writhe against him. "Fuck patience."

Suddenly he grabs my legs and pulls them away from him, and before I realize what's happening, he's flipped me over onto my belly. He leans toward me, his cock pressing against me from behind. He bends down so that his mouth is right against my ear.

"You will have more than your share of pleasure today. Don't you worry," he says. "But first, I need to go get a condom."

The thought of stopping, even for a second, makes me want to scream in agony. I writhe beneath him, lifting my ass against him. I don't want him going anywhere.

Roman groans in my ear and grinds against me.

"Don't tempt me," he says, his voice raw. "We need protection."

I almost tell him to fuck protection, to just risk it and bury himself deep inside of me, but I know he's right. Still, I don't know how he finds the strength to stand up. It's like our bodies are drawn together of their own will—logic and responsibility both seem far, far away right now. I let out a whimper of disappointment as he pulls back.

"I'll be right back," he tells me.

He leaves the kitchen, and I sigh and roll over onto my back. I don't bother pushing my skirt back down, though I wonder if I should. Right now, though, I don't care about being proper. I don't care that Roman is my boss and that this could make things even more complicated. I just know that I want him inside of me, over and over again. I want him to keep saying the things he's been saying to me. And I want to see that smile of his again, the real one that makes my insides turn to mush.

I throw my arm across my eyes and laugh. I've really lost it this time, haven't I? God, this is insane. I'm fluttery all over. I can't breathe or think or make sense of any of it. But I'm falling. Hard.

The sound of his footsteps returning sends a ripple of anticipation through me. I pull my arm away from my face and smile when I see him leaning over me again.

"Sorry to keep you waiting," he says. "I'll make it up to you."

He reaches down and pushes my hair away from my face. I close my eyes as his fingers move across my skin, temple to cheek to jaw to throat, exploring me inch by inch. Even the lightest of his touches wakes an overwhelming response in me, and a sound of impatience escapes my throat.

He laughs. "Don't worry. I won't torture you for long."

His fingers continue to move along my throat, following the same path they did that day in the fitting room. It's clear now that he's intentionally trying to drive me mad, and I'm beginning to think he's going to succeed when suddenly, his fingers pause.

"What's this?" he says.

It takes me a moment to realize what he's talking about, but when I do, my whole body goes cold.

The hickey.

I clap a hand to my neck, but it's too late. I didn't put any makeup on it this morning, and the concealer from yesterday would have worn off long ago. And there's no passing off a three-day-old love bite for a fresh one.

There's no lying my way out of this. And honestly, I don't want to lie to him. It's time he knew the whole truth about what happened with Rafe.

I sit up and push my skirt back down. "There's something we should talk about."

Roman's frowning. I don't even want to think about what's going on in his head right now.

He steps back and yanks up his pants. "Go on."

"I—I went out the other night," I say. "My brother called and said he spotted Raphael Fontaine at a club. I thought it would be a chance to practice some of the things you taught me."

Roman's mouth is a hard line. His expression—so open this morning—is guarded once again. "And?"

"And I ended up sitting next to Rafe in this diner," I say. "It was pure dumb luck."

He hasn't moved. He's completely rigid. "And?"

"And I tried to do as we practiced. And… it worked."

At least part of it did, but I have a feeling that right now he doesn't care about the fact that I didn't score an interview. I rush on.

"We didn't—I mean, I stopped things before we…" *How the hell do I explain this?* At the time, I thought Roman would be upset about the whole incident, but for different reasons. "It's not as bad as it sounds, I promise."

Roman still doesn't say anything. For a moment, I think he's just going to wait for me to tell him every little detail, but then suddenly, something seems to connect in his mind.

"Wait," he says, reaching past me for his laptop.

Oh, God, I realize. *The video.* I hadn't even gotten to that part yet.

"Don't," I say, sliding down off the counter and reaching across the computer. But he sweeps my hand aside.

"I thought it was just some shitty cell phone footage," he says. "I didn't even bother clicking on it."

"Don't watch it," I beg. "We just made out. It isn't as bad as you think."

"Then why didn't you tell me about it?"

His tone pins me where I stand. *I didn't tell him because I'm a coward. Because I didn't want to disappoint him.*

I don't try to stop him a second time from clicking on the video. He'll watch it whether I want him to or not. I just stand there in silence, listening to the scene I've been trying to forget—Rafe's moans and my own, then our humiliating exchange, then the two of us barging out of the stall. Roman's expression is blank throughout the entire thing.

When it's over, we both stand in silence for some time.

"Well," he says finally, and his tone is so cold that it sends a chill down my back. "It looks like I taught you well. You managed to seduce one of the Fontaines."

"Roman, I—"

"Did you secure an interview?" His voice is still completely emotionless.

"No, but I—"

"Then it looks like you still have some work to do tomorrow," he says. "Don't forget why we started these lessons in the first place."

In spite of his detached tone, there's still an accusation in his words.

"Roman, I didn't mean to—"

"You don't need to explain. I think we know where we stand now."

"Please, just—"

"I don't share, Felicia. No exceptions." He reaches down and grabs his shirt off the floor. "Now get your things. I've just remembered I have work to do today after all."

11

WELL, HERE GOES NOTHING

I'VE NEVER LOOKED this glamorous in my entire life—or felt as miserable.

The gold gown swishes around my legs as I walk, and the beads sparkle like diamonds in the late afternoon sunlight. My makeup is flawless, and my thick hair has been pinned into a flawless French twist. I debated skipping the salon appointment Roman made for me, but he had one of his assistants email me a reminder this morning, and it felt childish to refuse to go. Still, there was a knot in my stomach the entire time I sat in the chair, and while the results look beautiful, I don't feel as much like Cinderella as I expected. I feel a lot more like I'm going to throw up.

I've been here for almost three hours already, standing in my place behind the partition that separates the press from the red carpet. I've learned the hard way that they give priority positions to television reporters and the members of the press with cameras or other large equipment, but the crowd of journalists here today isn't nearly as large as it would be at a major film premiere or awards ceremony, so I'm hoping that when the limos start rolling up, I can elbow my way right up to the barricade. Right now, though, it's a waiting game—though there's only an hour and fifteen minutes left until the official start of the *Hollywood Saves!* dinner, so we should have some celebrity arrivals soon, thank goodness. My feet have started to throb in my strappy heels. Not to mention that the longer I stand here, the harder it is to keep from thinking about Roman and everything that happened yesterday.

He has no right to be angry at me, I keep telling myself over and over again. He and I aren't dating—we never were. We've hardly even had a real conversation about feelings—there was never an understanding between us, or anything else that should have prevented either of us from seeing someone else.

But how would you feel if you knew he was with another woman earlier this week? Honestly, the very thought makes me feel even sicker, but that doesn't matter. He had—*has*—every right to see someone else. To *sleep with* someone else, if that's what he wants. And I'm not allowed to complain. I never said a word about my burgeoning feelings, just as he never said anything about his before yesterday morning.

His words still echo through my head: *And I knew from the very beginning that you would be worth every bit of the trouble.* Apparently that was a lie, since he walked away from me over an assignment that *he* gave to me in the first place. He might not have sent me after Rafe himself, but he spent all week teaching me how to seduce other men. What did he expect? Is he still going to be angry if I come home with an interview today? Or will that only make it worse?

I shift my weight from one nearly numb foot to the other. A week ago, I was anxious but excited about this opportunity. Now, my enthusiasm has deflated. The whole thing feels anticlimactic, and even the idea of meeting more of the Fontaines leaves me feeling empty.

Don't think about him, I tell myself. *You're here, and you still have your career to think about. Focus on getting your interview.*

But that's hard to do when there aren't any celebrities here yet, so I find myself looking around me, desperate for anything that might take my mind off of Roman Everet. The first thing I notice is that I'm overdressed compared to many other members of the press. Most of the others are wearing simple, professional attire, so Roman was right—I'll definitely stand out tonight. I guess that's a good thing. Some of the other reporters look ruthless, as ready as I am to fight their way to the front of the group for the chance to ask a few questions. I've already been jostled and elbowed more times than I can count, and there's not even anything to see yet.

Even as I stand here, the man beside me shifts to let someone else through and ends up bumping me in the side, nearly knocking me over. I wobble on my heels, but a pair of strong hands grabs me before I can topple onto my face. I whip around.

"Hey, watch where you're—" The words die on my tongue.

I was expecting another reporter. Instead, I find myself staring right into Roman Everet's sharp hazel eyes.

"What…" I glance around, as if someone else might have the answer to the question I can't bring myself to ask. *What the heck is he doing here?*

"I'm sorry I'm late," he says coolly. "I was detained by a conference call."

I don't ask how he managed to get past security at this hour. Roman has his ways, I know. His press badge displays his name quite prominently, and I suspect he could get anywhere he desired at this event at any point during the evening. As usual, he's dressed to the nines, polished from head to toe. The Roman I saw briefly in the kitchen yesterday morning is gone, and in his place is the businessman I met in the conference room that first day.

"I… I didn't realize you were coming at all," I say. We haven't spoken since I climb out of his car at the *Celebrity Spark* offices yesterday morning. There are a hundred things I wanted to say to him then—a hundred things I *still* want to say—but none of them seem to be coming to my lips.

"I've been preparing you all week for this, haven't I?" His voice doesn't betray a hint of emotion. "I've spent a lot of money and time preparing you for tonight, and I'm here to protect my investment."

"Your… investment?" I can hardly say the word. My eyes tear away from his, unable to bear that gaze for a moment longer. "I thought…"

"You thought what, Felicia?"

Is he really going to make me say it? "I thought maybe you wouldn't want me to do this after all."

"Forgive me for giving that impression. At the end of the day, I want what's best for *Celebrity Spark*, and that means ensuring you've taken heed of our lessons. I haven't forgotten our original arrangement."

Our original arrangement. He means the fact that I only get to keep my job if I'm successful today. My ears burn. He'll probably get some twisted joy out of firing me once all of this is said and done.

"I see you've taken my advice about your hair," he says.

Is it just me, or did his voice soften slightly? I glance back at him. His eyes are on my exposed neck, and for a horrible moment, I think he's searching for the mark Rafe left. But as I watch, his gaze drifts slowly down my body—over my bare shoulders, across my breasts, down the whole length of me. He's silent throughout his visual assessment, but when he lifts his head again, I swear I see a flicker of desire in his eyes.

He still wants me.

And though he tries to hide it, now that I know it's there, the hunger is obvious in every line of his body. He still wants me, and my body responds to that knowledge with a sudden, sweet intensity.

"Do you like it?" I hear myself ask.

His eyes burn, and I feel an answering flame build in my chest. Roman reaches out and gently brushes his thumb against my throat. But even the barest of his touches has the power to send goose bumps rippling across my skin.

"I think Luca Fontaine will have a hard time resisting you," he says. "Assuming it's still Luca you're after."

His words are like a knife right in my gut. But before I can respond, there's a commotion at the far end of the red carpet and all of the reporters around us start pressing forward. The first limo has arrived.

There's no time to have this conversation right now. Members of the press start shouting for attention, calling to the couple that has just stepped out of the car. Camera bulbs flash. People jostle me from all angles, trying to get closer to the barricade. I know I need to fight too if I want any chance of speaking to one of the Fontaines.

Roman is right behind me. He's closer than he was a moment ago, pushed against me by the crowd, and the familiar heat of him against my back makes my knees feel weak. His hands fall to my waist, holding me steady, and I realize he's protecting me from the press of reporters, shielding me from the worst of the rush. Suddenly, I feel the heat of his breath against my temple.

"Move forward," he says right into my ear. "I'll help you get to the front."

I surge ahead, trying not to feel bad for elbowing the people who elbowed me a moment ago. Maybe I'm more ruthless than I thought, or maybe Roman's presence intimidates the others, because before I know it, I'm right against the barricade. Roman remains at my back, guarding me against those who are still fighting for position. I wish he didn't have to stand so close, and at the same time, I don't want him to be anywhere else. His body already feels so familiar against mine, so right. We never even had the chance to fully explore each other, and in spite of everything, I still ache for that chance. I'm as aware of him now as I've ever been, fully conscious of him—of his hands on my waist, of his breath stirring my hair, of his hips pressed right up against me. In our first lesson, he taught me about accidental touches, but there's nothing accidental about all the ways he's touching me right now.

His mouth grazes my ear again. It's the only way for him to make sure I hear him over the shouting.

"Are you ready?" he asks me.

Ready for what? To face Luca or Dante or Rafe or whichever Fontaine walks down the carpet? Maybe. To let *him* walk away? Most definitely not. But that's what happens at the end of tonight, isn't it? If I don't score an interview, I lose my job, and I never see Roman again. But even if I manage to succeed, then the new hierarchy at *Celebrity Spark* is already falling into place, and Roman will move on to the next deal, the next distraction. By his own admission, he's only here tonight to protect his investment. When someone like Roman puts in the work, he expects results.

And maybe it's my continued desire to show him what I've learned, or maybe it's a stubborn need to remind him that he set me up for this whole mess, but I want to do it. I want to get this stupid interview, one way or another.

"I'm ready," I say.

His hands tighten slightly on my waist, but he says nothing.

The shouts of the reporters around us have gone up in volume, and I realize the first of the *Hollywood Saves!* attendees have reached us. I tighten my grip on the digital recorder in my hand, wondering if my voice should join the chorus of calls, but I decide against it. I'm not here to get sound bites from sitcom actors or pop stars. I'm only interested in the Fontaines, and I don't want to be distracted by someone else when they get here.

But you are *distracted by someone else*, a little voice in my head reminds me. Roman's fingers still clutch my waist. His chest is still pressed against my back. But I can't think about how close he is, or how much I want to twist in his arms and throw my arms around his neck and beg him to stop fighting the desire I feel in his body. I need to focus.

It's only a moment later that the names reach my ears.

"Giovanna!"

"Charles! Can I ask you a question?"

"Just a word, Giovanna!"

"Charles! Charles!"

I suck in a breath and lean forward over the barricade, peering beneath the cameras and waving arms and down the length of the red carpet. There they are—Giovanna and Charles Fontaine, the couple that started my celebrity obsession. They're holding hands, and even from here, it's obvious from the glances they keep throwing at each other that they're still very much in love, even after all these years. They don't appear to be responding to any of the questions being thrown at them—their publicist is acting as a buffer and moving them along—but they stop for photos, and I have no doubt that the smiles they flash are genuine. At one point, Charles dips his head and says something in Giovanna's ear, and she gives a bright laugh and grins even more broadly. My heart beats faster and faster as the minutes tick by and they get closer and closer to where I'm standing. Giovanna is still striking, even though she must be older than my mother. Over the past year, she's started to let her dark gold hair go silver, and she's wearing a metallic silk gown that only draws attention to the new stunning shade—in addition to showing off her famous curvy figure. One look at her and it's no wonder she has such attractive children. And Charles is taller than I expected, and even more distinguished in bearing, but his easy smile keeps him from looking too stern.

"Are you all right?" Roman asks in my ear.

I realize I'm clutching the barricade for dear life. It takes me a minute to find my voice. "Yes."

They're close enough now that they could probably hear me. And Roman never said I had to interview one of the Fontaine brothers—no one could argue that Charles and Giovanna aren't A-list celebrities. I could talk to my childhood idols *and* avoid any awkward conversations with their sons.

"Giovanna!" I call. "Charles! A few questions?"

They don't even glance in my direction.

"Charles!" I yell again, waving my digital recorder this time. "Giovanna!"

"You're going to have to fight a little harder than that," Roman murmurs to me.

He's right. My cries are getting drowned out by the shouts of those around me. But even if Charles and

Giovanna *could* hear me, they don't seem to be responding to anyone. As I've already pointed out, the Fontaines are notorious for avoiding interviews.

Before I know it, the couple is out of earshot. And suddenly, my chances of pulling this off feel a lot lower.

I wasn't expecting my first red carpet event to feel so chaotic, so crazy. I wasn't expecting to have so many people pressed on all sides of me, or to have to shout myself hoarse just to get someone's attention. As I glance up and down the carpet, I realize that the celebrities who *do* stop to speak with reporters only seem to answer one or two questions before moving on. How the hell am I supposed to seduce someone here?

Panic rises in my throat. This is impossible. My career at *Celebrity Spark* is over before it ever really began.

Roman's hands move slightly on my waist and his breath stirs the hair next to my ear. "Are you all right?"

"Yes," I say, but my tone is clipped. I don't want to admit that I'm ready to give up, that I've realized how fruitless all of this is. If anything, his question makes me that much more determined to fight until the very end.

I don't have much of a chance to come up with a plan, though. Celebrities and socialites and Hollywood bigwigs continue to arrive and make their way down the carpet. Some get more attention than others, but the shouting never ceases, and the cameras never stop flashing. I recognize many of the faces that pass. I even spot some members of the Fontaine family who normally stay out of the spotlight—including Ellis Fontaine, the daughter of Charles' brother Harrison and cousin to Luca and the others. Rumor has it that Ellis has been spotted with a professional football player, but no one has managed to capture any photographs of the two just yet. Tonight, she's arrived by herself, and I'm wondering whether it's worth trying to ask her a few questions when suddenly I hear one of the names I've been listening for.

"Luca! Luca! Over here!"

"Luca!"

My stomach tightens as the shouts multiply. Luca was my original target, but I was hoping Dante might show up first. I had a moment with Dante back at Hallevern's—a *brief* moment, but a promising one, and it would have given me a starting point. With Luca, I'm facing the unknown. And he's getting more attention than anyone else in his family these days, so he'll be that much harder to pin down.

At least it's not Rafe, I tell myself. I'm not ready for that sort of awkwardness right now—either with one of the Fontaines *or* with the man behind me. I lean forward again and watch as Luca makes his way toward where I stand.

He's a charmer, that he is. And like the rest of his family, he's pretty damn breathtaking in person. His dirty-blond hair has been cropped close for *Cataclysm:*

Earth, enhancing the strong, sharp planes of his face. His body was always athletic, but he's clearly added some more muscle for this latest role—and he definitely has the build to pull it off without looking like a bodybuilder. He fills out his tux quite nicely. But as ever, it's hard to keep my eyes from his face and that million-watt smile. That smile could charm anyone, and it's out in full force tonight. He's certainly turning it on for the cameras.

Roman's voice in my ear pulls me back to where I stand. "Tell me who's with him."

I hadn't even noticed the woman standing beside Luca, but now that Roman has called my attention to her, I recognize her immediately. I'm sure Roman does too—he's probably just testing my celebrity knowledge.

"That's Stacia Fischer," I say. "She's been on a few network television series, but she's been trying to make the leap to the big screen." And no doubt she'll accomplish that soon—especially if she's making appearances with Luca Fontaine. I'm not surprised she caught his eye. She's quite lovely—tall and slender with that dark hair that Luca seems to love. The sort of dark hair that I thought, naively, might be my own way in, and I suddenly realize I have a new problem.

Luca brought a *date*. How the heck am I supposed to seduce someone with a beautiful woman on his arm? How am I even supposed to catch his attention?

Roman squeezes my side. "Do you have a plan?"

No. No, I don't. I should have anticipated this—men like Luca Fontaine don't go out alone, even after huge public breakups with their costars. Why didn't I prepare for this? Why didn't I ever ask Roman what I should do in this sort of situation? I couldn't even pick up a guy in a bar. This is an entirely different game.

Roman sees something in you, I remind myself. I remember all the things he called me yesterday—charming, beautiful, *irresistible*. He seemed genuine enough, but now that I'm standing here and watching Luca and Stacia get ever closer, I'm not so sure.

But Luca isn't the only Fontaine brother currently on the carpet. New shouts begin to reach my ears, and I realize that Dante has also arrived. Relief floods me, and I stand on my toes, trying to spot him through the crowd. But when my eyes finally lock on him, the bottom drops out of my stomach.

He brought a date too.

I'm frozen. I don't know what I'm supposed to do. If Roman wants me to fail, then he's definitely going to be pleased by this development. My mind has gone blank, and my knuckles are white around my digital recorder. All I can do is watch Luca and Stacia—and then Dante and his date, a pretty girl I don't recognize—move closer and closer. It doesn't help that Roman is still touching me, still right against my back, still able to send a shiver through me with just the tilt of his head and the brush of his lips against my ear. It's incredibly distracting.

But Luca is nearly here, and I have to try *something.*

I pull out of Roman's grip and lean over the barricade, adding my voice to those around me.

"Luca!" I call, waving my digital recorder. "Just a quick question!"

He hardly glances my way. Instead, never missing a beat, he grabs Stacia, swings her around, and tilts her back in a huge, dramatic kiss. If I thought things were chaotic before, it's nothing compared to the shouting that starts at the first touch of their lips. The camera flashes multiply, the voices get louder, and reporters jockey for position at the barricade, pushing Roman right up against me again.

"Are you two dating?" Someone shouts from my left.

Another comes from my right. "What does Emilia think?"

I could yell, too, but I know there's no point. Luca won't answer any questions. But he continues to put on a show, and Stacia seems more than willing to play along. The two are hanging all over each other, and Stacia laughs as he loops his arm around her waist.

I'm so absorbed in the scene in front of me that I almost don't notice that Dante has caught up with his brother. He doesn't look particularly amused by Luca's antics, but Dante always was the serious one. Now that he's closer, I get a better look at his date, but I still don't recognize her. She's very pretty—she'd have to be, to show up with one of the Fontaine brothers—with strawberry blond hair and big eyes. Dante hasn't had any big, public relationships like his brother, but maybe that's on purpose.

I lean back slightly against Roman. "Do you know who's with Dante?"

"No."

I guess it doesn't matter either way. She's still here with him, making my job that much harder. But I know I can't blame her for my mess—I should have known I wouldn't have more than the briefest of chances to speak with any of the Fontaines here tonight. Not one of them has paused to speak with any reporters, and gold gown or not, why would any stop for me? This is about more than my appearance or my ability to flirt. The Fontaines know how to manage their PR—even if the occasional bit of cell footage leaks through—and they're not going to break the rules for me.

I'm ready to throw in the towel when I look up again and find Dante staring right at me.

It's not a stare like the ones Roman has been giving me all week—dark and intense and full of desire—but rather one of confusion, and I realize that he recognizes me but can't seem to place *how*.

So I do the only thing I can—I smile and hold up my press badge, hoping he connects the dots. And it works—I practically see the light bulb going off in his head.

This is my chance.

I pull away from Roman and push my way along the barricade—only elbowing one person in the process—until I'm a little closer to Dante.

"You owe me an interview!" I call over the people around me.

The look he gives me isn't quite a smile, but there's a flicker of something in his eyes—humor? Appreciation?—that gives me hope. And then before I realize what's happening, he says a quick word to his date and walks toward the barricade. Toward *me.*

I'm so surprised that I almost turn and run just out of habit. But I'm not going to miss my chance. And anyway, Roman has just squeezed in behind me—I can sense his nearness in every part of me, even though I haven't turned to look—and I want to show him that I'm not backing down. A dozen mics and recorders are pointed at Dante, and he stops just out of reach. His date is beside him, and though she's smiling, she looks a little confused. He probably told her in advance that they wouldn't be talking to any reporters.

"I was wondering if we'd cross paths again," he says to me—*to me!*—and his voice cuts right through the noise around us. "I must admit, though, I wasn't expecting it to be so soon."

I'm surprised I've managed to keep my grip on my digital recorder. Inside, I'm freaking out. Dante

Fontaine wasn't just being polite back in the restaurant—he's actually making an effort to talk to me! He's looking at me expectantly, and I suddenly realize I'm gaping at him like a complete idiot.

Say something, Felicia! Anything! My mind plays through all of the awkward things I've said and done this week, and nerves rise in my chest. The sick feeling I've been fighting all afternoon returns in full force, but I fight it down.

Suddenly there's a touch on my back—a light one, but unmistakable all the same. Roman's placed his fingers gently against the curve of my lower back, and that gives me the strength I need to find my voice.

"I know this isn't exactly a good place to talk," I say over the shouts around us, "but I was wondering if sometime in the near future I might convince you to sit down with *Celebrity Spark* and talk about your work on *Cataclysm: Earth.*" I'm almost stunned to hear those words come out of my mouth. Old Felicia would have tripped over her tongue immediately, but New Felicia sounds so professional. Like a seasoned reporter.

"I don't normally give interviews," he says, but I can tell by his tone that he's just making me work for it.

And I intend to. "I know. Which is why I'm promising to keep it to ten questions."

A hint of a smile flashes across his features. "I'm afraid I can only give you three."

My pulse quickens. Is that an agreement? But three

questions is so few—I could never get a full cover feature out of that. He's playing hardball on purpose.

"I can do nine," I say.

"Five."

"Eight. And you get approval of the final piece before it goes to press." I'm honestly not sure if I have the power to grant him that, but I'll worry about the logistics later.

But before Dante can give me his answer, Luca is beside him.

"What's going on over here?" he asks. "Having a party without me?" He's still smiling, but I know he's just as confused as everyone else about why his brother is actually engaging with the press.

"I was just following up on a commitment," Dante says, inclining his head in my direction.

For the first time, Luca's eyes slide to me. At first, he just gives me a quick glance, but then he does a double take—and I feel my whole body flush as he gives me a much longer, much more appreciative look. I guess I'm Luca's type after all—though I'm sure the gown and the perfect hair and makeup are helping immeasurably.

Roman doesn't miss the way Luca is looking at me. His hand flattens on my back, his touch instantly becoming firmer and more possessive, but due to the crowd I don't think anyone on either side of the barricade notices except me.

Luca, meanwhile, is grinning at me, and a week ago

that smile fixed in *this* direction would probably have made me swoon. Not that I don't appreciate it now—I'm still a woman, after all—but it doesn't completely disarm me.

"I think you're on the wrong side of the partition, sweetheart," he says. "Are you sure you don't belong over here?"

I can't believe Luca is turning his charm on me. I want to laugh at the utter insanity of it—I now have *two* of the Fontaine brothers talking to me when they've been ignoring every other member of the press. I can't let this opportunity slip through my fingers—even if Roman has suddenly decided to do his best to distract me. His hand has moved from my lower back and down across my ass.

"Maybe you should come over onto *this* side," I say, trying to ignore the sensations Roman's touch is causing between my legs. "You've already bought your plate. You've made your donation. You've had your photo taken a hundred times to prove you were here. Doesn't part of you want to leap the fence and run off and do something crazy?" I don't know what's gotten into me, but I feel like a whole new person tonight. I'm talking to Luca Fontaine—practically *flirting*—and for the first time, the right words just seem to come to me.

Luca glances back over at his brother, grinning. "I like this one. Where did you find her?"

"That's a bit of a story," Dante replies.

"I work for *Celebrity Spark*," I chime in, trying to ignore the fact that Roman's fingers are moving still lower. "I'd love to sit down with you for an interview sometime." The last word is nearly a gasp, since Roman's hand suddenly grips and squeezes me. But neither of the Fontaine brothers seems to notice.

"No interviews," Luca says, still smiling at me. "I'm sorry, sweetheart, I really am, but they just aren't my thing."

Roman releases my ass, but his fingers are slipping into dangerous territory now. Even with the barrier of the dress between us, my body still responds to his touch, still remembers all the ways he caressed—and kissed, and licked—me just two short nights ago. My body doesn't care that my job is on the line, or that we're in the middle of a red carpet with people all around us. But *I* care, and I force myself to focus on Luca and Dante.

"Then what *is* your thing?" I ask sweetly. My voice is only the tiniest bit strained.

Luca's grin turns decidedly devilish. "That's a personal question, isn't it? I don't even know your name."

Roman's fingers have nearly moved between my legs from behind, and I suck in a breath and grab onto the barricade so I don't topple over. He's doing this on purpose—tormenting and distracting me while I'm trying to do exactly what I came here to do. But even though I'm barely holding it together, I try not to let it show.

"I'm Felicia," I say to Luca. "And your brother has already agreed to speak with me. Maybe you and I can come to our own arrangement."

He doesn't miss the flirtatious implications of my words. His eyes flash and his smile widens, but before he can respond, a man with an earpiece steps between the Fontaine brothers.

"What are you doing?" he asks Luca. "Stacia's already inside. I thought we said no interviews."

Disappointment fills me. I'm not sure whether the man in front of us is Luca's publicist or manager or someone else—I should probably find out, if I want any future dealings with this family—but I should've known his "people" wouldn't let him chat with me for long. *And I was just getting warmed up.*

"Well," Luca says, "I guess I can't keep my lady waiting." He shoots me a wink. "Nice to meet you, Felicia."

And with that, he lets the man with the earpiece escort him down the carpet. Dante is still standing in front of me, and he glances back at his own date.

"I'll tell my manager to expect your call," he tells me. He starts to go, then pauses and turns back to me. "I suspect Luca will come around as well, if you're persistent."

He doesn't wait for my response. He turns to go, and the other reporters crowd in around me, calling after him. I, meanwhile, am feeling a little dazed.

I did it. I actually did it. I snagged an interview with Dante—*and* a potential lead with Luca as well. But even as the realization is sinking in, Roman yanks me back against him. His lips are hot against my ear.

"Looks like you've won, my little seductress."

Heat courses through my body. He's no longer tormenting me with his fingers, but the damage is done. My skin is alive with sensation, my resistance quickly losing the battle with the desire building inside of me. But I'm not going to let him off the hook that easily.

"What the hell was that?" I snap at him. "I was trying to talk to them! And you were trying to… to…"

His strong arms still hold me firmly against him, and I feel the rumble of his bitter chuckle against my back. When he speaks, his voice is a growl.

"I was trying to remind you that you're mine."

His words send a little jolt of pleasure straight between my legs, but then I remember how we left things between us yesterday morning.

"I thought you were done with me," I say.

"I never said that. I only told you that I don't share." He leans in a little closer and lets his teeth graze my earlobe. "Not then, not now, Felicia."

"May I remind you that *you* were the one who spent the entire week preparing me for this moment?"

"And how does it make you feel?"

"What?"

"Making them want you, Felicia. Filling their shiny little heads with fantasies."

I'm feeling more lightheaded by the moment. "You don't know that they wanted me."

Another low laugh. "Still so naive, even after everything that's happened this week." One of his arms loosens and his hand slips down my body, retracing the path it took in the fitting room the first time I put on this dress.

"We're in the middle of a press line," I remind him breathlessly.

His hand glides lower. "No one is looking at us."

"But they might."

He ignores me. His hand presses against the place where my legs meet, and it's all I can do not to moan.

"Did you want him?" he growls in my ear.

"Him?"

"Luca. Dante. Raphael." His hand shifts. "Pick one."

His fingers are driving me mad. "I… I don't know."

"I think you do." He tightens his hold on my waist, and I can feel the hard length of him pressing against my back. "Tell me, Felicia."

What does he want me to say? That I don't find any of those men attractive? If I deflect the question, he'll only accuse me of lying. Roman bites down on my earlobe, and I suck in a breath at the sharp sensation before finally finding my voice.

"You know about my stupid childish fantasies," I tell him. "They're silly, but you don't just forget those things overnight."

"No? Then how many nights does it take?"

Something in his tone makes me pause. "What?"

"How. Many. Nights."

I try to twist around in his arms, to look him in the eyes, but he holds me too tightly. "How am I supposed to know that? Why does it even matter?"

"It matters because I'm going to make you forget them. Forget every single one of those damn Fontaines."

My heart is in my throat. "H-how?"

"You know the answer to that, Felicia."

My legs are shaking again, and I can hardly keep my grip on my recorder. I can feel the tension in his body, feel the need in his arms and his chest and even his mouth, which keeps nipping at my skin and neck.

"We… we're in a press line…" I say again, but even my resolve is weakening.

"You think that won't stop me from fucking you?" His mouth burns against my skin. "I'm going to drive every thought of every one of them out of your mind, one way or the other."

And I just might let him. But there's some reason left in my brain, and I hear myself beg, "Not here. Please."

He doesn't wait another moment. He releases his grip on my waist, then grabs my hand and pulls me through the sea of reporters. We're moving against the crowd, but that doesn't stop Roman. He forces his way through, dragging me behind him. I nearly stumble in my heels, but he doesn't let me fall. He leads me away from the carpet.

As we go, I hear a new round of shouts go up behind us.

"Raphael!"

"Just one picture!"

"Raphael! A question!"

Roman's hand tightens on mine, and his steps quicken. I'm more than happy to leave as fast as possible. I'm not particularly interested in facing Raphael right now. The video of the two of us hasn't gone viral yet—to my knowledge, at least—and I pray it gets buried by juicier celebrity news before more than a handful of people see it. And if it *does* start spreading... well, I'll deal with that when and if I have to. If the dating history of the Fontaine boys is any indication, Raphael will have another girl on his arm in no time, and everyone will forget about the random nobody he once tried to hook up with in a bathroom stall.

Everyone except the man pulling me through the crowd, perhaps. But no matter what happens now, I'm determined to show Roman that nothing and no one stirs me like he does. I don't know what's happening between us, but even though it's crazy, I can't seem to stop. Can't seem to slow down. Can't seem to deny him anything. I don't care where he's taking me—I will follow him, because I want to experience this madness for one more minute, one more hour, one more day.

At first I think Roman is leading me to his car, but then I realize he's taking me around the block to the back of the building.

"Where are we going?" I ask him.

"Somewhere away from all of this," he says in a gravelly tone that I swear I can feel deep inside of me. As soon as we're free of the crowd he pulls me closer, right against his side, and his hand moves down over my hip. I'm starting to wonder if he's just going to shove me up against the wall behind the dumpsters, but instead, he heads for a large metal door. It swings open as we approach, and someone in chef whites hauls out a bag of garbage. He's taken us around to the kitchens.

He walks through the door as if he knows exactly where he's going. The kitchen is busy—pots boiling, grills sizzling, people running to and fro—and everyone is so occupied with finishing up those $15,000 plates for the guests in the other room that they don't even notice us at first. We're across the room and nearly to the door before someone says, "Hey! You can't be back here!"

Roman doesn't miss a beat. "We wanted to avoid the paparazzi. I'm sure you understand."

The man who spoke looks startled. His eyes dart between the two of us.

"Y-yes, of course," he stammers. "Head right down the hall."

It's not until we're safely through the door that I realize what happened.

"He thought we were celebrities," I say.

Roman squeezes my hand. It's not *that* much of a stretch, I know, considering how we're dressed. But the idea that anyone might mistake me for someone famous brings me a rush of pleasure.

I can hear, down the hall, the buzz of sound from the event itself—the sea of voices, the soft string music, the occasional clanking of glasses. But Roman doesn't lead me there. Instead, he pulls me down another hallway.

"What's back here?" I ask.

"A dark corner," he says.

We're back in what appears to be the storage area of this particular facility, and Roman starts trying various doorways on either side of us. Most of them are locked, but finally one knob turns when he jiggles it. He doesn't even wait to see where it leads. He grabs me with both hands, and his mouth attacks mine as he pulls me inside.

We're in a closet… or something. We don't bother fumbling for the light, and all I know is that he's pushing me up against the wall, touching me everywhere, kissing me over and over and over again until I can hardly breathe. I'm touching him too, kissing him everywhere I can reach, tearing at his clothes in the dark.

Our first kiss in his kitchen was amazing. *This* is…

mind-blowing. All of the hunger we've built up, all of the tensions we've left simmering, all of our feelings have suddenly burst free, and I cling to him, trying to taste every bit of it on his tongue.

"No one else," he rasps against my mouth.

He doesn't give me a chance to respond, but I think he knows the answer either way. I'm jelly in his hands, melting against his body, and at the same time, my movements are as ravenous and desperate as his. A week ago, I could hardly even fathom the idea that someone like Roman might want someone like me. A day ago, I thought our brief, ill-advised *thing* was over before it even really started. But now Roman is touching me like he can't get enough, kissing me like he's starved for the taste of my lips, and I feel so reckless, so wonderful, so humbled and so *powerful* all at once.

"Roman…" I moan between his kisses.

His hands move up and down my body, from my breasts to my ass and finally down to my thighs, where he begins tugging my gown up my legs. My fingers fumble with the buttons of his shirt, and I manage to get it open about the same time he gets the gold dress up around my hips. I want to pull off his shirt and rip through his undershirt and press my hands against the warm bare skin of his chest, but neither of us seems to have the patience for that. Instead, we both go for his belt at the same time, and our fingers tangle in the dark as we get his pants open.

I hear him fish in his pocket for something before he lets his pants fall to the floor. A second later, there's the sound of a condom wrapper ripping open.

"You knew this would happen?" I ask him as I gasp for air.

His lips move down across my throat. "I knew there was only one way to solve our problem."

"Our problem?"

His answer is to bite down on my neck—not hard, but firmly enough to make me give a little cry.

"The problem of which man's marks you wear on your skin," he says before nipping at me again. "Of which man you think about when you touch yourself." He repositions himself in front of me, forcing my legs a little further apart. "Of which man makes you moan when he has you up against the wall."

He grabs my hips and lifts me up, pulling my legs around him in the process. Honestly, until he mentioned it, I'd forgotten all about Raphael Fontaine. And though Roman now has me in a similar position, this situation feels completely different. My encounter with Raphael was hot, but this is something else. My entire body aches, and I'm trembling from head to toe. But it goes beyond that. Those brief moments with Raphael were purely physical. Underneath the lust, they were empty. But right now I feel... well, it might be too soon to call it love, but there's an intensity to the emotions churning inside of me that I've never felt before, not with any guy. I yearn for Roman in more than just a physical way. I ache to know him deeper, to be vulnerable in front of him, to open myself to him fully.

He's poised at my entrance, and his breathing is ragged. He's barely holding back. And though it's dark, I can feel him looking at me.

"You want this," he says.

I can't tell whether that's a statement or a question, but either way, I can't leave it unanswered.

"Yes," I whisper. "Yes, more than anything." The need in my voice is plain.

"Good. I would hate to have to kill one of those Fontaine boys. They make the magazine lots of money."

"I told you I didn't—"

"I know. But that doesn't mean I still don't intend to drive them out of your mind, by whatever means necessary."

His body still doesn't move, but his lips brush against my jaw, my cheek, the bridge of my nose.

"And don't you think for one moment that our lessons are over," he says. "There are still many, many things I wish to teach you, but this time, your only target will be *me*."

"Show me," I plead.

He laughs. "Maybe we should start with patience."

"Says the man who dragged me into a closet because he didn't have the patience to—"

He silences me with a finger against my lips. "I can

stop, if you like."

"No!"

He laughs again. "Oh, Felicia. I'm going to enjoy this very much." He pulls his fingers away. "Not just making love to you, but everything that comes after."

My heart leaps. "What comes after?"

I can feel his eyes on me again, and there's something powerful about his gaze, even in the dark.

"I have some ideas," he murmurs, "but I think we'll figure out the rest together."

And then his mouth comes down on mine—not roughly, as before, but with a gentleness that makes me quiver. One brush of his lips, two, and then without warning, he buries himself in me completely.

I cry out as he enters me, but not in pain. He seems to understand, because he only gives me one more gentle kiss before the animal takes over again, before the controlled, perfectly polished Roman loses to the beast. He drives into me again and again, and I cling to him and bury my face against his neck. His mouth finds my throat once more, and he bites and sucks and teases my skin, covering Raphael's one faded love bite with a dozen of his own. I know I should stop him, I know I should care that he's marking me, but I don't. The pleasure is building between my legs, flowing out to the rest of me, and I can't think of anything else. We're connecting in a way we never have before—not just physically, but deeper. Beneath the hunger there's a hope and a promise, and I grab onto it with everything I have.

Our bodies move together, finding a rhythm. As we learn and adjust and spur each other on toward pleasure, even our breathing seems to fall into sync and I'm no longer sure how we waited even this long to join. From the moment I met him, I was drawn to him. I knew, deep down, that it could be like this between us. That this was *right*. And I never want to break this bond.

Somehow during our frenzied coupling, just before the sensation becomes too much to bear, he accidentally pushes me against the light switch. Fluorescent bulbs flicker on overhead, momentarily blinding me, but when I close my eyes he says, "No. I want you to look at me."

And I do. I stare into those hazel eyes as he buries himself in me, letting him see everything I'm feeling, everything I've been afraid to show him. I feel exposed and empowered all at once, and in his eyes—beneath those flecks of green and gold and other glorious colors—I see a need that mirrors my own. Not just a need for my body, or for pleasure, but a desire for something deeper, a connection both of us are only beginning to understand.

And my eyes are still locked on his when the ecstasy finally explodes through me, and we ride out the aftershocks together, I know there can be no doubt in his mind about who I want, now and for many nights to come.

TWO WEEKS AFTER THE MOST AMAZING NIGHT OF MY LIFE (SO FAR)

MY STOMACH GRUMBLES at me. I glance down at my watch, and I almost don't believe the time—I should have left work over an hour ago. But I've been so absorbed in polishing my latest piece that I completely lost track of how late it was. My interview with Dante Fontaine is tomorrow, and I've blocked off the whole morning so I can make sure I'm prepared. This is my chance to forge a major connection, to make sure *Celebrity Spark* is the publication Dante contacts whenever he needs to promote a project or wishes to arrange a "scandal" in the name of a little extra publicity. If I play this right and earn Dante's trust, I might be able to turn that into a working relationship with some of the other Fontaines as well. Tomorrow's interview could make my entire career.

A shadow looms over my desk, and I jump—and then look up into the eyes of Roman. My chest flutters. We've only been officially dating for a couple of weeks, but I have a sneaking suspicion that this lightheaded, giggly feeling will be around for some time.

"You're working late tonight," he says.

"What are you doing here? I thought you had some big meeting today."

"I did. It ended an hour ago, so I thought I'd come check in with Rachel."

Rachel Shanning has taken over as *Celebrity Spark*'s new Editor-in-Chief, and I love her already. She's sharp, driven, and I know she'll have a lot to teach me. She has some brilliant ideas for the launch of the magazine's new digital edition, and I'm excited about the publication's future.

"Are you ready for tomorrow?" he asks.

He's been helping me prepare, teaching me how to calm my nerves in professional situations and running through questions and practice interviews with me. His advice has been invaluable. Unsurprisingly, most of these sessions have been followed by "lessons" of a very different kind—if there was ever any doubt about who the current star of my sexual fantasies might be... well, Roman has made quite sure that my imagination wants for nothing, and that the Fontaine boys are far, far out of my mind the minute I'm off work. I have a feeling that after tomorrow's interview I'm going to be in for a bit of a treat, and my heart beats faster just thinking about it.

"I think I'm ready," I say.

"Good. Because I don't want you distracted tonight." He reaches down and grabs my hand, pulling me up into his arms.

I brace myself against his chest. "Why's that?"

His eyes gleam. "Because there are some very, very important things I think we should practice."

"Like?"

"Like this."

Before I can say anything, his mouth moves over mine, searching and teasing until I can't think anymore. I grip the lapels of his jacket and try not to sway in his arms.

"You shouldn't do that here," I say, pulling back and glancing around. "Someone might see. *Rachel* might see, and I want her to like me."

"She'll like you if I tell her to," he replies.

"But she won't respect me. And I want to make sure I'm here on my own merits."

"You got *Celebrity Spark* an exclusive interview with Dante Fontaine. Your merits are not in question."

But Dante is just the beginning. I still want that interview with Luca, too. And one with Giovanna and Charles. And I want to talk to Ellis about the rumors surrounding her love life. And… honestly, I want to talk to *all* of them. I'll probably take a pass on Rafe, just to avoid an awkward situation, but the rest of the family is fair game.

I glance up at Roman. He won't stop me from pursuing any of those interviews, but that doesn't mean he won't also try to take my mind off of the Fontaines the moment I'm in his arms. And honestly? I'm okay with that.

His eyes flash. "If you wish to discuss your merits, I believe the conference room is open. We might go over a few things in there."

Blood rushes between my legs as I remember the way he pushed me up against that table, and images of the things he said he wanted to do fill my mind. I quickly bend over my computer and begin saving my work. I don't intend to let anything happen here, but if the brief few weeks since I met Roman have taught me anything, it's that I tend to lose my head around him— and that neither of us seems to have any self-control around the other. Since that moment at *Hollywood Saves!* when we finally broke down and made love, we haven't been able to keep our hands off of each other. And it turns out that Roman has a lot more to teach me than just the secret to seduction.

I feel his eyes on me as I close down my computer.

"Would you be interested in getting some dinner?" he asks. "I believe I promised you once that I'd take you somewhere and let you try all of the desserts on the menu."

I glance down at my clothes. "I'm not dressed for anything fancy."

"I never said you had to be." He draws me toward his chest again. "If you prefer, we can pick up some snacks and a bottle of wine and go down to the beach."

My blush deepens. We both know exactly what will happen if we go down to the ocean. The thought of writhing beneath Roman on the sand sets off the butterflies again, but before I can say anything, my stomach rumbles. Loudly.

Roman smiles—one of his real, wonderful smiles— and kisses my hand. "I think we have our decision."

A few minutes later, I'm sitting next to him in his

car, watching the sunset through the window. This isn't our first real date, and I know it won't be our last, either. In fact, I have a very strong feeling that this is only the beginning.

I look over at Roman. He's still as polished as ever, but there's something… different about him these days. Something I can't quite put my finger on just yet, but something I'm very much looking forward to exploring. He glances over at me and smiles, and emotion swells in my chest. I'm falling hard for this one, no doubt about it. I'm already past the point of no return, and I can only hope that he's experiencing something similar in his own heart. Something a lot like… *love.*

Brrrrrrrinnggg!

The chime of his cell phone pulls me out of the moment. I feel that familiar tug of disappointment as he pulls it out of his pocket. No matter what has happened between us, I can't let myself forget who Roman is, or how important his work is to him. If I'm going to be with this man, I'm going to have to accept that his job will always come first.

But Roman presses the button on the side of the phone.

"Sorry," he says. "I meant to turn this off." And instead of sliding it back into his pocket, he tosses it onto the back seat. And when he looks at me again, his smile is as bright as the California sun.

The romance is only beginning…

Felicia and Roman's story doesn't end here—and you haven't seen the last of the Fontaine boys, either! *The Sweet Taste of Sin*, the next book in *The Fontaines* series, will arrive in Summer 2015.

Need more in the meantime? Felicia and Roman will appear in a recurring mini-series called *Rumors and Romance*, which will be available (for FREE!) exclusively through my mailing list. These episodes will explore Felicia and Roman's budding romance… and give you guys exclusive hints (and behind-the-scenes glimpses) of things to come for the Fontaine family! Learn more here: http://www.embercasey.com/newsletter.html

In the meantime, feel free to contact me at ember.casey@gmail.com (I love hearing from readers!). You can also find information about me and my books at http://embercasey.com.

Finally, I want to thank you for reading *The Secret to Seduction.* If you're so inclined, please consider taking a moment to leave a review. Even a couple of sentences can help other readers find books they'll enjoy!

BOOKS BY EMBER CASEY

ABOUT THE AUTHOR

Ember Casey is a twenty-something writer who lives in Atlanta, Georgia in a den of iniquity (or so she likes to tell people). When she's not writing steamy romances, you can find her whipping up baked goods (usually of the chocolate variety), traveling (her bucket list is infinite), or generally causing trouble (because somebody has to do it).

For more Ember Casey news, updates, and extras, check out http://embercasey.com. You can also reach her at ember.casey@gmail.com or join her new release list at http://www.embercasey.com/newsletter.html.

40144214R00171

Made in the USA
Charleston, SC
26 March 2015